Darkness

the

Color

of

Snow

ALSO BY THOMAS COBB

Crazy Heart

Acts of Contrition

Shavetail

With Blood in Their Eyes

DARKNESS

THE

COLOR

OF

SNOW

THOMAS COBB

WILLIAM MORROW
An Imprint of HarperCollins *Publishers*

DARKNESS THE COLOR OF SNOW. Copyright © 2015 by Thomas Cobb. All rights reserved. Printed in the United States of America. No part of this book may be used or reproduced in any manner whatsoever without written permission except in the case of brief quotations embodied in critical articles and reviews. For information address HarperCollins Publishers, 195 Broadway, New York, NY 10007.

HarperCollins books may be purchased for educational, business, or sales promotional use. For information please e-mail the Special Markets Department at SPsales@harpercollins.com.

FIRST EDITION

Designed by Jamie Lynn Kerner

Library of Congress Cataloging-in-Publication Data has been applied for.

ISBN 978-0-06-239124-7

15 16 17 18 19   OV/RRD   10 9 8 7 6 5 4 3 2 1

To Richard Shelton,
and in memory of Lois.

Darkness
the
Color
of
Snow

CHAPTER 1

PATROLMAN RONALD FORBERT SITS IN CRUISER FOUR, STARTING and restarting the ten-year-old Crown Victoria to keep the cabin warm. It will run for five minutes before it stalls out. He's just on the outskirts of Lydell, half a mile from the Citgo and two miles from the state line. It snowed early in the day, then melted, and now the melt is refreezing into black ice on the highway. He's on duty partly to hang paper on the drivers speeding to or from the Indian casino twelve miles away, and partly to slow down drivers who aren't aware of the icy conditions.

He sees the one-headlight car come over a hill a few hundred yards to the east, then disappear. He turns the cruiser back on and waits for the vehicle to come over the hill just east of him that hides him from view. When the car crests the hill, he lights it up with the radar gun, drops the cruiser into gear, and hits the light bar. As the car, a beater Jeep Cherokee, goes by, he recognizes it. "Shit."

He pulls out behind the Cherokee, his rear wheels spinning a bit as they slide over the ice and onto dry pavement, and begins to follow. When the Cherokee shows no signs of slowing down, he blips the siren a couple of times until it slows and moves to the right and off the pavement. He sees it fishtail just a bit before it straightens and comes to a stop.

He checks the radar. Sixty-eight in a forty-five-mile-an-hour zone. He calls it in to dispatch, gathers his book and Maglite, gets out and walks to the driver's-side door. He shines the light into the interior. There are four of them. Matt Laferiere is back to operating at full strength.

HE TAPS THE DRIVER'S WINDOW WITH THE FLASHLIGHT. "ROLL DOWN your window. Keep your hands where I can see them." He shines the light into the car through the open window, causing Matt Laferiere, the driver, to shut and shield his eyes. Next to him is Paul Stablein, always riding shotgun, and in back Bobby Cabella and a kid he doesn't know, the "virgie."

"Gentlemen," he begins.

"Forbert."

"Be nice to him," Paul Stablein says mockingly. "He called you a 'gentleman.' When has that ever happened? Good evening, Officer Forbert."

"You have a right front headlight out."

"OK. I'll fix it."

"And you were running sixty-eight in a forty-five-mile zone. We have black ice tonight. That constitutes a pretty dangerous situation."

"Thank you for informing us of that, Officer."

"You been drinking, Matt?"

"Of course not, Officer." Laferiere keeps hitting the "Officer" hard, in case anyone misses the sarcasm.

"Yeah, 'of course not.' I can smell it on you." He steps back and shines his light into the back. A busted thirty-can carton of Natty Lights is on the backseat. "You have an open container, and you're driving in the Cherokee. Of course you're drinking."

"Aw, Jesus. Come on, man. Leave us alone. We were on our way home. I'll fix the headlight tomorrow."

"License and registration," Forbert says.

"Oh, come on, Forbert. Nobody does forty-five on this road. That's not for locals."

There is something to what Laferiere says. Locals don't get papered for fifty, even sixty on this road. Warnings are the standard, and that is what Forbert is thinking now, even though sixty-eight pushed the standard pretty hard.

"Do you have any weapons in the car? Guns, knives, anything like that?"

"No."

"Are you sure? You tell me you don't have any, but if I find one, you're in a lot of trouble."

"Fuck you," Laferiere says. He leans over and fishes in his pocket for his license, then reaches over to the glove box.

"Let Stablein get it."

"You afraid there's a gun in there?"

"Wouldn't be unusual."

"If there was a gun in there, you'd be dead," Laferiere says. "You fucking loser."

"You threatening me, Matt?"

Paul Stablein opens the glove box, rifles through it, extracts the registration, and hands it to Laferiere, who hands it to Forbert. "Stick it up your ass," Laferiere says.

"Watch your mouth. I'm a police officer."

"You're a pussy loser with a badge, and we both know it."

Forbert lets that go and lights up the kid in the back. "What's your name?"

"Sammy."

"Sammy what?"

"Colvington. Sammy Colvington."

"Sam Colvington Junior?" The kid nods. "How old are you, Sammy?"

"Twenty-two."

"Yeah, right." Forbert puts the kid at sixteen, maybe eighteen, tops. "Where are you guys headed?"

"Home," Stablein says. "We're going home." Laferiere stares straight ahead, his jaw set.

The license and registration are both current. "I guess you'd prefer I didn't check for outstanding warrants?"

"I don't give a fuck what you do."

Stablein reaches over and pats Laferiere's arm. "Let it go, man. Let's just deal with Officer Forbert here, then go home." Then, to Forbert, "It would be cool, man, if you'd just let us be on our way. I'm not shitting you. We're on our way home."

"He been drinking?" Forbert nods toward Laferiere.

Stablein raises his hand and wiggles it from side to side. "You know."

"Yeah. I know. How about you?"

"Less, man. Less."

Forbert shakes his head. "Speeding, DUI." He shines a light on the kid, Sammy. "Providing alcohol to a minor, and you've got a headlight out. I should put you all in jail."

"That is fucking *it*," Laferiere says, throwing a big stress on the "it." "Give me a beer."

Cabella looks at Stablein, who shakes his head no.

"Now, goddamn it."

"Don't do it," Forbert says. "Don't get in deeper than you are."

Laferiere turns and reaches to the backseat. "Did you fucking hear me? Give me a beer. Now."

Cabella pulls a beer from the cardboard case and hands it to Laferiere.

"Don't be stupid," Forbert says.

Laferiere pops the top of the can and takes a long swallow, gulping until he drains it, then throws the can out the window.

"All right," Forbert says. "I want everyone out of the vehicle. Now." He hears a door open, and Stablein slides out the passenger's side. Then Cabella opens his door, steps out, and Sammy Colvington follows him. "Everyone's out, except you, Matt. Open the door and get out of the vehicle."

Laferiere slams his shoulder into the door and pops it open, making it hit Forbert on the right hip and knocking him to the ground. Forbert falls hard, drops his flashlight, the license, and the registration. As his hands slide across the ice at the side of the road, he can feel the small stones tearing at his hands.

Laferiere starts to laugh. "Sorry, shithead. I didn't mean to do that. I mean, really."

Forbert guesses that's true. The door of the Jeep does stick sometimes. He reaches down and feels his leg. His pants are torn, and he can feel blood dripping from his leg, as he starts to rise.

"You think this is funny, Matt? You think this is funny? You just assaulted a police officer."

"Hold it, hold it," Paul Stablein says, coming around the front of the Jeep. "Let's calm down. All of us."

"You get back there," Forbert says. "And sit down. All of you. You," he says to Laferiere. "You are going to jail."

"The fuck I am."

"You want to add resisting arrest to it? Are you fucking nuts? Get your hands on top of the vehicle."

Surprisingly, Laferiere does it, leaning into the Jeep with both hands on top of it. Forbert comes up behind him and takes Laferiere's right arm, pulling it down and snapping a cuff on it. Laferiere takes his left hand down, spins, and tries to backhand Forbert, who gets his left foot between Laferiere's feet and pulls Laferiere toward him as his body swings awkwardly, tripping him and sending him down, heavily, to the ground. Forbert lunges onto Laferiere's back and grabs the cuffed right wrist and tries to pull it back. Laferiere is bucking and trying to get traction with his feet.

Forbert hangs on to the right wrist and tries to get the left, but he has no leverage. Laferiere begins to crawl on his knees back down the road, away from the car, carrying Forbert with him. Finally, twisting in his heavy winter coat, Forbert slips off Laferiere's back. Laferiere struggles to rise, and Forbert comes up with him. Forbert is hanging on to the cuff on Laferiere's right wrist while Laferiere throws ineffective punches with his left hand. They are now playing a kind of tug-of-war with Laferiere's right arm. Laferiere is able to start Forbert struggling to his right. Forbert starts to move faster to his right, pulling Laferiere's arm hard across his chest.

Then they are doing a weird dance, moving in a circle, both of them with Laferiere's cuffed right wrist as the locus. They begin to move faster, each trying to wear the other down, until Forbert just lets go of Laferiere's wrist and sends him spinning, then stumbling across Forbert's outstretched leg and into the road where he slips and falls face-first. Forbert is calculating his next move as Laferiere rises to his knees and is suddenly brightly lit.

The car that has just come over the rise hits Matt Laferiere a glancing blow from the back and sends him airborne. It seems like seconds after the shatter of glass that Forbert hears the dull thud as Laferiere is sent pinwheeling into the back of his own Jeep.

The white car spins and straightens, travels a hundred yards down the road before the brake lights come on. Then the brake lights are out and Forbert is standing there, trying to get a plate number. The car vanishes over another hill. He has a J 6. A New York plate, he's pretty sure.

Forbert walks over to where Matt Laferiere is semi-kneeling at the back of the Jeep, his head canted upward and resting on the rear bumper, illuminated by the headlights of the cruiser. He reaches down to check Laferiere's pulse at the carotid artery when he realizes that Laferiere's head has been impaled on the Cherokee's trailer hitch and is split open. There's no need to check for a pulse. He's dead.

From behind him, he hears someone vomit, and then he's choking back vomit himself. The three others from the car have come up behind him to see what has happened. "Goddamn," one says. Then, "Goddamn, goddamn, goddamn" rising to a keening. There is nothing more to say.

"Back," he says, turning. "Get back."

"Dude," Bobby Cabella says. "Is he dead?"

Forbert pushes Cabella back and turns to Stablein and Colvington, who are six feet behind him. "What did you see?"

"You killed him, man."

"No. No. He fell."

"That's right," Stablein says. "I mean, I didn't really see it, but he fell. Out on the road. He's dead? Oh, fuck, man. Oh, fuck."

Cabella says, "That's right. He fell. I know that. You were trying to arrest him, and he fell on the ice."

Forbert switches on his shoulder mike. "Officer needs assistance. Route 417, mile eighty-two. Hit and run with fatality. Repeat. Officer needs assistance. Fatal accident at Route 417, mile eighty-two." He turns to the three now gathered together behind him, lighting cigarettes. "I was trying to arrest him. He resisted."

"Yeah," Stablein says. "You were trying to handcuff him."

Forbert looks back at the body. The right arm twisted behind Laferiere still has the cuff on it.

"It just happened, man. That's all. It happened."

"Did you see the car?" Forbert asks.

"That hit him? Yeah. It was a Camry. A white Camry."

"Maybe an Accord," Cabella says. "Going like a hundred miles an hour. Right over the hill. Never stopped. Didn't even slow down."

"White," Forbert says. "It was white."

"Yeah, man. White. For sure."

"Anyone catch the plate?"

"We were back there, man. Didn't see it. Couldn't see it."

"New York," Forbert says. "It was New York. A J and a 6."

"OK. You guys are witnesses. That's it. No charges. You're just witnesses."

"That's cool. Witnesses. We saw it happen. It was really fast."

Forbert hears the siren in the distance. It will be a couple of minutes before the car gets here. "Really fast," he says. "Really fast."

CHAPTER 2

GORDY HAWKINS HEARS THE MARIMBAS OF HIS PHONE FIRST IN his dream, then in his waking. "Chief," Pete says. Gordy bolts up. No one, especially not Pete, calls him Chief unless it's really bad.

"Chief, there's been an accident. You need to get up here. Route 417, quarter mile west of the Citgo."

"Bad?"

"Fatal. Hit and run. Officer involved. Ronny Forbert."

"Forbert? Dead?"

"No, no. He's OK. He was making an arrest when it happened. He's OK."

"A few minutes, Pete."

"Sorry to wake you, Gordy, but you need to be here."

"Right. Right. A couple of minutes."

Gordy turns on the edge of the bed to tell Bonita he has to go. He's momentarily startled to see her side of the bed still made. It's been more than six weeks since she's been there. Again he feels the hollowness inside him. He can't quite get used to it. He gets up, goes into the bathroom, and gets dressed.

HE CAN SEE THE GLOW OF THE LIGHTS FROM A LONG DISTANCE. THE Citgo is still nearly half a mile ahead, and the accident's a quarter mile beyond that. Every official vehicle in the town must be there. He's seen hundreds, maybe thousands, of accident scenes in his life. There is still something surreal about them at night, especially after being awakened, the lights, the bursts of flashlight on the suddenly destroyed, the responders moving in and out in their fluorescent coats. It never ceases to be strange.

He comes over the rise in the road and sees the flares with their ultra-red glow. Someone, John, he guesses, is directing traffic around the flares. Gordy goes around him. It is John, who nods grimly and points to a spot behind another cruiser. "So what do we have?" he asks Pete Mancuso, who is keeping onlookers who have stopped at the scene from getting in the way or getting a good look at someone's death.

"Hit and run. Fatal." Pete nods to where a couple of volunteer firefighters are holding up a blue tarp to shield the scene from passing traffic. "That was the point of impact." Pete motions toward a spot in the road littered with bits of glass.

"Skid marks?"

"Not really. Mostly black ice through here. If we had skid marks, they wouldn't tell us much."

"And Ronny?"

"Over there." Gordy turns and sees Ronny Forbert's back as he leans on his cruiser. "Pretty shook up," Pete says. "Otherwise, fine. Some scrapes and scratches."

"OK. What happened?"

"Traffic stop. Speeding. Driver DUI, uncooperative. Ronny tried to arrest him. There was a struggle, driver fell into the road and got hit by a westbound, speed excessive."

"All right. Everything is under control?"

"Roger that. The fatality is Matt Laferiere."

"Oh, shit."

"Yeah. Oh, shit. He was out with his homies. They're over there. The stories pretty much match up. Nothing seems too weird."

"Except that it's Matt Laferiere."

"Except that. We knew this day was coming. Here it is."

"What's Ronny saying?"

"Pretty much the same as the others. He tried to make an arrest. Laferiere got uncooperative. There was a struggle, and Laferiere wound up in the middle of the road. Hit and thrown into the back of his own vehicle."

"Ronny put him in the road?"

"No one seems to know. Not even Ronny. You want to see the body?"

"Do I need to?"

"Probably a good idea. It seems calm now, but given the nature of shit and fans, I don't think it's going to stay that way. Ronny says that Laferiere assaulted him before the attempted arrest."

"Shit."

"Headed for the fan, Gordy. Headed for the fan."

"Jesus Christ," Gordy says when they make their way around the tarp. The body is belly-up next to a body bag on the ground by the left rear wheel of the Cherokee. His arms are at his sides, palms up. Laferiere's head is split open.

"I hate when the insides end up on the outside," Pete says.

"This the way he was found?"

"No. He was belly-down, head, or what was left of it, resting on the Jeep. Went headfirst onto the trailer hitch." Pete indicates a large and dark pool of blood under the bumper of the Jeep. "EMTs moved him. We got pictures first. It seems like the more gore, the more questions that are going to get asked. Lots of questions here."

"Dead on impact, no doubt."

"No doubt. Though no one knows unless the M.E. can make some sense of what's left. The early thinking is that the H and R vehicle clipped him on the right side and threw him up into the Jeep. The impact with the Jeep did the killing. I'd guess that's pretty much right."

"What about the hit-and-run vehicle?"

"White. Maybe a Camry, maybe an Accord. Not new. Ronny got only a couple of figures off the plate—a *J* and a 6, New York."

"Not much to go on."

"Nope. I think this one's one big, fat, ugly bitch. Like I said, fans and shit."

"Ronny's clear on this?"

"Probably."

"Not certainly?"

"His story is OK. Laferiere wouldn't get out of the vehicle, and when he did, he hit Forbert with the door of the Jeep, knocking him down. There was a struggle when Forbert tried to cuff him, and then Laferiere ended up in the road where he met the Camry."

"You're not convinced."

"I'm never convinced."

"Understood."

"It all makes sense. I would be surprised only if Laferiere wasn't drunk and uncooperative. Ronny's probably clear on this. Should have called for backup, especially considering the circumstances."

"Obviously."

"How many times do you have to learn that lesson?"

"How many times it take you?"

"The usual. Too many. You need to take a look at the passengers over here."

"The usual posse?"

"Almost. We got a new one. A joker in the deck."

Gordy gives Pete a questioning glance.

"Sammy Colvington."

"Shit."

"Yeah. I would guess his father is going to be the fan."

GORDY TAKES ONE MORE LOOK AT THE BODY. WHEN IT ALL COMES down, the human body is a frail thing in a world of things that are strong, fast, and very unfrail. People can't seem to grasp the concept until they actually see what a car does to a human body when it hits it. Gordy knows Matt Laferiere well. He was a big bull of a kid, stocky and muscular, not bad looking, either. Now he looks as fragile as a dropped and stepped-on doll. He nods to the EMTs to lift the tarp back over the body. "Let's go talk to Ronny," he tells Pete. "The kids can wait."

Ronny is leaning up against his cruiser, talking to an EMT who peers at him like he's about to spill some secret. Pale, Ronny stares straight ahead as if the EMT isn't there. His uniform sleeve is ripped and hanging, and his trousers torn at the thigh. He's smoking a cigarette.

"How is he?" Gordy asks the EMT.

"OK. He's a little shocky. A couple of pretty good scrapes and scratches. Don't see any signs of concussion, but he needs checking overnight."

Gordy looks at Ronny, questioning.

"I messed up, Gordy. I really messed up."

"Never mind that right now. How are you feeling?"

Ronny puts the cigarette to his lips. His hand is shaking. Gordy's never seen him smoke before, and he has to suppress the urge to bum one from him.

"I'm OK. Don't need to go to the hospital."

"You need to get checked out. When did you start smoking?"

"High school. Haven't done it for a while."

"It's a good idea to take it up again," Pete says. "It'll provide you with a whole bunch of entertainment in your later years."

"You need to get checked out," Gordy says.

"No. No. I'm fine. I messed up is all."

"You remember what happened?"

Ronny looks at Gordy as if he asked the question in French. "I pulled them over for speeding. There was an open container and a strong smell of weed. They were all drinking. I got those three out of the car, but Matt wouldn't come out. When he did, I tried to cuff him. He fought me. We ended up on the ground, then he was on the road. The car came over the rise and hit him. It didn't stop. Didn't even really slow. It just sped up and got out of here."

"You call for backup?"

"No time. It just happened real fast. I wasn't even intending to arrest him, but he started to fight me. I didn't get the cuffs on him. Just one. I had to subdue him. There was no time."

"The car door. When did he hit you with the car door?"

"The car door? Right. He hit me with the car door. Knocked me down. I tore my pants. Right before, I guess. I don't really remember how it all happened. It was really fast. But right before."

Gordy nods. It's always fast. Really fast. You learn procedures to make sure that nothing gets out of hand. Once it gets out of hand, you're in it, and there isn't going to be any help.

"I want to transport him to the hospital," the EMT says.

"In a while. He's going, but you hang on for a bit."

"He could have a concussion. He needs observation. There's road rash on his arm and leg."

"He'll go. I promise. Just keep your shirt on."

Down the road to the east, Patrolman John North is waving cars on. Still, a few of them stop. Mostly they're gawkers, wanting to see the gore. You only have to see this kind of gore once to never want to see it again. "Pete. Get these people out of here."

Pete Mancuso is a hulking man, well over six feet, three hundred pounds plus. He had been a defensive tackle at LSU, not a starter, but on the team, nonetheless. Gordy is six feet, going quickly to fat and completely gray, but Pete seems to dwarf him. Pete is the sergeant, but often does the dirty work by virtue of his size.

"Ronny. Hang on," Gordy says. "I want to talk to the others. Don't go to the hospital yet."

"I'm not going to the hospital."

"Yes, you are. Only not right now. I'll be back in a minute or so."

PAUL STABLEIN, BOBBY CABELLA, AND THE COLVINGTON KID ARE SITting on the ground some ten yards off the road behind the Jeep. They're all smoking and staring into the distance, not looking at the body under the tarp. Gordy walks up and kneels in front of them. "You're all right? All of you?"

Stablein nods and Cabella mutters a weak "Yes."

"All of you?" Gordy looks at Sammy Colvington. The kid just nods in return.

"Just because you're not bleeding doesn't mean you're all right. Anyone need to see an EMT or a doctor?"

"We're OK," Stablein says.

"All right. Good. Let me know if at any time you think you may not be OK. You can get up if you want. Just don't do anything stupid. There's been enough stupidity tonight."

"What's going to happen to us?" Colvington asks.

"Haven't really decided yet. Be on your best behavior. Maybe things will work out for you. Maybe we'll take you back to the station. Or maybe we'll turn you over to your parents. A lot depends on how you answer my questions. Have your parents all been called?"

"We didn't really do anything," Cabella insists.

"You weren't drinking? You weren't smoking some weed? Before you answer, the car is full of empties, and I can smell the weed. You were drinking. Don't lie to me. It's the worst thing you can do. You've made enough mistakes for one night."

"A few beers," Stablein says. "We're not drunk. He gave me a couple of tests after it happened." He nods toward Ronny Forbert. "I passed."

"Laferiere drink all that beer?"

"A lot of it."

"I'll accept that for now. We're going to put you all on the Breathalyzer. All three of you. Maybe draw a little blood. It's what we do when there's been an accident with alcohol related. A bad accident."

"GORDY," JOHN NORTH, PATROLMAN, SAYS. "THERE'S A PARENT." JOHN put his hand on Gordy's shoulder as if consoling him.

"Laferiere?"

"No. Sam Colvington. You want to talk to him?"

"Not especially. But I will."

Sam Colvington is standing back behind Ronny Forbert's cruiser, inside the tape barrier. He's rumpled, a big parka over jeans and work boots. Just out of bed, no doubt. "What the hell happened?" he asks Gordy.

"Hit and run. One fatality. Your boy is fine. Unhurt. That's about all we have right now."

"Sammy was involved?"

"Indirectly, Sam. Indirectly. Nothing very serious. He was at the scene. That's pretty much the limit of it."

"Who got killed?"

"Can't really say until the parents are notified, but Sammy's all right. Not a scratch. He's over there. You can talk to him."

The three boys are still sitting, passing a cigarette back and forth, looking miserable. Sammy Colvington starts to look more miserable when he sees his father coming toward him.

"Are you all right?"

Sammy nods.

"You're sure?" Sam reaches down, takes the cigarette from Sammy's mouth, and tosses it away.

"Matt Laferiere is dead."

"That's not information to be shared," Gordy says. "Sammy and I have talked, and we're just about finished. I want to give him a Breathalyzer, then he's done here. You can take him home."

"No Breathalyzer," Sam Colvington says.

"Have to," Gordy says. "We need the whole picture of what happened. I doubt that the results are going beyond my desk. At this point, I don't see any reason to charge Sammy with anything. And I think he needs to go home and get some sleep. As soon as John's done with the test, you can take him."

"I said, 'No Breathalyzer.'"

"Sam, you don't want to do this. If you refuse the Breathalyzer, he gets charged. We draw blood. He goes to court. I promise you I'll do everything I can to keep the results under wraps. But if you refuse, I can't do that. I'll have to take him in, and it will be on the public record."

"Are you drunk?" Colvington asks Sammy. Sammy waves his hand back and forth. Maybe, maybe not.

"That sounds right to me," Gordy says.

"If this gets out, it will be your job," Colvington says. "I can make your life miserable."

"Like I said, I have no intention of bringing charges. I can't promise that won't happen as the investigation moves forward, but right now, I don't see it. That's all I can tell you."

Colvington turns away in obvious disgust. Gordy takes that as assent.

"Pete, get John on the Breathalyzers."

"John's gone to get the Laferieres. But Steve's here. I'll get him on it."

"Good. Then search the vehicle. You guys," he says to the three waiting on the ground. "You're going to have to blow into the Breathalyzer. Then we'll release you to your parents or someone else who can take you home. We're pretty much done with you."

IT'S ANOTHER HALF AN HOUR BEFORE JOHN PULLS HIS CRUISER BACK into the accident scene. He gets out and opens the back doors.

Gordy watches Roger Laferiere get out, followed by his wife, Gayle. Roger is a tall rangy man, dressed in jeans and canvas coat, cap pulled down tight on his head. Gordy has never seen him without a cap on. He walks with a pronounced limp, the product of an industrial accident some years earlier. Gayle is also thin, nearly gaunt. She's wearing jeans and a Giants sweatshirt. Gordy hopes she's got plenty on underneath it. There's still a chance of snow tonight.

"Roger, Gayle. Sorry to be seeing you under these circumstances."

"Where's my boy?" Gayle asks.

"On his way to the hospital."

"He's hurt?"

Gordy looks over at John, who looks down and shrugs apologetically. Gordy is nonplussed. How did John not tell them? How did they not ask? "I'm afraid it's worse than that."

"Dead?" Roger asks.

"There was an accident. A hit and run. I'm afraid Matthew didn't survive. It was instantaneous. I don't think he suffered at all." Gordy grimaces at the inadequacy. But what is there to say that's not inadequate? He's delivered hundreds of these messages, all inadequate. "I'm very, very sorry for your loss." The Laferieres exchange looks of incomprehension.

"You said he was at the hospital," Gayle says.

"He is, but I'm afraid he didn't make it. He'll be examined and pronounced dead, then sent to the morgue."

"The morgue?" Gayle repeats as though she has not heard that Matt is dead.

"Yes. I'm afraid so. There will be an examination, and then they will turn the body over to you. I hope that won't be very long."

"Can we see him?" Gayle asks. Her voice is the calm, steady voice of someone who is not going to accept this yet.

"I wouldn't advise it. It was a terrible accident."

"They're not going to cut him up."

"There'll be an autopsy. It's the law."

"No. No. You can't do that."

"I'm afraid we have no choice. This was a hit and run. It's a criminal case. He was hit by a hit-and-run driver. There's going to be a trial."

"You have the one that hit him?"

"Not yet. We will. There will be a trial, and the person who hit him will go to jail. That's pretty much certain. But an autopsy is part of that. The law."

"When can we see him?"

"Again. I don't advise you to see him. He was very badly hurt. I don't think you want to see him that way."

"When can we see him?"

Gordy nods sadly. "Tomorrow, maybe. But think about it."

Roger glares at Gordy, then turns and walks to the Jeep. There is still blood, hair, and tissue on the Jeep. Gordy isn't sure what other matter has been left behind.

"Chief," Steve Holt says. "Can I see you for a minute?"

Gordy excuses himself and walks over to Steve.

"Thought you might want to see the Breathalyzer results." He hands Gordy a sheet of paper—Cabella .11, Colvington .14, Stablein .093. "What do you want to do with these guys?"

"Let Colvington go home with his father. Keep the others. If no one shows up to take them home, take them back to the station. Don't charge them yet."

And then Roger Laferiere is in front of Gordy, again. "He says that Ronny Forbert was in on this."

"Who says?"

Laferiere points to John North, who has been shepherding the Laferieres around the scene.

"Officer Forbert was making the arrest when the accident occurred."

"They was friends."

"Yes, I believe that's true."

"Nothing worse than friends that go bad on each other."

Gordy starts to say something, then stops. That's pretty much the truth. Affection often stirs violence into the stew of disagreement. Gordy nods. "John, take the Laferieres home, please."

"We'll stay."

"No. There's no reason. We're just going to collect some evidence and get this cleaned up. I'm sorry, but there's nothing you can do here. John, take the Laferieres home."

"I'll drive the Jeep," Roger says.

"No. Can't let you do that. It's evidence. When we're done with it, I'll have it delivered to you. You go on with John." He watches them go to John's cruiser, Gayle in the lead, striding hard, fast, angry, and straight ahead. Roger follows, limping slowly behind, shoulders down. Farther to the east he can see the amber lights of the wrecker coming for the Jeep.

"Chief," Pete says. He's carrying a bundle wrapped in cloth. "You need to see this." He unwraps the bundle. There are two handguns—a Colt 1911, .45 automatic, and a .357 Magnum. There's ammo, too. "Under the seat, driver's side."

"God," Gordy says. "When you think it can't get any worse, you find out it could have been. Bag those."

"YOU'RE SURE YOU'RE ALL RIGHT?" SAM COLVINGTON ASKS HIM.

"Yeah, I'm OK," Sammy says.

"That Forbert lay hands on you?"

"No. He told me what to do and I did it."

Sam, sometimes "Big Sam," considers this as he drives them back into Lydell city limits. Then he shoots out his right hand fast enough that his son has no chance to duck or block the blow that catches him on the cheek and nose, making him see sparks in the darkness. "You dumb shit," his father says.

Sammy puts his hand up to gingerly touch his face, the burn of the blow just starting to spread across it. He turns his head toward the car window so that his face will be protected if his father sends another shot his way. He can just make out the outlines of bare trees flashing past the car window.

"You're riding around in the middle of the night with that bunch of punks, drinking beer and smoking grass. You're lucky you're not dead. You're lucky I don't kill you."

Punks. For a second Sammy sees an image of Matt, Paul, and Bobby, in leather and torn denim. Bright Mohawks and lots of piercings. "Matt's dead."

"Yeah. Good riddance. That guy is a piece of shit. Always was. What the hell are you doing riding around with a bunch of guys who are older than you?"

Being cool, Sammy thinks. Being not your son. Being anyone but Sam Colvington Jr. "Just hanging out," he says.

"Hanging out. Shit. I ought to stop this car and beat the crap out of you. Then you can hang out. See how you like it. You know what you've done to me tonight? You've damned near ruined me. You've lowered me in the eyes of the community. I'm a community leader. I'm on the town council. When Martin runs for state office,

I'll be the next president. At least, I was going to be. But all anyone thinks now is that I can't even control my own kid."

"Sorry," Sammy says. Then he thinks, You can't control your own kid. You'll never be able to control your kid, because I'm not a kid anymore.

"You know what those guys are? You know?"

"Punks," Sammy says.

"Bums. They're fucking bums. They don't have real jobs. They just 'hang out,' drinking beer and smoking grass and riding around town being bums. Is that what you want? You want to be a bum?"

Yeah, Sammy thinks. I want to be a bum. I want to hang out with guys who get me, who aren't saps to the system. Guys who don't walk around with their noses up Martin Glendenning's ass. You're goddamned, fucking right I want to be a bum. He says, "I don't know. Matt's dead."

"Get over it," his father says. "It's no loss."

CHAPTER 3

(DAY ONE)

RONNY FORBERT SITS IN THE WAITING ROOM OF WARRENTOWN Hospital, drinking a Coke and picking at the leg of his trousers, working at the flap of fabric where they tore. A nurse has given him a couple of safety pins to keep the torn fabric from flopping around, but his fingers keep going to it, maybe after the scabbed, scraped skin under the bandage. On his arm, he has more safety pins, more bandages, and more scraped skin. He has a headache, and he feels like he had exactly the fight he was in last night.

He finishes the Coke and goes back to the small snack bar, buys another and a banana that has a little too much brown on it. He keeps looking at the entrance door to the emergency wing, the way everyone else does, waiting for someone to take them out of here.

He slept in the emergency ward last night. Or, rather, he didn't sleep in the ward last night. Either someone kept coming in to ask

the same questions over and over, or he was listening to the scream-
ing of an obese man who kept demanding dinner because he knew
his rights and he had been there for more than four hours. When
someone brought him a sandwich, he became enraged and threat-
ened to sue the hospital because he was entitled to a hot meal.

Just shut the fuck up, he thought, listening to the ranting, his
jaw clenching and teeth grinding as he lay behind the curtained
enclosure, then caught himself. He had watched someone die just a
few hours ago. That's where anger led, to violence and destruction.
He wanted no more of it.

EVERY TIME THE DOOR TO THE OUTSIDE OPENS, EVERY HEAD TURNS
to it. Then all but one turn back to what they had been doing, or
not doing. Finally, it is Ronny's turn to rise as Pete Mancuso makes
his way through the door. Ronny sets down his Coke can and rises
to meet Pete.

"How you all doing this morning?" Pete asks.

"Good. A little sore and tired, but OK."

"Good. Let's get out of here. I hate hospitals. I was worried I was
going to have to wait until you got checked out."

"No. That happened about an hour ago. They try to push them
through the door as fast as they can."

"That's fine by me. You eat yet?"

"I had a Coke and some sweet rolls and a banana."

"What? Are you on the Gordy Hawkins diet?"

"I could use a couple more pounds."

"Too bad Gordy can't give you some of his."

"You're not skinny, Sarge."

"That's Pete, not 'Sarge.' And I was a defensive lineman at a major college. This is what I'm supposed to look like. It's my natural state."

"LSU Tigers."

"You been studyin'. Let's get something to eat, then head back to the office. I think you've got kind of a busy day. You up for that?"

"Yeah. I'm fine. Just some road rash."

"That's not the 'fine' I'm worried about. You watched someone die last night."

"Yeah. I'm good."

RONNY WAITS UNTIL THE WAITRESS HAS FILLED THEIR COFFEES AND taken their orders. "Can we stop at Dunkin' Donuts for some good coffee?"

"Dunkin' Donuts don't have good coffee. We have to go to Starbucks for that. Besides, I've lived my life not conforming to clichés. No Dunkin' Donuts."

"Pete, how did you come to be named Mancuso?" It was not the question he had wanted to ask. He couldn't make himself ask the real question yet.

"The usual way. The way you got to be named Forbert. It was my daddy's name. What you want to know is how did a black man come to be a Mancuso. My daddy, a good Eastern Italian, went to Louisiana in the seventies to find work on the oil rigs. His name was Pete Mancuso, too. While he was down there, he met a genuine Creole queen who weaved a spell he would never be able to break. When the jobs ran out there, he brought the whole family back up here. And that's how you got a fine ebony Mancuso in Lydell."

"Did your grandparents object? I mean, interracial marriage and all?"

"Hell, yes. But probably not the way you're thinking. My mother was Creole, and Creole is special. Creole's got long bloodlines and regal history. My grandfather, my momma's daddy, was furious that she took up with some white Eyetalian Yankee polluting our fine gene pool. He turned his back on her and wouldn't even talk to her when she announced she was getting married to Pete Mancuso."

"Did he ever talk to her?"

"One night, she and Daddy was sleeping. I was there then, too, but I don't remember it, only the hearing of it. The doorbell rang and my daddy went downstairs, and then he came back up to bed holding a yellow envelope. A Western Union telegram for my momma. You can bet she opened that envelope with trembling hands."

"Why?"

"Back then, a telegram in the night could only mean bad news. Now it means that someone's gone your bail. Anyway, my momma opened the telegram and read it. It said, 'So, Lavinia [stop] Just how cold IS a well digger's ass? [stop] Love Dad.'"

"You ever meet your grandfather?"

"A couple times. He died before I turned ten."

"Am I going to get fired?"

"Probably not. Gordy and I haven't discussed it, but I would guess you won't. The only thing we can figure that you did wrong was failing to call for backup, and I know that I take some of the blame for that. The one time you did, I went two feet up your ass, which was my mistake. I think you'll be getting some time off."

"A suspension?"

"Likely. A week, maybe. But maybe not. I don't know. That's entirely up to Gordy. He'll discuss it with me, but he will do what he thinks is right. I would probably go to the long end of that, just to keep it in your memory, but Gordy won't ask me. He'll tell me."

"I really fucked up."

"You fucked up. That's enough."

"When someone gets killed, you really fucked up. I really fucked up."

"Let me go back and clarify myself here," Pete says. "You made a mistake. Matt Laferiere and the driver of the hit-and-run car, they fucked up. Not you."

Ronny lets out a long exhalation. "I killed Matt Laferiere."

"No. The hit-and-run driver killed Matt Laferiere. You were an agent in a complicated accident. Stop feeling sorry for yourself. That's probably the worst thing you can do right now. Take your medicine when Gordy gives it to you and pull yourself back together and be ready to come back to work when Gordy says you can.

"And more. Call your father and that fine girlfriend of yours. Set their minds at ease. Lydell is a small town. About now, everyone in town is aware of what happened last night. Don't let your loved ones spend more time than they need to worrying about you."

EVERYONE JUST LOOKS UP WHEN RONNY AND PETE ENTER THE DOOR. Expressionless, no one says a thing until Pete says, "The prodigal has returned. Bandaged." Then there are smiles and "how are you feelings" enough that for several seconds he is just repeating, "Fine, fine, fine." Sue, the day dispatcher, comes out of her closet-sized cubicle and gives him a hug, then the men shake his hand and pat his shoulder. He is welcomed back into the world.

Gordy stays at his desk in his office, watching the scene from his open door, smiling, and when the other expressions of welcome are finished, he motions Ronny to come in. "Close the door," he says when Ronny is inside.

"I'm OK," Ronny says.

"Good. That's good. I'm glad to hear it. Sit down."

"I fucked up. I know it."

"It was a serious breach of procedure. Make no mistake about that. But don't take too much responsibility for what happened. It was an accident. There were lots of factors involved—alcohol, drugs, bad weather, a speeding driver on a road with terrible sight lines. But as soon as you saw you had four potentially unruly drunks on your hands, you should have called for backup. Immediately. But your mistake was a part, not the whole. And frankly, there's no guarantee that calling for backup would have made any difference. Probably not. Things happen, and they happen fast. Nevertheless, you made a mistake. There are consequences from that."

"I know. Pete told me."

Gordy says nothing for a moment. "Five-day suspension, without pay."

"Pete thought I might not get suspended."

"Pete was wrong. It's a stiff penalty for failure to call for backup, but there was a fatality involved." Gordy puts up his hand to stop Ronny from responding. "I know. I just said it probably had little or nothing to do with the accident. But we live in two worlds. One world is a world of cause and effect. Excessive speed on a bad road leads to bad consequences. But what we do afterward can lead to bad perceptions in the political world.

"I don't have to run for election, or campaign, but I'm still part of the political world in Lydell. I serve at the pleasure of the town council, as you do. The town council also appropriates all of the funds for the department—your salary, Pete's, mine. All of it."

He picks up a pencil. "We have to ask the council for pencils, for Christ's sake. So the town keeps a close eye on us. In large part, we are the government of Lydell. I can't risk the perception that we let things slide here. So I'm suspending you, because that's the punishment for failing to follow procedure, and I'm suspending you for five days to let everyone, including you and the council, know that I'm serious about following procedure."

"All right."

Gordy regards him for a moment with the look of a parent disappointed in his child. "I'll need your weapon, too."

"Why?"

"Because you're on suspension. You're still a cop, but you're not. You have no need to carry a weapon." He holds out his hand, waiting for Ronny give it up.

When he does, Gordy extracts the magazine, checks the chamber for a live round, then holds the gun up and squints at it. He turns it in his hand a couple of times.

"What's wrong?"

"Nothing. Trying to read the serial number."

"I can read it for you."

Gordy paws at his desk for his glasses. When he finds them under some papers, he puts them on and turns on the desk lamp. He studies the numbers then writes them down. When he is done, he picks up the form he has been writing on, tears off a copy, and hands it to Ronny. "Your receipt," he says.

"Why do I have to give up my gun?"

"I told you. For the next five days, you're not a working cop. You're a cop, but not a working one. You're not authorized to carry a weapon. Also for your own safety."

"My safety?"

"Standard in cases where the officer is involved in a fatal."

"You think I'm going to kill myself?"

"No. But we try to deal with all possible events, not just the likely ones. It's procedure, Ronny. Procedure."

"Any other procedures?"

"You're going to have to fill out a report. You can wait until tomorrow, but no longer than that. OK? Let me know when you're ready."

"I'll do it now."

"Are you sure? You don't want a little time to think about it, to get it all straight in your head?"

"It's straight in my head."

"All right. Remember, this is the official version of what happened. If you make a mistake, it could come back to haunt you. I'm going to advise you to wait, to think it through a couple of times. Come back and do it tomorrow. Write it out, then let it rest a few hours before you read it over. A suggestion, not an order."

"But it's what you want me to do?"

"Yes. It's my suggestion to you."

"Tomorrow then?"

"Yes, tomorrow. Things will be better tomorrow. Take today and pull yourself together. Talk to your loved ones. Reassure them that you're all right. Reassure yourself. Get your thoughts in order and come back tomorrow."

Ronny nods as if Gordy has just given him a lecture on quantum physics. He turns and goes back into the main office. He can feel the absence of his weapon on his right hip. He feels off balance.

GORDY FEELS SORRY FOR THE KID. HE REALLY DOES. HE DOESN'T want to make more of this than it is, to make Ronny feel worse than he does. He doesn't want to freeze him up with the enormity of what has happened. This is going to be with Ronny the rest of his life.

It was 1963, Fort Bliss, Texas. Gordy was a private first class in the MPs. He liked the job. It seemed like something important, even when his primary job was pulling drunk soldiers out of bars in El Paso and Ciudad Juarez, though, officially, they never crossed the border. It was also often an interesting job, with changes of scenery and assignment. Usually. Not this night.

Gordy was in a patrol on watch over a convoy that had rolled in from the east. The cargo was top secret, which meant that it was more than likely nuclear. They were in an especially tense part of the Cold War, just months past the Cuban missile crisis. Everyone was moving nuclear weapons around, searching for the strategic upper hand.

That was the thinking. All Gordy had been told was that no one, no one, was to go near the convoy. They were authorized to shoot on sight. Gordy was walking the southern perimeter, a good assignment considering it was cold in that southern Texas way when the clear sky made for a sharp and brittle night. Walking was far better than taking up a stationary position.

He saw the shape moving in front of him, heading south toward the fence. He immediately ordered whoever it was to halt and identify. Instead the shape lurched forward, doing an awkward run as it carried something in its arms. He again ordered it to halt. It did not, and Gordy fired.

There was not enough light to see exactly what happened. The shape went down, and Gordy moved cautiously forward, M1 at the ready. He came to the spot where the shape had gone down and found no one. He headed south, flashlighting the ground, occasionally illuminating spots of blood. He found the hole cut in the fence, and found blood on the fence as well. He went back to where he had seen the person fall. There were two other MPs there now, standing over nothing but a box of nails spattered with blood.

They spent most of the night searching for the source of the blood. It was, almost surely, a Mexican who had come across to steal supplies from the base. Nails. They found the blood trail and followed it through the hole in the fence. But they found no one. Whether he, the wounded man, had made it back to the river and up into Ciudad Juarez, or had moved east into El Paso, or had died somewhere they could not find, no one knew.

Gordy has dreamed about it for years. There was a lot of blood. But it was reasonable to believe that the man had survived. Still, he didn't know. He pulled a tour in Vietnam, again in the MPs, moving up the ranks. He never fired another shot at anyone, not as an MP, not as a cop back in the States. People ask occasionally if he ever killed anyone. He doesn't know. He only knows that the dreams will start up again.

He wants Ronny Forbert to have some certainty, some clarity. Ronny was involved in a death, but he did not cause the death. Once Ronny has that clearly embedded in his mind, he will be all right. It will also take a long time.

SAMMY COLVINGTON IS HAVING BREAKFAST. MOSTLY HE'S SWIRLING Cheerios through milk, mashing the occasional one with a spoon against the side of the bowl. It's a strange thing. He's hungry but he doesn't want to eat. He takes a spoonful of cereal and puts it in his mouth. He chews a couple of times, then forces himself to swallow. He reaches for the sugar bowl and spoons more sugar into the cereal.

"You all right?" his father asks.

He shrugs. "Guess so."

"Hungover?"

"Not really," he lies.

"You thinking about what happened last night?"

"Yeah," he lies again. Mostly he's trying hard not to think about last night.

"You better think about it. You need to get your story straight. I talked to Martin Glendenning this morning. He's concerned. He wants you to get your story straight. He needs you to tell our side."

What's "our side," he thinks. He saw a guy die last night. His friend. He saw his friend die. Where are the sides to that? For his father and Martin Glendenning, it's all about sides. There are always two sides to any story. Where do they get this shit?

He's sick of his father, and he's sick of Martin Glendenning. Half the kids at school think he's a stuck-up rich kid because his father is on the town council. The other half think he's a complete asshole for the same reason. Fuck them both.

But Sammy keeps running it through his head. It's like a dream. He can't shake it, but he can't quite hold on to it, either. The more his father keeps at him to remember the details, exactly what happened, the less sure he becomes about it. He isn't sure he saw exactly what happened. It was all very sudden and he was drunk. He remembers the lights, the way the headlights of the car suddenly lit the whole scene, Matt trying to scramble up, having trouble getting his feet under him, then the amazing sight of Matt flying through the air and the horrible thump at the end as he hit the Jeep.

Had he seen the fight between Matt and Forbert? Some of it. He knows they were struggling. He remembers their arms tangling and untangling. But the car hid much of what went on. He saw Matt go out onto the highway, and he saw the lights suddenly appear over the hump in the road. He has lots of pictures in his head. One- or two-second film clips. But he can't put them together in the right way. His father keeps assuring him that he will be able to, but he was drunk last night. Very drunk. It was all messed up. Messed up bad.

"Matt's dead," he says.

"Matt was a piece of shit, and he got killed by an even bigger piece of shit. You remember that."

Maybe Matt was a piece of shit. Maybe he's a piece of shit, too. But Matt Laferiere and the others were the only ones who didn't treat him like a piece of shit. Even though he was the "virgie," Matt and the others treated him right. Like he was someone. This is so fucking messed up.

RONNY DOES WHAT PETE TOLD HIM TO DO. HE LEAVES THE STATION, feeling the emptiness on his right hip where he keeps his weapon. As he climbs into his truck he suddenly feels a great weariness. He parked the truck here a little over twelve hours ago, but it seems he hasn't been in it for weeks.

His truck is his favorite possession, certainly his largest and most expensive. It's a Dodge 1500 four-by-four. He bought it the day after he graduated from the academy, the day before he was hired on full-time as a Lydell cop. He struggles to make the payments, but he won't consider giving it up for something cheaper. It is the first nice, new thing he has ever owned.

His apartment is cold. Usually coming off the night shift, it takes a couple of hours for him to settle down enough for sleep, so he keeps the heat low, only turning it up when he gets home. It's a small apartment, the upper floor of a two-story garage that belongs to Nathan Greene, the pharmacist, who lives in the house in front of the garage. The furnishings are sparse. Most came with the apartment. The only thing that's his is a forty-inch flat-screen TV that sits on the stand they threw in to sweeten the deal.

He thinks about having the TV attached to the wall, but he likes knowing he can just pick it up and take it with no hassle. He could, if he wanted, be completely out of the apartment in two hours.

He kicks up the heat and makes a pot of coffee, though he is not particularly fond of it. It's Starbucks Sumatra, Vanessa's choice, pre-ground in deference to him and her only contribution to the apartment, though she stays over at least once a week. He stays at her place about the same, maybe more, especially if he has the weekend off. He prefers his place because it's closer to the station, and he wants to be ready to respond in a hurry if there is an emergency, but hers is nicer. The only emergency they've had in the months he's been on the force was last night, and he was right in the middle of it.

He calls Nessa while the coffee brews. At just two rings he gets voice mail. "Hi. There was a bad accident last night," he says. "I was involved in it. I'm OK. I spent the night in the hospital, but I'm OK. Call me." He clicks the call screen off, relieved that he didn't have to tell Vanessa he had killed her old boyfriend, but still dreading the conversation.

He goes into the bedroom to shower and change his clothes. He tries to keep the bandages on his leg and forearm dry, but it's impossible. He'll have to go to the drugstore later and get gauze and tape, but for now he pats them dry and hopes they'll stay on to keep the wounds from bleeding into his pants and shirt.

Both his pants and shirt are ripped. That looks like another hundred or so dollars. Maybe the dry cleaner's can mend them, but he's afraid they'll never look right again. He puts on a T-shirt and his other pair of tactical pants, then a sweatshirt. He takes out his dress shoes, which are shined to a high luster, and wears them, though they look ridiculous with the pants. He checks his boots to see how much damage they took last night. They're badly scuffed, but he's sure he can salvage them.

He goes back to the kitchen, pours a cup of coffee, and carefully wipes up the drops that spill and the bits of grounds around the pot. Then he takes a paper towel and rubs the surface of the coffeemaker, removing a couple of smudges. He takes the coffee into the living room and turns on the TV. ESPN *SportsCenter*. He's not a big sports fan, of any kind. But he lives in a world where it seems everyone is a sports fan. So he watches ESPN and tries to remember things. The Steelers are the most important. They're going to make the play-offs. And the Patriots, too. The Jets and the Giants don't have a chance. He can use that when he finally gets back to the office.

There's a stack of *Law and Order* magazines on the coffee table. He studies these, too. It's a continuation of his AA in criminal justice. He sorts them by date, then restacks them on the coffee table, newest issues on top.

When his coffee cup is empty, he takes it back to the kitchen, rinses it, washes and dries it, and puts it back in the cupboard. There are four mugs there, in different but complementing colors. He keeps them in a line, each handle just touching the mug to its right. Then he pushes the coffeemaker back on the counter and aligns it with the toaster. He reaches into the cabinet under the sink and takes a bottle of 409 and a sponge and washes the counter and the sink, working on the faucets and handles. Because they are old and scratched, he pays particular attention, bringing up a shine where there is still chrome plating left. Then he takes the 409 and heads into the bathroom and goes to work on the shower, sink, and toilet. Later he will sweep and mop the floors. He does this every day. It will take him two hours, which means he will be done by eleven. It is going to be a long five days.

When he comes back into the bedroom, he sees the boots he had set aside. He gets his polishing kit from the closet, carries it and the boots into the kitchen, where he unlaces the boots. He pours a bowl of water from the faucet, takes a rag, wets it, and begins wiping the shoes to get off the dust and mud. Then he takes another rag, coats it with saddle soap, and scrubs each boot to get the grit and salt off. When that's done, he opens a can of polish, sets a match to it, and lets it burn for a few seconds before he puts the lid back on and douses the flame. Then he takes a cloth, dips it in the now liquid polish, and begins rubbing it into the leather. That done, he buffs the boots, then starts the process over again. He does this until he has five coats of polish buffed to a high shine. He washes the bootlaces in the sink and drapes them over the kitchen faucet to dry. He has used up forty-eight minutes.

He checks his phone. Two calls from Nessa, one from his father. He swipes the screen and turns the phone off, puts it in his back pocket, then pulls it out again and dials Nessa's number. He wants and dreads to talk with her. It rings twice and goes to voice mail. She's in class. "Hi," he says. "It's me. I'm home. I have the day off. Give me a call. I guess you heard what happened. I'm OK. Give me a call."

He's trying to repair his pants, but he has no skill with a needle and thread. He will have to take them to the dry cleaner's, who will send them to a tailor in Warrentown. Or buy a new pair. The shirt has to go to the cleaner's as well. Buying a new uniform will take more money than he should be spending right now. He lays out the torn uniform for the dry cleaner's.

When the phone rings he answers it immediately, expecting Nessa. He's surprised when he hears his father's voice.

"Are you all right?"

"Yeah. I'm fine. A little road rash, nothing more."

"That's good. I was worried when I got your call. I had heard there was an accident, but I didn't hear any details."

Ronny is relieved to hear his father sounding sober. "Matt Laferiere got killed last night."

"Yeah. I just heard that. I know he was your friend. I'm sorry."

"Not so much anymore. Friend, I mean. We didn't have much in common."

"Still. It must be hard. But you're OK. What happened?"

"I was trying to arrest him. Drunk and disorderly. We fought. He ended up in the road and got hit by a hit-and-run driver. Dead at the scene."

"Well, glad to hear you're OK. I have to get back to work. Big remodel north of Warrentown. Don't know where people get the money, but glad they do."

His father is a finish carpenter and master cabinetmaker. He had wanted Ronny to join him in the business, but Ronny couldn't take the idea of a life of sawdust and cutoff fingers for almost no money at all. Just living from one bottle to the next.

THE LAFERIERES LIVE ON TWISTED ROOT ROAD, A DIRT ROAD THAT was once a wagon trail. There was contention about whether it was an actual town road, but the town has been plowing it for as long as

Gordy can remember, so he guesses it is. There are only two houses and the ruins of a nineteenth-century spring factory on the road. The Laferieres live just beyond the ruins.

It's a rambling mess of a place that sprawls over two acres. The center of it is a double-wide trailer that has been added on to three or four times. The additions jut out at odd angles. Roger Laferiere is a decent builder, but a terrible architect. There are three outbuildings, two of which seem to be chicken coops and the other a tack room or shop. There are junked cars, trucks, and tractors scattered about and old farm implements rusting into the ground. There has been an epidemic of thefts of farm equipment, but this stuff is far too old to be part of that.

Gordy parks the cruiser next to the house, or whatever it is, and walks to the front door and knocks. It's a chore he's performed many times before. There's no answer. He knocks again, waits a bit, and turns toward the cruiser. There is a beaten but intact Ford F150 between the house and the chicken shacks, so he assumes that at least one of the Laferieres is home. He walks between the cruiser and the truck, toward the shack, calling, "Hello."

"Chief."

He turns to see Roger Laferiere walking from the direction of the shop building. Roger's dressed just as Gordy had last seen him, and as he always sees him—jeans and boots, a barn coat covered in grease and torn at both sleeves (in summer this is replaced by a cotton long-sleeved shirt). He always wears a battered, billed plaid cap.

"Good morning, Roger."

"Not a goddamned thing good about it." Roger puts a cigarette to his lips and lights it. Out of habit, Gordy guesses, Roger extends the pack toward Gordy, who waves it off.

"Well, no. Of course not. I'm so sorry, Roger."

Roger nods and tilts his head waiting to hear more from Gordy.

"Mostly, I'm here to offer my condolences, something I should have done more of last night. I'm terribly, terribly sorry for your loss."

Roger nods, starts to say something, then stops.

"I also have some information for you. The autopsy is being performed this morning, and they should release Matt's body to you by late this afternoon."

"They cut him up?"

"I'm sorry. It's the law. There's no way around it. I can't do anything to stop it."

"Why do they do that?"

"Like I said. The law. This is a criminal case, and there will have to be evidence presented in court."

"Against who?"

"Whoever killed him. The driver of the car. We don't know, yet, who that is, but we will soon."

Roger again starts to say something and stops. He takes the cigarette from his mouth and crushes it into the ground with his boot.

He hears a woman's voice behind him. "It was Ronny Forbert who killed him."

Gordy spins around to face Gayle Laferiere, who has come up behind him. "Gayle. I came to express my condolences."

"Ronny Forbert is who killed him. He wasn't driving the car, but he killed my boy."

"No, Gayle. That's not true. There was a struggle, sure. But Ronny did not kill your son."

"We'll come to find something different. We got a case against this town on this."

"No, Gayle. I don't think you have a case. It's a clear-cut hit and run."

"Martin says we have a case."

"Martin? Martin Glendenning?"

"He said so. And he knows. He's president of the town council. He says we got a case against you, the town, and Ronny Forbert."

"He told you that?"

"He was just here. He told us that. Ronny Forbert is an incompetent moron, and he got the job on the police force because he was your pet."

"Gayle, none of that is true."

"Martin says it is."

"I can't believe he would say that. Martin's wrong about a lot of things, but on this one he's really wrong. You need to talk to a good lawyer."

"We're going to do that."

"I also came to tell you that you can claim Matt's body this afternoon."

"They cut him up," Roger says.

"Of course they did. Goddamn you, Gordon Hawkins. Why won't you leave my boy alone? You tormented him when he was alive and now you're still at it when he's dead. I suppose you're on your way over to the hospital right now, just so you can piss on his body. Goddamn you, Mr. Hawkins. This ain't over. Not by a long shot."

IT'S SO MESSED UP. ALL DAY AT SCHOOL KIDS KEEP COMING UP TO Sammy, asking him about the accident. He doesn't want to talk about it, but everyone wants to know.

"Did you see it happen?"

"Yes," he says, but he's not sure he really did. See it. He's not sure he actually saw the car hit Matt. He saw it drive away, but he's not sure what he actually saw. His vision was partially blocked by the car. He saw something. He saw something, saw Matt come flying, but even now he's not sure. He lies. "I saw the whole thing. Really messed up. Really, really fucking messed up."

"It knocked his head off, didn't it? You saw that, didn't you?"

"No. It smashed his head." This he saw, afterward. It was the worst thing he has ever seen.

"You saw his brains?"

"Yes." He has a clear image of blood and gore. Maybe his brain in all of that mess. He remembers Matt's teeth scattered in the blood. Maybe an eye. He doesn't want to talk about it, but everyone else does.

"Really? His head smashed to pieces. Whoa, dude. How fucking cool."

No. Not cool. Just fucked up. Really fucked up. He starts telling the story. Matt flying through the air until he hit the Jeep head-first. His head smashed open like a Halloween pumpkin. At first he thinks he is going to throw up again. But as he keeps telling the story, he feels better, like it was something from a movie, something he saw in some movie. He keeps telling it and telling it.

In class, he can't concentrate. He tries to draw it on lined paper in his notebook, but he can't. There's too much. He walks out of class.

"Hey, Colvington. Tell me, man. Tell me what you saw."

Just messed up. Completely fucking messed up.

WHEN GORDY GETS BACK TO THE OFFICE, MARTIN GLENDENNING IS talking with Pete. He can't quite read Pete's expression: angry, disgusted, but more than that.

"Gordon," Martin Glendenning says when he sees Gordy. "How are you doing this morning, Gordon?"

Gordy just stares at Martin for several seconds, then shakes his head. "How do you think I'm doing? I just talked with the Laferieres."

"Tragic," Martin says. "It's just a tragedy. What a horrible thing. For the Laferieres. For you. For all of us. All of Lydell."

Gordy starts to turn his back on Martin and walk into his office. He gets two steps and turns. "Martin, did you tell the Laferieres they should sue the town, and me?"

"Gordon. Of course not. Of course I didn't. I spoke with them. Expressed my condolences. The town's condolences."

"The Laferieres said you told them to sue the town."

"No, Gordon. I did tell them that there might be legal ramifications about what happened. But no, I didn't tell them to sue. Why would I do a thing like that? I mean, the poor people. They're dealing with enough right now."

Gordy just glares at Martin and then turns away again.

"Gordon. We need to talk. About what happened."

"I think there's been enough talk right now. I don't want to talk about it."

"But Gordon, you're the chief of police. I'm the town council president. We need to discuss this." Martin shakes his head. "This is a major incident. The town is going to have to answer for this. We must talk."

"Not now. Not now."

"Gordon, you can't hide from this. There are serious issues here. You know that."

Gordy keeps walking.

"We need to talk about the whole Ronald Forbert issue."

Gordy stops. "What Ronny Forbert issue?"

"What issue? He's a rookie patrolman. He got a man killed last night. Your Ronald Forbert. The Ronald Forbert you hired. That issue. This casts the town in a very bad light, Gordon. We could get sued over this, Gordon. Lydell could be ruined once and for all over this. Your mistake.

"We have a whole town of young men. Good, able young men, who would have loved to join the police force. Good students, never in trouble. But you had to have Ronald Forbert, when we could have done something good with that position."

"Like give it to the kid of one of your cronies? Trade it for something you need?"

"We're going to get sued over this, Gordon. You just wait and see. We'll get sued."

"If we get sued, it's because you're putting the idea in the Laferieres' heads, Martin."

"That's ridiculous. I could lose my job. We could both lose our jobs. I like my job. Not sure you feel the same way about yours, Gordon."

Gordy turns to Pete. "I'll be in my office. I don't want to be disturbed." He walks into his office and slams the door behind him. He sits at his desk and starts picking up pieces of paper at random, looking at them, putting them in new piles without reading them.

Several minutes later there's a knock on the door and Pete comes in. "Sorry, Gordy. I know you want to be alone, but Channel Eight is on its way for an interview. You want me to handle that?"

"No. Let me know when they're here. Is he gone?"

Pete nods. "Sorry, Gordy. And yes, he's gone. For now."

"That asshole."

"Trouble with assholes is that even natural-born ones figure they got to keep on practicing. Tough thing when the town council president is so pumped up on ideology, he hasn't got a clue what's really going on."

Gordy shakes his head. "It's not ideology. The ideology just happens to coincide with what's good for Martin Glendenning right now. If he could get rid of the police department, it would benefit his side businesses. For Martin the power of government is the power to screw up his enterprises."

"And throw him in jail," Pete says.

"One of these days, maybe, we'll do that."

RONNY FORBERT IS STILL CLEANING, TRYING NOT TO THINK ABOUT it, not to think about anything, when his phone rings. He hopes it's Nessa, but it's his father again. He looks at his watch. Three o'clock. He tries to figure. His father could be drunk again, but he's working, over in Warrentown. He figures it's not likely, and he answers it.

"Ronny. Are you all right? I heard there was an accident."

"You heard that from me. We talked this morning."

"No. I was working. Over in Warrentown."

"I called you."

"No. I was at work. Are you all right?"

"Yeah. Yeah, I'm all right."

"It was a bad accident. Guy got killed."

"I know. Matt Laferiere. I was there."

"But you're all right."

"I'm fine. Some scratches. I was arresting him when he got hit by a car. A hit and run."

"Did you fuck up, Ronny?"

"No. I was arresting him. He got hit by a car."

He can hear the slurring, now. "I feel real bad, Ronny. You fucked up, didn't you?"

"No."

"It's not your fault. I know that. It's my fault. I know that. Entirely my fault."

"It's not your fault. You weren't even there."

"I'm a terrible father. I know that. It's really all my fault. You wouldn't be such a fuckup if I had done a better job of raising you. I don't know what your mother was thinking, just running off and leaving the two of us. She was a better parent than I was. I did my best, but it wasn't very good. I'm sorry, Ronny."

"It wasn't your fault. It wasn't my fault. It was an accident. Hit and run. And it has nothing to do with you."

"You're my son. I should have done a lot better for you. This is my fault." His father begins to cry. "We're just a couple of losers, Ronny. And that's all my fault."

"You're drunk."

"No. No. I mean I had a couple of drinks, yeah. But I'm not drunk. I'm just so sorry I got you into this mess. You should be working with me, but there aren't any jobs. I mean, you're a good carpenter. I could have helped you out."

"I don't need your help."

"You're going to get fired, aren't you?"

That stops Ronny. "No. I'm not going to get fired. It wasn't my fault."

"You can come back. You can come home. I owe that much to you."

Ronny hangs up.

IN THE MIDDLE OF THE OFFICE, A YOUNG WOMAN, BLOND, IN A DOWN parka, skirt, and running shoes stands talking to Pete. Gordy recognizes her face from TV but can't place the name.

"Renee Lawson," she says, sticking out her hand. "Channel Eight *Newswatch*. Would you mind doing the interview outside? It's cold, but the light is great, and I love the look of this old building."

"It is that," Gordy says. Then adds "old." He pauses for a reaction, gets none. "Wherever. It's fine, either way." He follows her outside. The video guy, a big, heavyset guy with long graying hair tied back in a ponytail, and a graying beard, nods and continues to make adjustments to his camera.

"This won't take long," Renee assures him. "We'll get out of here and let you get back to your work. Mostly we want to just get the basic facts of what happened last night. It was a hit and run, right?"

Gordy nods. "A hit and run. Right."

"Do you have the driver?"

"Not yet."

"Maybe we can get you some help on that. So, I'll ask for details on the accident and then on the car that ran. Give me all you can, and we'll run a crawl asking for help and giving your phone number. We'll post it to the website, too. Maybe someone will call in with info you can use."

"That would be great."

"And I'll need info on the victim. Can you give me that?"

"Some. Name, age, that sort of thing. He was an adult and his family has been notified, so we're clear on that." He gives her a sheet John North has printed out with basic media information.

"Fantastic. And the officer involved?"

"Yes. One of our officers was on the scene."

"I'll ask about that. And the road. There have been a lot of deaths on this road, right?"

"Four fatalities in the last seven years. Five. Five now."

"How do you pronounce these names?"

Gordy goes over them with her.

The big video guy leaves his camera, comes up to Gordy, offers his hand. "Alex. Alex Fernandes. Can I borrow his attention for a little bit, Renee?"

Alex takes a step back and hands Gordy a sheet of white paper. "Can you hold this up for me? Just under your chin?" Gordy looks at the paper. Blank on both sides.

"Good, man. Just a little lower. An inch, maybe. That's it. Right there. Look to your left. Your other left. OK. Now to your right. That's perfect. I'm just going to mike you. Mind unzipping your jacket for just a second? I know it's cold. I'll let you zip it right back up." Alex attaches the little lavalier mike to Gordy's collar then runs the wire down the front of Gordy's shirt and hooks a transmitter on Gordy's belt. "OK. You can zip back up. I'm ready, Renee."

Renee looks up from the media sheet. "Is there anything you want to bring up, Chief?"

Gordy thinks. There must be something. He shakes his head. "We just want to catch this guy."

"OK. We'll do our best for you. If there's anything else you want to say, just let me know. We will edit this back at the station. Likewise, if you fuck up, just start over. OK? So just relax and, whatever you do, don't fuck up." She smiles. "A little joke. Keeps things loose."

"Renee Lawson, Channel Eight *Newswatch*. We're here in the small town of Lydell, just off Route 417 where a horrific hit-and-run accident occurred last night. With me is Chief Graham Hawkins of the Lydell Police Department."

"Gordon."

"Pardon?"

"My name is Gordon. You called me Graham. Fucked up."

"With me is Chief Gordon Hawkins of the Lydell Police Department. Late last night, during a traffic stop on Route 417, twenty-one-year-old Matthew Laferiere was struck and killed as he was being placed under arrest by Lydell patrolman Ronald Forbert. Chief, what can you tell us about the accident last night?"

"It was a hit-and-run fatality in the early morning around twelve thirty, just about a mile and a half west of the state line. The young man was struck and killed during a routine traffic stop by a white vehicle, maybe a Honda Accord or Toyota Camry that was headed west on 417."

"So there was an officer involved?"

"There was an officer on the scene. I wouldn't say that he was directly involved, but he was there. He made the stop."

"And what can you tell us about the victim?"

"He was Matthew Laferiere, age twenty-one, of Twisted Root Road in Lydell, a graduate of Warrentown Regional High School. He was the driver of the vehicle the officer stopped."

"And he died at the scene?"

"It was instantaneous, yes."

"Any more information on the car that hit him?"

"Witnesses say that it was a white sedan, probably an Accord or Camry, in the 1990-to-2000 range. This vehicle will have taken significant front-end damage, probably to the right side of the vehicle—right front fender and headlight."

"And you're asking for help from the public, right?"

"We would appreciate any help we can get. If anyone sees a

vehicle that fits that description, we would appreciate a call to the Lydell Police Department."

"And that number is running across the bottom of the screen right now, and will be available on our website eightearlyandlate .com. What about the officer involved?"

"The arresting officer is Patrolman Ronald Forbert of the Lydell Police Department."

"And he's a rookie, right?"

"He's been on the force for almost a year, first as a probationary patrolman, and on active duty for six months."

"And I understand he's on suspension."

"Yes. A preliminary investigation indicates that Patrolman Forbert performed his duties in a responsible and correct manner."

"Well, why a suspension if he performed correctly?"

"A procedural matter. He did not call for backup in what we would consider a timely fashion. He didn't get that done. He missed on just that one thing."

"He was also injured in the accident."

"He received some scrapes and scratches."

"Wasn't he fighting with the victim?"

"He was placing him under arrest. There was some resistance. That's all I can say about that right now. There is an investigation under way."

"Is it likely that charges will be brought against the officer?"

"No. He was performing his duty. There won't be charges brought."

"But he struggled with the victim."

"The victim resisted. There was a struggle. All indications are the officer acted appropriately."

Renee Lawson turns away from Gordy toward the camera. "There you have it, a hit-and-run fatality in the small town of Lydell. If you have any information that will aid Chief Graham Hawkins and his staff on this investigation, please call the Lydell Police Department at the number on your screen. Renee Lawson, Channel Eight *Newswatch*."

"Gordon."

"Pardon?"

"Gordon, not Graham."

"Police Chief Gordon Hawkins. We'll get that in editing."

RONNY'S PHONE RINGS AGAIN. HE CHECKS IT. VANESSA. "HI," HE ANSWERS.

"Are you OK?"

"I'm fine." He wonders for a second if he should change his voice mail message to simply, *I'm fine.* "How are you doing?"

"I'm fine. Busy. Finals and all. But you're all right? You're not hurt?"

"No. I'm not hurt. You heard what happened last night."

"Some of it. Matt's dead."

"Yeah. Matt's dead." He can't think of anything else to say.

"I'm glad you're OK. I was worried."

"No. I'm OK."

"Well, what did happen last night? Are you OK to talk about it?"

"Can you come over?"

"I have a big lab tomorrow. It's part of the final."

"I don't really want to talk about this on the phone."

"If I come over, I can't stay."

He pauses for a long time. "Coming over and not staying is better than not coming over, I guess. I think I need to talk, just not on the phone."

"All right. I'll be there in a hour. Maybe two."

"Fine."

GORDY WALKS INTO A COLD HOUSE. HE THOUGHT HE HAD STOCKED and banked the woodstove to keep it going all day. But the cold was not as bad as the emptiness of the house. He goes out the back door and walks into his woodshop. There, inside a toolbox, he fishes out the bag of M&M's he had hidden out here so that he wouldn't have to eat them in front of Bonita, whose diabetes left such treats forbidden. He opens the bag and pours out a handful. They're frozen, of course, but he's become fond of frozen M&M's. He's not sure why he still keeps them hidden in the toolbox. He wishes he had Bonita to talk to. Without her, he feels untethered. He had always brought his problems to her.

They had been together for forty years, since they had met in Texas when he was an MP stationed at Fort Bliss. She was a student at UTEP, and he was taking two classes, using the army's long way toward a college degree. They met in English class. The United States was conducting small operations in Vietnam, sending advisers from the army to train South Vietnamese soldiers in what was looking more and more like the beginnings of a civil war. Arguments about the U.S. role in Southeast Asia were just beginning, and he had impressed her with a quiet, reasoned defense of the U.S. presence there, and, even more, an ability to listen to the arguments of the other side with a calm, steady respect.

She caught him one day after class. "I like the way you make your point in class. It makes you seem smart." He was taken aback. He had noticed her, thought her pretty, smart, and quiet. He was surprised that she would approach him, the army guy, who wasn't quiet, and who was in a constant battle to show these kids that he was as smart as they were.

He smiled. "Maybe I am smart."

Yes. She nodded thoughtfully. "Yes, you could be. But I kind of doubt it, and you're certainly wrong."

"About what?"

She smiled. "Most things."

"I guess that's better than *everything*."

"You could probably work your way to that."

"How can I convince you that I'm not stupid? Wrong, maybe, but not stupid."

She shook her head and tsked. "I doubt you could prove it. But you can try if you want."

"How about dinner and a movie?"

"What movie?"

"That new one with Peter Sellers. *Dr. Strangelove*."

"Good choice. Probably just dumb luck, though."

"You can explain it to me afterward."

She smiled more broadly, then. "I'll do my best."

"Me, too."

That began an interrupted arc of their lives together that included two tours in Vietnam for him, a twenty-four-year career as a teacher for her, and after the army, a career in police work that took them to the Northeast and finally settled them in Lydell, seventeen years ago.

Bonita had retired, in part due to a general decline in her health as her diabetes became less and less manageable. Gordy kept looking for police work that was less dangerous and less stressful, going from Boston, to Providence, to Salem, New Hampshire, and finally to Lydell where he spent ten years moving from patrolman to sergeant and finally chief of police.

He had given up on showing her that he was as smart as she was. He wasn't. He'd figured that out early on. Teaching elementary school was a necessary and important job, but he had always thought that her intelligence was being wasted there, though he couldn't think what she might do that would be more important. Living with her raised his appreciation of teachers, though. They didn't get credit for being as smart and hardworking as they were.

In school he had pretty much thought that teachers were fakes, reading a couple of chapters ahead in the textbooks, spending their summers hanging out and taking long vacation trips. He guessed a lot of people felt that way, and a lot of them never quite outgrew it. He had always been proud of Bonita, even though he knew she could have done better. In a lot of ways.

He had watched her fight against the diabetes, struggling to control her weight, finding odd times in the morning and afternoon to exercise, watching her diet, trying to avoid taking the insulin injections. She fought hard, and the disease made its gains slowly, but it gained on her. Daily insulin injections started when she was in her fifties. Then came the fatigue, as if all of her fighting had finally sapped her strength so that she wouldn't recover it. Then the neuropathy, slowly, steadily crippling her until it eventually took her legs at the knees.

And what legs they had been. When he first noticed her in English class, he noticed how demure she was, but it was impossible to ignore the legs, long and coltish. Even under a full skirt they couldn't be ignored. Early on it took him a while to say anything because he didn't want to appear overly lecherous and scare her off, but in the springtime, when she showed up for an evening date in Bermuda shorts, he told her she had beautiful legs.

"I do, don't I?" she said.

"I thought it would embarrass you if I said that."

"You didn't think I knew? They got your attention, didn't they?"

"I didn't think you knew."

"You're sweet," she said. "Dumb. But sweet."

THE KNOCKING ON THE DOOR WAKES HIM UP. RONNY LOOKS AT THE TV where *Monday Night Football* is in progress. He has fallen asleep, waiting for this. He gets up quickly and goes to the door. Vanessa.

"Sorry I'm so late," she says. "There was an optional question on the final. I thought I better do it."

"You think you needed an extra question?" he asks, momentarily relieved to be on this sidetrack of the conversation.

"No. I did well. I know that. But what if he decides that he's only giving A's to the people who choose to do the optional question as well. See what I mean? You could get screwed for doing too well. I mean, if you figure you did well and skipped the extra question. I had to do it."

"Yeah, I guess. Sounds pretty bizarre, though. A little paranoid?"

"Who isn't? I mean, you've got to be. At least sometimes. How are you?"

"Fine. I'm good."

"But you got hurt."

He pulls up his sleeve and shows her the bandage. "Road rash. A week or two and it will be gone. Some on my leg, too."

"You poor thing." She steps in and gives him a hug. When she steps back, he tilts his head to kiss her, but she is already moving to the side to put down her things.

"You want some coffee? Anything?"

"No. I'm afraid I can't stay. I have another final in the morning. I'm going to have to study for it tonight."

"Why?"

"Because it's a final. I have to do well."

"But you will do well. You're smart. You do all your work. You will."

"Thanks. I wish I could believe that."

"You've got a 4.0."

"Because I work hard. That's why. Besides I'm here for you, not to argue over grades. You're really all right? It must have been awful."

"Yeah, I mean, I wish it had never happened."

"It must have been horrible. You saw it all happen?"

"I was right in the middle of it. I was trying to cuff him when he got hit."

"Then you're lucky you didn't get hit."

"Yeah. I guess. I don't feel very lucky. I got suspended for five days."

"They suspended you? Why?"

"Because I didn't call for backup. You're supposed to when you think there may be trouble, and I had a car full of drunks. Trouble. I should have called."

"But you didn't kill Matt. You weren't the cause."

"No. He fell in the road and got hit by a hit-and-run driver. I didn't really do anything to cause his death. If there had been another officer there, maybe Matt wouldn't have tried to resist arrest. That's the thinking. That's why I'm suspended, and I see their point. But I figured I knew all those guys and I could handle them. I wasn't really even going to arrest Matt, probably. Not until he started fighting with me."

"You had a fight?"

"Not really. He knocked me down with his car door. The next thing I knew he was out in the road and the car came right over the hill."

"Was it awful?"

"I hope I never see anything like that again."

She came in to him and hugged him again. "I'm so sorry. What a terrible thing to happen."

"It's a little rough. I really wish it hadn't happened."

She reaches out and touches his face, her fingers tracing along his jaw and cheek. "I feel so bad for you."

"I wish you would stay. I'm pretty tired of being alone. I could use some company."

She shakes her head slowly, then rests it on his shoulder. "I'm sorry. I have to study. You know that." She lifts her head and looks him in the eye. "Can you understand that?"

"I guess."

"I know this is very hard for you, because it's very hard for me. I'm doing my best not to deal with this right now. My boyfriend is in a terrible accident in which my ex-boyfriend dies. I'm not ready to deal with that. Let me get through my last finals, and then I'm right by your side. All the way."

He nods, not in comprehension, but in submission.

She leans in and kisses him. "I'll tell you what. I can't stay. I really can't, but how about I give you something to help you sleep tonight? Go get ready for bed. I'll be right in. Don't argue. Doctor's orders."

When he is in bed, she comes in and leans over the bed, kissing him. He puts up his arm to embrace her, and she gently but firmly pushes it down. As they kiss, she slips her hand under the cover and fondles his erection, then pulls down the cover and his boxer shorts, and takes it in her mouth.

She works slowly at first, lots of licking, then moving her mouth up and down along it. His hand is brushing at her sweater, and she reaches back under her sweater and pulls up her bra and guides his hand to her breasts. His body is tensing and relaxing rhythmically and she quickens the pace, urging him on. His hand comes away from her breasts and goes to the back of her head, where he tries to slow her, working to make himself last. She reaches up and moves his hand back to her breast and quickens the pace again. She is in full control now, pulling him on. He can do nothing but go where she is taking him, and she puts her hand flat on his belly as she feels his body start to spasm and the first jet of semen comes into her mouth and she rubs his belly, holding him, gentling him to the end of the orgasm as she would gentle a horse.

"Feel better?" she asks.

He nods and laughs a weak laugh as he languishes on the pillow and says, "Yeah. I feel pretty good."

"That's good. You go to sleep now. Tomorrow things will be better. Tomorrow I'll be over in the afternoon. We can have dinner and other good things.

"I'll let myself out."

CHAPTER 4

RONNY WAKES WHILE IT IS STILL DARK. HE'S SWEATING AND DIS-oriented. He gets out of bed. It's three thirty, and he makes his way into the living room, turns on the light, and goes to the thermostat. He never turned it back the night before. He sets the temperature down to sixty, then pads back to bed.

He stays awake in the dark, replaying the accident in his head. He will have to write his report in the morning, and he wants to get it right. This was not his fault.

WHEN HE GETS UP, HE WANTS TO GO TO EDNA'S AND GET BREAKFAST. This is not a good idea. He knows that, but he can't stay in the apartment where he has no food other than bread and peanut butter, and no one to talk to. He turns on the TV, then goes to the kitchen and makes a peanut butter sandwich. Back in the living room, he clicks the remote until he gets to Channel Eight.

"Brian Semple, Channel Eight Weather. We're in for a few days of frigid weather here, with temperatures staying in the high teens and low twenties, going down to zero and below at night. But no real snow. There may be some scattered snow showers, but nothing to be concerned about. You can put the shovels away for a little while. I say 'a little while,' because way up in Canada, there's a storm forming that may be headed our way at the end of the week. Too early to tell, but I'll keep an eye on it for you."

Ronny finishes his sandwich only to realize that now he's really hungry. He hasn't eaten a full meal since yesterday morning. He grabs his coat, hat, and gloves and goes out the door. When he walks out to the truck, there is a thin layer of snow—a dusting. Sitting in the truck, waiting for the heater to blow hot, he feels a sense of comfort and pleasure in the one thing that is truly his.

BUT ALONG WITH THE COMFORT AND PLEASURE HE FEELS, THERE IS an undertone of unease. He owes $487 a month on the truck. Being suspended for five days will make that amount harder to raise. Worse, it reminds him of just how vulnerable he is. If he were to get fired, he wouldn't be able to keep up those payments, and the truck would be gone. He doesn't want to think about this. Gordy has told him that he won't be fired, and he believes that. He has to believe that.

When he pulls into Edna's, the parking lot is nearly full and he has to park at the very end of the lot and walk back. There are a few swirls of snow, but when he looks up he realizes that it's not snowing. The wind is just blowing the earlier snow off the roof of the diner.

Inside, the tables are pretty well taken, but there is room at the counter. He is halfway to the counter when he realizes that the noise level, which is always high in the mornings at Edna's, has dropped off. He is aware that he is an object of interest this morning. He continues on to the counter smiling and nodding as he passes the tables.

Diane greets him with a smile, a "Hello, Officer," and a pot of coffee and a mug. She greets him the same way every morning. He drinks the coffee while he waits for his order. He likes Edna's coffee better than the Starbucks he keeps at home for Nessa. He guesses it would be considered weak by people who didn't drink it all the time, but it suits him fine. He doesn't really like coffee very much.

He can feel people watching him as he waits. He wishes he had bought a paper from the machine outside, then remembers that there is always a stack of abandoned papers at the end of the counter. He walks down and picks up a couple of sections. He's got Sports Monday from the *New York Times*, and he thumbs through it, pausing to read the scores from yesterday's games. When he finishes, he couldn't pass a simple quiz on who won and who lost, who still has a chance at the playoffs and who doesn't. He goes back and starts the section over, trying to retain the information so he will have something to talk about at the station.

The second section, which he starts after his eggs, bacon, potatoes, and toast have arrived, is the front page of the *Warrentown Clarion*. It seems an odd combination, the sports section from the huge city and the front page from the small town that's bigger than the town he lives in.

He's on page two.

> **Fatal Hit and Run on Route 417.** A driver pulled over for speeding in Lydell was struck and killed by a hit-and-run driver Sunday night. Matthew Laferiere, 21, was pronounced dead on arrival at Warrentown General Hospital. Mr. Laferiere was being placed under arrest at the scene by Lydell patrolman Ronald Forbert. A struggle ensued and Mr. Laferiere slipped on road ice and was hit by a vehicle described as a white late-1990s, early-2000s Toyota or Honda. Passengers in Mr. Laferiere's vehicle, Paul Stablein, 22, Robert Cabella, 21, and Samuel Colvington, 17, were unhurt. Patrolman Forbert has been suspended pending the results of an investigation. Arrangements for Mr. Laferiere are listed in the death notices, section B.

He folds the paper up and places it beside him. He's now more self-conscious than he was when he first came into Edna's. He's aware that someone is standing to his right. He turns to find a smiling face and an extended hand. "I believe we've met before. Martin Glendenning, president of the town council."

Ronny, who knows exactly who he is, nods and extends his hand.

"I just wanted to say hello and extend my condolences on the loss of your friend, Matthew. He was your friend, wasn't he?"

"Back in the day. Yeah. We knew each other for a pretty long time."

"Well, I'm sorry for your loss. And you? Are you doing all right? I understand you were sent to the hospital Sunday night."

Ronny shakes his head. "Nothing. It's really nothing, just some scrapes on my arm and leg. I'm fine."

"Well, I'm certainly glad to hear that," Martin says. "And you're doing all right, otherwise?"

"Yeah. Fine. I'm fine."

"That's good. That's great to hear. If there's anything that I can do to help you through this trying time, please let me know. I'll do whatever I can. I want you to know that I'm on your side, so if you have any problems, let me know."

"Thank you. I appreciate that."

"No. Thank you. For the job you're doing for our town." Martin smiles a big smile. "You might be underpaid, but you're not under-appreciated." He claps Ronny on the shoulder. "Remember. Anytime. Keep me posted."

"Thank you."

Ronny goes back to his eggs as Martin Glendenning wanders around the diner stopping to chat and laugh, when it occurs to Ronny. My side? Who's on the other side?

WHEN RONNY WALKS INTO THE OFFICE, EVERYONE IS THERE—GORDY, Pete, Steve, and John. There must have been a meeting this morning, or an important football game last night. He can't tell because the talking stops when he walks in. There is a pause, long enough to be noticeable, then they greet him, ask about his health. When that's done, things lapse back into silence again.

"I'm here to write my report," he says.

Gordy gets up. "You feel ready to do that?"

"Yeah," he says. "I do. I haven't really remembered anything more about what happened that I haven't already told you. I'll just have to write about that."

"That's fine," Gordy says. "Write it just as you remember it. You call your dad?"

"Yeah."

"Vanessa?"

"Yeah, her too."

"And you're feeling OK?"

"Yeah. I am. A little bored, but I'm OK."

"Good. Good. Sorry about the bored part. Maybe you could start *War and Peace*."

"I don't really read."

"Well, watch movies. Take long drives, go to the gym. Whatever eats up the time. You'll be back to work in no time."

"Really?"

"Yeah. Really. I told you, you're suspended, not fired. You've already got one day down. Come on. Let's get that report done."

Gordy takes him over to the desk Ronny shares with John North and says, "Excuse us." John gets up and pulls out the chair for Ronny in an exaggerated impression of a waiter. Ronny sits, taps the computer back from sleep mode, and pulls up the template for reports.

REPORT LYDELL POLICE DEPARTMENT

Case Number

"I don't know the case number."

"Seventy-three twenty-one," Pete says.

Case Number 7321

Date: December 18, 2010

Reporting Officer Ptl. Ronald Forbert

Preparer Ptl. Ronald Forbert

Incident: Death of Matthew Laferiere by hit and run driver on Route 417, Lydell, during traffic stop for speeding.

Detail of Event

At approximately 24:30, December 16, 2010, I was on patrol on Route 417, specifically clocking traffic for speeding vehicles. Lit approaching vehicle, a 2001 Jeep Cherokee with only one headlight, traveling at 68 mph, per radar. I pursued vehicle and stopped approximately half a mile from spot of first sighting. The driver was Matthew Laferiere, age 21. There were three passengers, Paul Stablein, age 22, Robert Cabella, age 21, and Samuel Colvington, age 17. I observed a strong smell of alcohol, and located a nearly empty 30 can case of Natural Light beer in the backseat. I also detected the presence of marijuana by smell.

I ordered the passengers out of the vehicle and they complied. I ordered the driver, Matthew Laferiere, out of the vehicle and he did not respond. He appeared to be intoxicated. I ordered him out a second time, and he pushed the driver side door open, striking me on my right side and knocking me to the ground. I got up and ordered him to place his hands on top of the vehicle and notified him that I was placing him under arrest for Driving Under the Influence. I placed a handcuff on his right wrist and pulled his right arm down, behind his back, and attempted to place the other cuff on his left wrist. He resisted and there was a short struggle. Mr. Laferiere slipped on a patch of ice, stumbled, and fell out onto Route 417. A west bound vehicle, white in color, a sedan, came over the rise at high speed and struck Mr. Laferiere and knocked him into the parked Jeep Cherokee. The white vehicle spun, slowed, then continued westward on Route 417 at great speed. I recorded only a partial license plate number J 6 New York.

Mr. Laferiere was observed to have sustained acute head trauma and was unresponsive. I immediately called for backup and an ambulance. He was deceased before the ambulance arrived and pronounced dead at the scene.

Actions Taken

I immediately called for backup and an ambulance. He was deceased before the ambulance arrived. The three passengers in the Jeep Cherokee were Breathalyzed and released into the custody of their parents. All three were over the legal limit.

Summary

Matthew Laferiere was struck and killed by a hit and run driver at approximately 24:30 on Route 417 at mile marker . . .

He looks over to Pete. "What was the mile marker?" Pete did not even look up. "Three eighty-one."

Mile marker 381. Mr. Laferiere was struggling with arresting officer before stumbling and falling into road and being struck. Hit and run vehicle continued traveling west bound on Route 417.

Ronny sits back, looks over what he's written, and calls Pete over to look at it. "Anything else I need to put in?"

Pete scrolls the screen up and reads over it. "I don't think so. We have the Breathalyzer results to back up the observation of intoxication on the other three, and we'll be getting a tox report on Laferiere. Save it and send it to Gordy. Let him look it over before you go."

"Should I put the Breathalyzer results in?"

"Yeah, that's a good idea. Hang on a sec. OK. Here they are. Robert Cabella, .11, Samuel Colvington, .14, Paul Stablein .093. All legally over the limit. Put that in that paragraph, or better yet just type it at the bottom of the report as an addendum."

Ronny does that then checks over the report. He puts in a comma, then takes it back out. He reads it over until Pete tells him to stop. He prints it out, and starts to read again, then hands it to Pete who is now standing at his back with his hand out.

"Anything else I need to do today?"

Pete shakes his head. "Hang around for a bit until Gordy says you can go. Then you're back on your own."

Ronny nods.

"It ain't no fun being on suspension, is it? Everybody hears 'five days off,' and it sounds good to them, but it's a bitch."

"Yesterday was all right. I've just got to get through with today, tomorrow, the next day, and the next day."

"Stretches out before you like a bad cold, doesn't it? Well, like a bad cold, it goes away, too. This time next week, you'll barely remember how bored you were."

Gordy comes out of the office. "That looks OK for our purposes.

Print out a copy for yourself. Maybe a couple. You may need to write a deposition at some point. It will be helpful to have this handy."

"A deposition?"

Gordy shrugs. "There could be some legal proceedings farther on down the road. Maybe. Maybe not. But it could happen."

"I could be charged with something?"

"No. You didn't do anything. You won't be charged with anything. Once you finish your five days, you're good. There might be civil actions, though, from the Laferieres."

"I'm going to get sued?"

"No. You're not. The town might, though. Might not, either. It doesn't look like there's much here to base a lawsuit on. Don't worry about it. You're sure you're all right?"

"Yeah. I'm fine."

"Good. Then you need to go home. You're on suspension, and you can't be hanging around here."

Ronny nods glumly. "See you guys."

"HE'S TAKING THIS HARD," PETE SAYS.

"Of course he is. Seeing someone get killed is a hard thing."

"And blaming himself?"

"All we can do is assure him that he's not to blame. When we can get the driver, it will be easier. Then there will be someone to blame, and he won't be pulling it onto himself. He's a stand-up guy, we know that. He's going to go over it and over it. We're going to have to prove to him that it wasn't his fault. I think kids of drunks tend to get pretty good at blaming themselves for things they don't have a lot of control over. But the kid's got a good head and a good heart. We saw that at the fire."

THE FIRE HAD BEEN ON THE FOURTH OF JANUARY, 2006, ALMOST FOUR years earlier. Gordy had been asleep for more than two hours when the phone rang. It was another call that began, "Chief." He got out of bed and went to his closet to dress. "Gordy," Bonita said. "What is it?"

He hadn't wanted to wake her, and he was doing his best to dress quietly, in his closet, in the dark. He fumbled in the drawer for his underwear, turned them around several times before he found the front. He pulled them on, nearly losing his balance and falling heavily into the side of his closet. "A fire," he said. "The gazebo. The gazebo is burning."

"You're going?"

He took a shirt from a hanger and got it on, then felt in the dark for his pants. "It has to be a set fire," he said. "That's what Laurie just said. 'A set fire.'"

"Why do you have to go? It's so late." Bonita was still recovering from the amputation of her foot, an effect of her diabetes. She was not doing well, and was heavily medicated.

"My job," he said. "It's my job. Do you need anything before I go? Another pill? Do you need another pill?"

"No," she said, still groggy.

"How about the bathroom. Do you need to go to the bathroom before I go?"

"I'm all right. I have the wheelchair if I need to get up."

"Be careful. You're still a little unsteady getting in and out of that thing. Don't take a fall."

"I'm sleepy. I'll go back to sleep. You be careful, too. The roads. The snow."

"I'll be careful, and I'll be back as soon as I can."

He got his boots and coat in the living room, found his keys, and trudged out the door to the cruiser. It was slow going. The cruiser, a Crown Victoria, heavy and rear-wheel-driven, didn't have snow tires. In an effort to cut costs, they had outfitted the cars with all-weather tires that didn't do very well in snow, rather than switching between regular tires and snow tires. The snow was light, now, lighter than it had been when he went to bed, but many of the roads, including his, would still be unplowed, as public works concentrated on the main roads before they did the mainly residential streets. He backed out of the driveway slowly, turned the car on the road, and, even going slowly, felt the back end slip and slide in the few inches of snow that covered the road.

A mile away he could see the glow of the fire through the bare trees. He pushed on, taking it slow, letting the car wobble on the unplowed pavement until he reached Hunter Road, which, also unplowed, had deep tire tracks from other vehicles that kept the old Vicky pointed straight ahead.

The gazebo was nearly gone when he got there. The roof had fallen in and the supporting columns were leaning, all completely engulfed in fire, despite the water the volunteer fire department was spraying, which froze before it reached the burning timber.

He found Pete next to the fire truck. Pete had the earflaps of his hat down and the fur collar of his parka pulled up. Gordy was wearing a similar parka, but he had put on a ball cap, Lydell Police, instead of his winter hat. His ears were already cold. "What happened here?"

"Call came in about forty minutes ago. Plow truck spotted it. Took almost half an hour for the fire truck to get here. Whole thing was engulfed. It's gone. Letting it burn, now. There's not going to be anything to salvage."

"Anyone hurt?"

"No. Just a big old fire."

The gazebo was less than a year old. It had been a town project. Built by Public Works with a little money from the state and a lot of volunteer labor, the gazebo sat in a small field off Route 232. The town's one lumberyard had donated much of the materials. Public Works mowed the field once a week in spring and summer, and the town had its first park. The local papers played it up big, an example of a community coming together to improve itself in an economy going to hell.

"Know what caused it?"

"Not only what, but who." Pete walked over behind the fire truck and came back with a red plastic gas can. He held it up so that Gordy could see the initials in black Magic Marker. R. Laf.

"Roger Laferiere? He helped build this thing."

"Well, not Roger. But his kid. That's what I think. Of course someone could have stolen the gas can, but I figure this is kid work. Nice of him to leave this for us."

"Anything else?"

"Beer cans. Tire tracks." Pete walked Gordy over to a scattering of Natural Light beer cans. "Kid beer," Pete said. "Lots of footprints, more than the fire crew made. Kid party. Got your four-wheel drive, your beer, can of gas, matches, and there goes the gazebo. Pretty much a Matt Laferiere special."

"Son of a bitch," Gordy said.

"Yep. Son of a bitch."

"All of this hard work," Gordy said. "And now, nothing. And for what? A few minutes of entertainment for some bored, drunk kids."

"Mother was right," Pete said. "Can't keep anything nice."

"Anyone looking for the kids?"

"John went out. He's going to cruise around for a while, then make his way over to the Laferieres'."

"Yeah. They wouldn't go home right away. Must have stayed around to watch it burn. No point, otherwise."

"No point anyway. No point at all. Just stupid destruction for the sake of destruction."

"We'll haul them in in the morning. We don't need Spenser to solve this one." He nodded toward the gas can.

"The stupidity just goes on and on, doesn't it?"

"Can't stop it."

THE NEXT MORNING, WHEN GORDY GOT IN TO WORK, PETE AND JOHN had Matt Laferiere, Paul Stablein, Bobby Cabella, and Ronny Forbert in the office. Laferiere, Stablein, and Cabella were familiar figures to Gordy. They had been hauled into the office half a dozen times, together and separately. The charges, when there had been enough evidence to charge them, were misdemeanors—possession of alcohol, rowdiness, vandalism. Kid stuff.

Forbert, though, was new. While the three others sat slumped in chairs, looking alternately bored and cocky, the tall, skinny kid stood against the wall, behind the others, doing a bad job of hiding his nervousness. Like the other three, he was dressed in a flannel shirt, jeans, unlaced work boots, and a hooded sweatshirt, as if it weren't cold enough to put on a coat.

"So, you gentlemen had a party last night."

Laferiere shrugged.

"Didn't you?"

"School's out. We hung out last night."

Gordy walked over to the skinny kid. "I don't believe we've met. I'm Police Chief Gordon Hawkins."

"Yeah. I know."

"And you are?"

"Forbert. Ronald."

"Well, Forbert, Ronald. I hope I don't come to know you as well as I know these other three. I know them pretty well." Gordy turned back to Laferiere. "I know you hung out last night. Over in the park. By the gazebo." He watched Forbert straighten and stiffen.

"We were there for a while." Laferiere was always the spokesman. He was pretty good, admitting to enough that he wasn't easily tripped up on a lie he didn't need to tell.

"I know that, too. You left a lot of beer cans there."

"We'll pick them up."

"No need. We picked them up for you. They're evidence, now."

"And you're going to test them for DNA. CSI: Lydell. No need. We were drinking beer in the park."

"That was just the start," Gordy said. "Like your little party. We're more interested in what came later."

"We went home."

"Yeah. Eventually. But first you poured gasoline on the gazebo and burned it down."

"I heard that," Laferiere said. "But it wasn't us. We just hung out in the snow for a while, then went home."

"No, Matthew. You didn't. You burned the gazebo. And you were kind enough to leave us with evidence for that, too. You're not very good at cleaning up after yourselves. We found your father's gas can." Forbert was shifting his weight from leg to leg as if he had to pee.

"My father burned the gazebo down?" Laferiere asked with a smile.

"Doubt that, since he helped build it. No. You burned it down."

"Nope. Didn't do it."

"Why don't you just admit that you did it, and we'll move on?"

"Move on where?"

Gordy turned and nodded toward the holding cell to their left, the only lockup Lydell had. It was primarily for drunks to sleep it off before they got shipped over to Warrentown for arraignment. Gordy thought it would do the whole bunch some good, and Forbert was looking at it like it was Attica.

"Bread and water?" Laferiere smiled again.

"Oh, no. We'll get you a nice lunch before you head off for Warrentown and your arraignment. Want to try it out for a while? Your dad's going to be here in a bit. You can wait for him there."

"You're taking my dad out of work? He's going to be pissed off about that."

"I'm sure he's not going to be a happy guy. I think he's got a lot to be pissed off about."

"He usually does."

"All right," Gordy said. "Pete, lock them up until Roger and the rest of the parents get here."

Pete walked to the holding cell, unlocked it, and swung the door wide. "All right, gentlemen, single file into the cell. Empty your pockets on the desk there." Laferiere rose slowly and shuffled over to where Pete held the door open.

"Shit, man. It's cold in here."

"Maybe you'll find something to burn. You guys know how to make a fire."

"This sucks."

"So much in life does," Pete said.

ROGER LAFERIERE ARRIVED FORTY-FIVE MINUTES LATER.

"Roger," Gordy said. "Thanks for coming. Sorry to interrupt your day like this."

"What did he do?"

"These four had a little party last night in the park. They burned down the gazebo."

Roger Laferiere had the haggard face of a man struggling with way too many problems, one who was never surprised when another arose. It was like he collected problems, which he probably did. He was tall, well over six feet, and bone-thin. His face was weathered and unshaven, and it didn't register much, though his eyes were always moving, looking for the next bit of trouble that was going to stick to him. Gordy thought of him as a kick dog, always expecting the next kick, but not sure where it was coming from. He looked like he might bite and run.

Roger took a couple of steps toward the holding cell where his son sat on the edge of the cot. "You do that?" Matt Laferiere didn't look up. He just shrugged.

"You sure it was them?"

Gordy reached down to the floor next to the desk and picked up the empty gas can. "This yours?"

"Shit," Roger said.

"Yeah. Shit."

"What are you going to do?"

"Honestly? I haven't really figured that out yet. I thought we would wait for the other parents to get here and see what we can hash out."

Again, Roger Laferiere nodded, as if the whole situation was completely out of his control. Gordy guessed this was only one of many things Roger found out of his control. He had that look. He was a receiver. Things happened, and he accepted that. He had no power to change or avoid what came at him.

"Why don't you have a seat, Roger? The others should be here shortly." Gordy pulled a chair out from one of the desks in the office. "Again. I'm really sorry to have to pull you away from things I'm sure you'd rather be doing. I hope this won't take too long, though the situation is pretty serious. I can't just let the boys go on their own. You want some coffee or some water? Just ask Steve here. He'll get you anything you need."

Roger nodded, still glum.

GORDY MADE HIS WAY BACK TO HIS OFFICE AND PETE FOLLOWED HIM. "So what are you thinking?" Pete asked.

"I don't really know. What about you?"

"It's arson. They're going to have to be charged."

"And then they get sent to jail."

"Yeah. If that's what the judge decides. It'll be up to the judge."

"It's an option."

"But not one you like."

"It seems like giving up, Pete. We'd just be passing the problem on to someone else. It's a town problem. I'd like to handle it in town."

"A stretch in prison would teach them a lesson."

"What lesson, though? What does jail teach anyone, except how to be a crook?"

"That's what happens when you commit a felony, Gordy."

"Yeah. They have committed a felony."

"How many times has this bunch been in here? We haven't managed to teach them anything on our own."

"I know. I can't really argue with that."

"But you're going to handle it?"

"Pete, I just don't know. I don't know. Personally, I would like to kill the little shits. But I can't do that. We have to figure something else out."

"No such thing as a bad boy?"

"No. There is such a thing. We have prime examples in the holding cell. But these boys are more a nuisance than anything else. It's when they grow up into bad men that we really have to start worrying about them."

JACK STABLEIN WAS THE NEXT TO ARRIVE. HE CAME IN WOOL SLACKS and a camel-hair topcoat. Underneath it, a sport coat, sweater, and tie. He sold cars in the next town over. He had youthful good looks, though he was no longer young. He had a good smile and a firm handshake. Gordy guessed he was pretty good at selling cars. He looked over to the holding cell where his son sat on the cot next to Matt Laferiere. Bobby Cabella and another kid, one he didn't recognize, sat on the floor across from the cot.

"Chief," he said. "How are you doing?"

"Not bad, but I was better before the gazebo burned down last night."

"I heard about that." He nodded toward the cell. "Them?"

"Pretty sure. They haven't confessed to anything, but we've got good evidence."

Jack turned to the cell. "Paul, you do that? You burn down the gazebo?"

Paul Stablein shrugged, much as Matt Laferiere had.

"I asked you a question."

"I think I want a lawyer."

"Son of a bitch. You're not getting a lawyer, not yet. What you've got is me. You do it?"

"It was kind of an accident."

Matt Laferiere turned to Stablein. "Shut up."

"I didn't say anything."

"You said something. Just shut up. All of you. They're playing us. They don't have any evidence."

Jack Stablein turned back to Gordy.

"We have the gas can they used to start the fire. It's Roger's. Have you met Roger?" Gordy motioned toward Roger Laferiere, who was sitting on the desk chair, not saying anything. "I want to get all the parents here before we start talking about this. Maybe you two can chat."

"I walked away from a customer ready to buy for this. I can't hang around here all day," Jack said. "How much is this going to cost me?"

"I have no idea," Gordy said. "This is a case of arson."

"You're charging them with arson? Paul, don't say another word. Not until there's a lawyer here."

"It's arson. Whether they're going to be charged is something we haven't decided yet. It's the logical and correct thing to do, though."

"Son of a bitch."

Gordy smiled a small smile and motioned to the chair Pete had pushed next to Roger Laferiere's. "We want to hear from everyone before we decide how we're going forward with this. The others should be here soon. Mostly I want to hear it from them." Gordy motioned toward the cell.

"Not without a lawyer," Stablein said.

"If we get lawyers in here, we're going to be forced to charge them and let the lawyers do their thing. I'd rather not work that way. Talk to Roger."

Gordy went back to his office to think more, mostly unsuccessfully, about what they should do with the four boys. None of the options seemed good to him. He hated the idea of sending kids to correctional institutions. It was a waste. More, it was surrender. But mercy didn't seem like such a good option, either. There was no real way to forgive these kids for what they had done. It was an insult to the town, and the town had gone through enough already.

In five minutes, Pete was at the door. "Cabella and Forbert are here."

"Bring them in. Their chairs, too."

The fathers entered in single file, Jack Stablein first, with clenched jaw, then an almost equally annoyed Frank Cabella in khakis and red polo shirt embroidered Auto Depot. Frank, Manager. Then one he didn't know, obviously Karl Forbert, followed by the still-glum Roger Laferiere.

"Gentlemen. Thanks for coming. Again, I'm terribly sorry to take you away from your busy day. But we have a serious problem we need to talk over." He rose and extended his hand to Karl Forbert. "I don't believe we've met. Gordon Hawkins, police chief."

Forbert just nodded. "Karl Forbert."

"As I think you know," Gordy said, "the gazebo in Henry Stuhl Park burned down last night. We're sure that your sons are the culprits. I would really like to just write this off as a juvenile prank, but I'm afraid I can't. That gazebo was a point of pride in this town. A lot of people put a great deal of time and money into that structure. I know Roger and Karl both worked on it. This is going to cause a lot of ill will in the town."

"What evidence do you have that they're the ones who did it?"

"A lot. We have Roger's gas can that was left at the scene. We have plenty of tire tracks that will match the tires on Matt's Jeep. We have eight empty beer cans from an empty thirty-pack we found in the Jeep this morning. And we have their admission that they were in the park last night."

"That sounds a long way from airtight," Jack Stablein said.

"Maybe, maybe not. That's for lawyers to figure out. But it's enough to satisfy me that we have the right guys. It'll probably convince a jury, too. But we'll see about that if it comes to that."

"I'm going to beat holy hell out of Bobby," Frank Cabella said. "He's just turned into a little shit since he's been hanging around with the Laferiere kid."

Gordy saw Roger look up, a flash of anger in his eyes, but then he looked back down, even more glum, if that were possible.

"No. No beatings. Beatings don't solve problems."

"This one will. I'm going to give him a beating he will remember every day for the rest of his goddamned life."

"I don't doubt that he will. But I don't really want to have to arrest you for battery, either."

"It's my business. I'll do with my son as I please."

"No," Gordy said. "I'm sorry, but no you won't. If we're talking about sending a kid home for a beating, I'd rather send a kid to juvie where he'll get beaten by someone his own age. No. No beatings. And I'm not kidding about arresting you. If I find out you battered your son, I will arrest you."

"OK," Jack Stablein said. "It's time for the lawyers. I want to call mine."

"As I explained, Mr. Stablein, if you call a lawyer, I have no choice but to charge your son with a felony. I do that, it's out of our hands. It's in the courts then. I asked you here to talk this thing through, to see if we can come to an agreement. I think that's the best way to handle this. It's a Lydell issue, and I'd like to deal with it at this level. But if I have to charge them and send them to Warrentown, I will."

"What are you thinking?" Karl Forbert asked.

"I'm thinking a lot of things, and I don't, frankly, have a good answer. I want something that fits the crime. I'm just not sure what it is."

"I don't have a lot of money," Karl Forbert said. "I'm a carpenter, and there's not a lot of work right now. I can't afford to reimburse the town for what my son did."

"No one's confessed to anything," Jack Stablein said.

"But we know they did it."

"That's not an admission. They haven't said they did it."

"Look. I don't want you to answer this question. But think about it for a minute. Do you have any real doubts that they did it? Really?"

To Gordy's surprise, no one said anything. The four of them, including Stablein, just sat and stared at the walls.

"It's a tough one," Gordy said. "The whole town is hurting. Jobs are scarce. We're all suffering in one way or another. But there will have to be reparations. We can't go to the town and ask for volunteers to build another gazebo when they all know it was maliciously burned. That can't happen."

"You want us to rebuild it?"

Gordy thought for a minute. "No. I want them to rebuild it."

Cabella shook his head. "I don't know about the rest, but Bobby couldn't build a dog pen."

The other three laughed. That was good. The laughing was good, Gordy thought.

"They could if someone showed them how."

"Ronny can build," Karl Forbert said. "I could show the others how, but if a job comes up, I have to take it. Making a living is tough enough without a second, unpaid job."

"You didn't burn it down, Karl. You shouldn't have to rebuild it, or even supervise it. None of you. They burned it down. I want them to do it, without help from you."

"But they can't do it themselves."

"Let's not underestimate them. We have a building inspector and a public works director in the town. They can supervise. They can show them what to do, and apparently Ronny knows how to build."

"It's going to take a lot of material. It's going to be expensive, and the price of lumber is way up. No one's building, but the price of lumber hasn't come down. It's up."

"Yeah. I know that," Gordy said. "I want them to pay for it. I want them to supply the labor and all of the materials."

"Maybe Ralph over at Lydell Materials could give you a break on the lumber—sell it at cost."

"That's not fair to Ralph. He would probably do that, but that's still taking money out of his pocket. He donated a lot of the material in the first place. He's not responsible for replacing it. They will have to buy lumber at retail."

"How?"

"They'll have to get jobs. There are always things to do if you look hard enough. This is a crime of boredom. They were hanging out, drinking and smoking a little, maybe. They have too much time on their hands. Let's take some of it off their hands. Let them learn what it means to work and struggle to get something done."

"I don't know," Frank Cabella said. "This seems pretty difficult to pull off."

"It would be easier than putting in six months or a year in juvie or worse. They could be charged as adults, and then they would have to do adult time."

"I don't want Paul doing jail time."

"Can't blame you," Gordy said. "They won't come out of jail better boys."

"I don't see that we have a lot of options here," Stablein said. "I'll agree to it." He looked around at the other three.

"It's a pretty good deal," Cabella said.

"OK. Fine," Forbert said. Roger Laferiere just nodded.

"All right," Gordy said. "We have a deal, then. Let's just make sure we're all talking about the same thing. They will rebuild the gazebo. They will do it themselves, with supervision from the town. If they don't do it, I'm going to press charges. Those are their only options. Build the gazebo or be arrested."

The fathers nodded their agreement.

"And no one helps them. In any way. No money." He looked at Stablein. "No doing any of the work for them." He looked at Forbert. "I want them to have a sense of accomplishment at the end of this. Are we agreed? All right then, let's go back into the main office and let them know."

"THIS IS YOUR LUCKY DAY," JACK STABLEIN SAID.

"I'll handle this," Gordy said. "We're going to offer you guys two options. Your fathers and I are in agreement. You can rebuild the gazebo you burned down last night, or I will arrest you for arson, a felony, and you'll be bound over for arraignment in Warrentown. Those are your choices. There will be no others, no compromises. If you take the first option, and you'll be fools if you don't take it, you'll spend every afternoon, every Saturday on the gazebo. You'll build it yourselves with no help except directions from the building inspector or the public works director. You will buy all of the materials. When it's rebuilt, you will be released with nothing on your record."

"How are we going to buy materials?" Bobby Cabella asked.

"With your own money. That will probably entail getting some part-time jobs. I don't know. Frankly, it's your problem, not mine. You find money for beer and weed . . ." Gordy glanced at the fathers. "So you can find money for lumber."

"How are we supposed to get jobs if we have to work here every afternoon?"

"You'll work here every day from three to five. After that, you can go to your jobs."

"There aren't any jobs," Matt Laferiere said.

"Shovel snow, wash cars, have bake sales, gather beer cans along the road. I don't care. The town will buy the initial materials, but you'll pay us back. You won't be released from pending charges until you've rebuilt the gazebo and paid for it."

"This is messed up," Matt Laferiere said.

"It is," Gordy agreed. "And you're the ones who messed it up. Now you're going to clean up your mess."

"They probably don't have tools," Karl Forbert said. "Can Ronny use mine?"

"Sure. If you can't borrow tools, you can use the town's tools from public works. You want the offer?"

The boys looked at one another. Stablein, Cabella, and Forbert all nodded. Laferiere stayed on the cot and stared ahead at the wall. "He doesn't have enough evidence."

"Oh, but I will. You all are going to sign confessions that will go into the file. When you're done, I will destroy them."

"I'm not copping to anything, and I'm not signing anything," Laferiere said. "He just admitted he doesn't have enough evidence."

"You want a lawyer?" Roger asked.

"Hell, yes, I want a lawyer."

"How are you going to pay a lawyer? I'm sure as hell not paying for one," Roger said. Gordy smiled.

"I'll get a public defender. I'm not rebuilding that thing, and I'm not getting a job."

"You other three going to take the offer, or are you going to jail with him?"

The three looked at one another. "Don't take the deal," Matt Laferiere said. "Don't sign anything."

"Work or felony arrest?"

Forbert spoke first. "I'll take the deal."

"Me, too," Bobby Cabella said.

Stablein looked at his father, who nodded. "Yeah," Stablein said, "I'll take it."

"I've got three to work this off. One arrest?"

"Take the deal," Roger said.

"No."

"I'm going to have three signed confessions that the four of you did it," Gordy said. "Now, what kind of magic is a public defender going to work against that? You're going to jail."

"Take the deal," Roger said. "If you don't, you ain't coming home tonight or any other night."

"Fuck," Laferiere said. "What choice do I have?"

"Exactly," Gordy said. He motioned for Pete to unlock the holding cell. Gordy walked over to the supply cabinet. "I'm going to give each of you a pad of paper and a pen. You will write down exactly,

exactly, what happened last night. If I like what you write, you can sign it and go home."

The boys sat at opposite sides of Pete's and John's desks and began writing. Gordy collected the signed statements. "Be at the park at nine Saturday morning. We'll get started then. You're free to go. Get your belongings from Sergeant Mancuso as you leave."

The boys shuffled out of the building, their fathers behind them. Karl Forbert turned around and came back and shook Gordy's hand. "Thank you," he said. "You didn't have to do that. I really appreciate it. Ronny's a good boy, but he doesn't have a mother, and I work as much as I can."

Gordy said, "I think this is the best thing." He looked beyond Karl to where the Forbert kid stood, still on the steps of the police station. He watched as Matt Laferiere turned back, climbed two steps, and shoved Forbert's shoulder. "You pussy. You folded. He didn't have anything on us. We would have walked on this. You're shit."

Ronny Forbert stared straight ahead.

TWO WEEKS LATER IT HAD STARTED TO SNOW HEAVILY IN THE MID-afternoon, and Gordy had left for home early to stock the house with wood and water in case they lost power. The roads were still passable, even in a high-mileage Crown Victoria. He wished he had taken the Explorer, but they would need it tonight. There were always a couple of cars that had to be pulled out of a snowbank on snowy nights. Or kids, or old folks who wandered off in the snow. Gordy swung by the park to see what progress had been made. No one was there, but he could see they were breaking up the old concrete pad on which the gazebo had rested. There were piles of broken concrete, one still holding the remains of a burned six-by-eight post that had made one of the corners.

It pleased him to think of the boys out there with sledgehammers and iron bars in the afternoon, just a little snow coming down as they hammered the concrete until it cracked, then wedged the pieces out with long iron bars. This was work, but real, honest work. He smiled to think of them going home, sore in the back and shoulders, their hands red and starting to blister.

He got back into his cruiser and headed down Wolf Den Road toward home, looking forward to getting a good fire going in the woodstove and taking the rest of the day to watch the gathering snow with Bonita until it got deep enough that he wouldn't be able to get out until DPW came and plowed him out.

He saw the boy trudging down the road, hood up, hands stuffed in his pockets. He pulled up to him and stopped. It was Ronny Forbert. He rolled the window down. "Need a ride?"

The boy stopped and looked at him, shook his head, and said, "No. I'm OK."

"Yes. You need a ride. It's starting to really come down now."

The boy looked again, as if he was calculating which was worse, walking down a dirt road in a snowstorm or riding next to a cop. Finally, he turned and came around in front of the car. Gordy leaned over and opened the door for him. "It's going to be a big one. No sense walking when you can ride."

Forbert climbed in. "Guess not. Thanks."

"Seat belt," Gordy said, and Forbert reached behind him for the belt, pulled it across himself, and buckled it. "Your friends just leave you?"

"They were going the other way."

"Could have given you a ride, though."

Forbert just shrugged.

"Not too happy with you, are they?"

"Guess not."

"You did the right thing. It's a tough thing, I know. But Lafe-riere was wrong. You were right. You guys weren't going to make out well by going to court. Chances are you would have ended up in juvie for a few months. Or worse. Doubling down on a weak hand is a bad bet. Always."

"I don't want to go to jail."

"No, it's not a nice place. A lot of times the tough guys figure they're going to do all right. They figure they'll be the toughest guys there, but there's always a few guys tougher than you are. Jail is miserable." He looked over at Forbert, who still had his hands in his pockets, leaning forward, trying to hold the heat in.

Gordy reached over and pushed the heater control up all the way. "That's not a lot of clothes for a snowstorm."

"It was OK this morning. Kind of warm."

"Then the snow comes."

"Yeah."

"It was brave, too. What you did. You stood up to Laferiere. I know he's the leader of your little group. It's tough to take a stand that challenges the leader, even when he's clearly wrong. I admired that."

"They think I'm a pussy."

"They're wrong. You're the strong one, and in a minute or so you'll be the warm one, too."

"Thanks for picking me up."

"Hated to see you walking through the snow. You got a coat?"

"At home. It's kind of small and beat up. I don't like to wear it to school. Mostly, the hoodie is OK."

"So, where are you in school?"

"Junior. Another year to go."

"You going to graduate?"

"Yeah. I'll graduate."

"Good. Not a great time to be looking for work."

"I know. I'm looking for a job, like you said."

"Any luck?"

"Not really. I'll do some shoveling and stuff. If this keeps up, there won't be any school tomorrow. I can shovel half a dozen driveways or so. It'll be a couple hundred bucks. Lots of people have snowblowers, though. Not as much work as there was a couple of years ago. I have some neighbors who are old. Retired. I can't charge them as much as I need to, but I can earn some."

"Tell you what. If there's no school tomorrow, call me. I'll put you to work at the station and at my house. I've got a snowblower, but I would rather have you push it than me. And I already have a job."

"That would be cool."

"Just call the station when you've got your neighbors dug out. I'll come out and pick you up. You going on to college?"

"I don't think so. Maybe the junior college. I have to get a car, though. I can't keep on borrowing my dad's truck."

"And what would you major in in college?"

"I don't know. Maybe I'll join the army."

"I was in the army, right out of high school. Couldn't figure out what to do. I ended up an MP. That's how I became a cop."

"They teach you stuff in the army. Computers, mechanics, engineering. Stuff like that."

"Lots of places teach you stuff. I believe colleges are pretty good at it."

"Yeah. I could do that. I don't know. I'm getting kind of tired of school."

"I know. You get tired of it. Then, later, you wonder why. I think going to college is the way to go."

"You in Vietnam?"

"I was there. One tour in Phu Bai."

"You kill anyone?"

"Not there. Mostly I did a lot of guard duty. Broke up a lot of fights, threw drunks in the stockade."

"It must be hard to actually kill someone."

"Harder than you can imagine."

"Who'd you kill?"

"I don't know. I guess I don't even know if I killed him. I was stationed at Fort Bliss, outside of El Paso. MP. I was guarding some trucks heading west and stopping at Bliss for the night. Secret stuff. New weapons systems, I think. In the middle of the night I saw this guy rummaging around in the secure area. I yelled for him to stop, but he picked up something and made a run for it. I fired one warning shot that made him start running in a zigzag. The next shot, I hit him. He went down hard, but then he got up and went on.

"We searched for his body the next day. We found more blood, but we never found him. Maybe he made it back into Mexico. Maybe he drowned in the Rio Grande. Maybe he lived. Maybe not. I'll never know. But I'll never forget it, either. It'll catch me at odd times, and I'll think about it, wondering if I killed him or not. I hope not, but I can't shake the fear that I did. The worst thing that ever happened to me. And that's just one of the things that can happen in the army."

"A lot of the guys want to join up and go over and kill hajis."

"I know that. A lot of them get their wish. The lucky ones don't."

"You went."

"I bought the big lie. There's always a big lie. This one is 'They're trying to take our freedom.'"

"That's a lie?"

"A big one. Don't die for it. Don't kill someone for it."

"It's just down here." Forbert pointed down the road. "To the right."

"Here?"

"Next mailbox."

The driveway was long, winding back into the woods. "You shovel this driveway?"

"Yeah. It takes a while."

They pulled up to the house. It was a sixties ranch-style, with snow building up on the roof and around the edges. Gordy could see it had once been yellow, but now was mostly gray where the paint had peeled off and the wood had weathered. It looked like it had never been a great house, but once was a lot nicer than it was now. It was like a lot of houses in Lydell, neglected for lack of time, money, and the inclination to keep it up. Twenty years ago, houses were better kept, but that was a time before everyone had two jobs just to afford the things they needed, or thought they needed.

"Well, if you shovel this out, no one can say you're afraid of hard work. This is a job."

"We've got a snowblower, but it's old. It works sometimes, but a heavy snow will stop it dead. It's almost easier just to shovel it."

"Well, you call me tomorrow. I'll find you some work. It'll be easier than this, and we'll pay you for it."

GORDY PICKED RONNY UP IN THE LATE MORNING. THE FORBERTS' driveway was clear and easy. "Looks like you put in a full day already."

"It wasn't so bad. Seven inches, pretty light and fluffy. I got the snowblower working. It wasn't too bad."

"You had lunch yet?"

"No. But I'm OK."

"I'm not. Let's get lunch." Gordy backed the cruiser down the long drive again. He looked over at Ronny, who wore an old canvas coat over his hoodie. "Reach behind the seat there. I brought you something."

"This?" Ronny held up a navy-blue nylon quilted police jacket with a fur collar.

"That. It's warm. I grew out of it a couple of years ago. I quit smoking and put on some pounds. Can't even zip that one up, now. It's yours. You got gloves?"

Ronny pulled out a pair of soaked leather work gloves that looked really worn.

"There's some dry ones in the trunk. You can use those."

At Edna's on Route 23, Ronny ordered a burger and fries, Gordy a chef's salad. "You still trying to diet, Gordy?" Diane the waitress asked.

Gordy patted his belly. "Still working on it. Still working."

"I can put you on the no-pancake list. The no-ice-cream list, too."

"Oh, no. Don't do that. You've got to attend to your pleasures. I'll just use willpower."

"You got some?"

"More than you can imagine, Diane."

When she had gone back to the kitchen, Gordy said, "She gets on me about lack of willpower. But I've quit smoking, and I've quit drinking. I have lots of willpower. And I'll get away from the sugar, too. One of these days."

"Good morning, Gordon." Martin Glendenning stood at the side of their booth. "Fighting crime?"

"Calories, mostly."

"Have you heard? I'm going to run for the town council in the special election next month. Be your boss one of these days."

"I heard. Good to get it from the horse's mouth, though. Think you can win? This here is Ronald Forbert. He's going to be doing a little work around the station."

Martin looked at Ronny and nodded. He reached down and fingered the shoulder of Ronny's new jacket. "Are you a new member of the police force, Ronald?"

"Chief Hawkins gave it to me," Ronny said.

"Well, wear it in good health. Chief Hawkins is a good and generous man. He's been our chief for a long time. Do what he says. He'll keep you on the straight and narrow. Won't be able to play with matches if you're a member of the Lydell Police.

"To answer your question, Gordon, I can win, and I will win," Martin said. "We have to make some changes in Lydell. I think I'm the man to do that."

"What sort of changes you thinking about? Am I going to still have a job?"

"Nothing is going to be off the table, Gordon. I have to be honest about that. Nothing. We're getting killed with taxes here. Lydell's going down fast. I think everyone knows that. We're going to have to look at some big changes just to keep the town alive."

"Would that include doing away with the police department?"

Gordy knew that Martin wanted to disband the police department and turn protection over to the state police. And a lot of others did, too. There were opposing sides—those who wanted to keep the town going and those who were content to let it die. Those were mainly the old rural stock whose parents let the school system go and be merged into Warrentown. And then the fire department, which they defunded until it became all volunteer. And now they were after the police department, which they considered an expensive nuisance. Martin saw it as a danger to his enterprises.

"Oh, I don't know, Gordon. If we didn't have a police department, the state police could patrol the town. It would save a lot of money. But it's just a thought."

Diane reappeared with their orders.

"Good morning, beautiful. How's your day going?" Martin asked.

"One minute it's great, and the next it goes right into the dumper," Diane said with obvious distaste.

"Way of the world, gorgeous. Way of the world."

"You fellows need anything more here? All right on your Coke there?" she asked Ronny. When Ronny nodded, she turned, a sharp pivot, and headed back to the kitchen.

"She don't like me much," Martin said.

"Would have been my guess," Gordy said.

"Used to like me a lot."

"Way of the world, Martin. Way of the world."

"Well, all right, then. You wanted me to let you in on my plans. Don't suppose I'm going to get your vote?"

"Martin, I do all I can to stay out of the politics. Every election, there's a fifty–fifty chance I'm going to piss off my boss. Those aren't good odds, so I pretty much stay on the sidelines. I work with whoever the town chooses."

"Fifty–fifty chance of getting in good with the boss, too."

"Same odds. Just like flipping a coin."

"Well, that's true, but sometimes you just have to roll the dice."

"Only if you don't mind losing. Me, I mind losing. That's why that new casino down in Franklin won't see a lot of me.

"You know Martin?" Gordon asked when Glendenning had left. "He runs the gravel pit out on Weller Road. Farms some, too, though I don't see him farming much beyond some corn in the summer and pumpkins in the fall. Deals a little farm equipment on the side."

"I've seen him around."

"Yeah. It's hard not to know people in a town like Lydell. Well, eat up. We better get to work before Martin fires me and you, too."

In the afternoon, when Ronny had finished clearing the sidewalks, Gordy went out to check. The walks were completely free of snow and water, and had been sprinkled with sand. The edges of the path had been cut clean. Amazingly clean. The angles where the sidewalk turned and split were cut sharply at ninety degrees. He had never seen anything quite like it. Gordy guessed that was what you got from a carpenter's son.

"TELL US, SAMMY. TELL US WHAT YOU SAW. YOU SAW MATT LAFERIERE get killed, man. You saw him dead." That was the worst thing he had ever seen, the worst thing he hoped he would ever see. You shouldn't see someone you knew like that. Dead. Really messed up. He had seen Matt Laferiere's brain, and his teeth scattered among the gore.

"It was gross," he says.

"I heard that his head was, like, smashed. You see his head smashed?"

He just nods.

"You see the car hit him, dude? You see that?"

"Yeah," he says, almost believing that it's true. He wants to just get away from this, get away from the questions, but more people are coming up. "Sammy's telling the story. Sammy's telling what he saw."

"Did the cop really throw him into the road as the car came at him?"

He looks around at the kids, guys and girls both, crowding in, waiting to hear the story. Waiting for the story he said he wouldn't tell. They're paying attention to him, wanting to hear what he saw. What he saw and none of them did. He likes the way everyone's eyes are on him.

"Yeah," he says. "I saw it. He just grabbed him by the arm and threw him out into the road. The car was coming fast. Matt didn't have a chance. The car just rammed into him, sent him into the back of the Jeep."

"Did he, like, fly through the air?"

"Yeah. He did. Like nothing you ever saw. Headfirst right into the Jeep. Totally smashed his head."

"God. That's cool, man. That cop killed his ass, man."

"Yeah," Sammy says, though he doesn't know why.

RONNY HAD LEFT THE STATION WITH NO PARTICULAR DESTINATION in mind. He doesn't want to go back to the apartment. He knows that. So when he gets to Route 417, he hooks a left and heads northwest toward Warrentown. Two miles down the road he pulls off onto a narrow dirt road that leads toward Stark's Pond. It's a place where he's spent a lot of time.

When Ronny moved out of middle school into the regional high school that combined the tenth through twelfth graders from the three towns south of Warrentown, including Lydell, he lost his best friend, Max, whose parents moved to Vermont. They were only forty-some miles apart now, but since neither had a car, and neither had parents willing to drive the forty miles a couple of times a week, and they were now going to separate schools, they may as well have been in separate countries.

Ronny and Max had been bound by a love of the outdoors, especially the woods and the animals that lived there, and a vague but aching longing for girls, though neither was adept at attracting them. They had stayed young for their ages, preferring to play in the woods where they seemed separated from the rest of the world by miles and years.

In summers they would fish and swim in Stark's Pond and when it got too cold for that, they tracked game—deer, fox, raccoon, pheasant, grouse, and the occasional coyote, which often turned out to be someone's wandering dog. Neither had a real gun, so they didn't hunt, just tracked. Or they sat in makeshift blinds, smoking stolen cigarettes or pieces of grapevine, fingering stolen magazines, masturbating and waiting for bear that never showed up. Left alone long enough, they reverted to earlier childhood games of war, or Indians and settlers, popping up from behind their makeshift shelters to fire BB guns at marauding trees and falling back behind cover. They would stay from the time school let out until it was too dark to see before heading back to their homes.

But while they played, they learned. Finding the nests of deer, the burrows of raccoon and fox, and learning the seasons by the plants that appeared, from the skunk cabbage that came up in the woodlands when the snow was still on the ground and frost in the air but warmth underneath, to the rotation of goldenrod, joe-pye, and jewelweed that signaled the coming of winter, and the long, sloppy V's of geese making their way south in the late fall.

Alone at the regional high school, Ronny would slip out between third-period social studies and fifth-period English to smoke the cigarettes he stole from his father along the unpaved service road that came into the back of the cafeteria. There were always other kids out there, singly or in small bunches. He was a moderately good student who fit with neither the grade chasers nor the misfits. One day, one of the kids in a familiar group waved him over.

"Hey," the smallest one said. "I know you. Forbert. You're from Lydell. I remember you from middle school. Bobby Cabella."

"Yeah. We had gym together a couple of years."

"Right. Mr. Porous Morris. What a fag that guy was. You got smokes?"

"Not today."

Cabella produced a pack of American Spirits, shook one out, and held up a blue Bic lighter. "Lydell, man. We stick together."

"Thanks."

"This here is Matt Laferiere, Steve Woodrow, Paul Stablein, and Larry Morrel. We're all Lydell."

"Yeah. I know. Hey, guys."

"What's going on," Matt Laferiere asked. "What are you into?"

Ronny was slightly surprised and pleased that Matt Laferiere, the leader of the misfits, was actually talking to him.

"Just stuff. Nothing special. I just come out here to get away from the crap. You know? How about you guys?"

"We're just figuring out ways to burn the school down," Paul Stablein said.

"The kitchen," Ronny said. "Fires always start in the kitchen. Nobody will suspect anything."

"The kitchen," Matt Laferiere said. "I like that. This guy thinks. I like that. He's all right."

He was all right. Matt Laferiere had said so. That made him proud in a way he had never felt before. Matt Laferiere was, he thought, the coolest guy in school, always walking with a measured pace, smiling, nearly a smirk that said he knew just how cool he was. And he dated Vanessa Woodridge.

Ronny stood in awe of Vanessa Woodridge. She was pretty, though probably not the most beautiful girl in school, but she was cool, always well dressed, always somehow more grown-up than the others. Grace, he guessed. She had grace and money. Nothing seemed to touch her.

Cabella bumped Forbert's chest with his elbow. "We know, dude. We all know. Lots of shit. Lots of shit to get away from."

"That would be right."

"Listen, dude. We're usually hanging out here before school, at lunch and for a while afterward. Matt here's got wheels. After school we take off and hang out. Always got smoke, usually some frosties, and sometimes some weed. We do all right. You ought to come along sometime. We have a pretty good time."

"That would be cool."

"All right then, dude. See you after last class."

HE HAD GONE WITH THEM THAT AFTERNOON, CRUISING THE MAIN street of Lydell in Matt's Jeep Cherokee, a beater four-by-four, and then out 417 into the country where they rode the back roads, drinking beer that Matt always seemed to have in abundance and smoking a little weed.

It became a routine, going out every afternoon after school, and then, after dinner, they would appear in Ronny's driveway and honk the horn. Ronny would tell his father he was going out for a little while. His father, usually into his second or third Heaven Hill in front of the TV, would raise his glass. "Do your homework?"

"Yeah. Did my homework."

"Behave yourself and get home early."

"SO WHAT ARE WE GOING TO DO?"

"Let's get Ronny laid."

"Right. That's the plan. With who?"

"Katie Montierth."

"Yeah, Katie Montierth. Let's head over there."

They drove quickly back to the state highway, then headed north. Ronny was feeling excited but apprehensive, too. Were they really going to do this? When they got to Ramshead Road, they went half a mile and pulled up outside a ranch-style house with a wooden fence in front. There was a porch light on, and lights in several windows.

"OK. We're here. Go to it."

"What?"

"Go up to the door. Knock. Say you want to see Katie."

"Yeah. Then what?"

"Tell her you want to fuck her."

"No. I can't do that."

"She won't care. She'll either say yes or no."

"No. Not even take her out or anything?"

"She won't care. She likes to fuck. Just go up and ask her. No. Tell."

"I'm not going to do that."

"Shit. Well, ask her if she wants to go for a ride. Maybe she'll fuck all of us."

He got out of the car because he didn't see any way he could not at least do that. If he refused, they would drop him. It would be the end of everything.

He knocked on the door. He heard voices inside, raised. Finally a woman in sweatshirt and jeans came to the door, barefoot.

"Hi. Is Katie home?"

She looked at him like he was a piece of garbage that had gotten accidentally blown up against the door. She turned and walked away but left the door open. He stood outside the storm door and waited. "Katie," he heard. "Someone for you."

"Who?"

"I don't know. Some boy. Deal with it."

Katie appeared from around the corner of the living room, also in sweatshirt and jeans. "What?"

"I'm Ronny Forbert. I've seen you at school."

She cocked her head, like a bird trying to get a good look at something. "Yeah. I've seen you."

"We were riding around. Me and Matt and Paul Stablein and Bobby Cabella. We thought you might want to hang out for a while."

"Matt Laferiere?"

"Yeah, Matt."

"You got booze?"

"Yeah. Beer."

"That's it?"

"We got some weed, too."

"You and Matt."

"And Paul and Bobby, too."

"All right. Hang on. I'll be out in a minute."

He stood by the door after she had shut it in his face. He heard the voices again, loud and angry. He heard Katie say, "Just out. I'm just going out." Then something he couldn't quite make out.

A man's voice. Then, Katie's. "I'm just going to go hang out for a while. I'll be back later."

Then Katie opened the door and came out. "OK, Ronny Forbert, let's hit it."

Katie crawled into the backseat next to Bobby Cabella, and Ronny slid in next to her. Matt gunned the Jeep in reverse, backed into the driveway, peeled out, and headed back down Ramshead Road to the state highway.

"I don't seem to have a beer," Katie said.

Bobby Cabella leaned over the backseat, snagged a beer, and handed it to her. "We're getting a little low on beer now that there are five of us."

"Katie, you got any money?" Matt asked.

"Nope. Didn't figure I needed any money. Is that what you guys wanted, another contribution to the beer fund? What a bunch of douchebags."

"Paul. How much we got? Come on, guys, let's fork up all the money."

They fished in their pockets and handed up a few damp bills and a handful of change. "Not enough," Paul said.

"Shit." Matt leaned into the driver's-side door and fished two bills out of his pocket. "How about now?"

"Still not enough."

"Barry. Barry's always got money."

"Hate to do that," Matt said. "Lot of risk, not much money."

"Well, what else are we going to do?"

"You sure that's all of it? Anyone holding out?" No one was.

"Crap. All right. Let's go get Barry."

"Yeah," Katie said. "Like we need another douchebag. I don't see a shortage of them in here."

"You want beer?"

"I'm here, aren't I?"

"Then we got to go get Barry."

They went up the road, onto Route 417, and pulled in to the side of the Citgo gas station.

"All right," Matt said. "Here's how this is going to go. Paul, you and Bobby go in first. Ronny, you stay here until I tell you to go. Then you go in, make a lap around the store, and come back by the counter. Paul, you do the buy, and Bobby, you do the handoff. Virgie, you take the handoff. They don't know you. Come right back to the car with the handoff. Paul and Bobby will be behind you."

"What's the handoff?"

"Just take what Bobby hands you and get back here."

"What are you going to do?"

"I'm going to drive. Just do what you're told. Don't fucking hesitate. Just do it."

Paul and Bobby got out of the car and went into the store. Katie got out, too.

"Where are you going?" Matt asked.

"Front seat." She looked at Ronny. "No offense, Ronny Forbert."

"Don't get in the front seat. Stay back where you are."

She went around the back of the Jeep, opened the front passenger door, and slid in, right up next to Matt.

"All right. Go in. Remember, take a lap. If there's someone at the counter besides Paul and Bobby, take a second lap. Pretend you're looking for something. If there's no one, walk past the counter, as close as you can get to Bobby without looking like an asshole faggot."

Ronny walked into the store. Paul and Bobby were standing

behind a woman at the counter who was fishing through her purse, probably looking for exact change. Neither Paul nor Bobby looked at him. He walked up the candy aisle, picking up candy bars and then putting them back. Then he walked to the back of the store and down the next aisle and stopped at the shelves of motor oil and flat fix. He read labels on plastic oil bottles.

He saw the woman at the counter turn and start for the door. Paul and Bobby moved up. "I need a cigar," Paul said.

"What kind?"

"One of those in the purple wrapper."

The clerk turned his back, went back to the cigar display, and looked until he saw the cigars in the purple wrappers.

"Just one?"

"Yeah, just one."

Paul examined the cigar as the clerk started to ring it up. "Anything else?"

"No. Hold it. Hold it. This is one of those grape-flavored faggot cigars. I don't like these. You got any White Owls?"

The clerk turned back to the display, put the purple cigar back, and picked up a pack of White Owls. "I got this five-pack."

"No. I just want one. What do you have in singles?"

Bobby shot a quick glance over to Ronny and made a slight nod. Ronny started down the aisle as the clerk named off the brands of single cigars.

"I like those in the plastic tubes. They're fresher," Paul said.

As Ronny came up behind him, Bobby reached out his hand and tucked something into Ronny's belly, like a quarterback handing off a football. Ronny took it and headed for the door. He couldn't tell what it was, only that it was plastic.

He headed for the car, still holding it under his coat. He climbed into the backseat and saw Paul and Bobby strolling out of the store. They got into the car as Matt threw it into reverse, gunned it, and headed back to the highway.

"Give it here," Paul said.

Ronny pulled it out of his coat. He could see it was a plastic tube of money.

There was a printed label: Save a Kid. Give Your Change to the Barry Fund.

"How much?" Matt asked.

"There's some bills, quite a few coins. We're good."

"Should we have taken that?" Ronny asked. "I mean it's for poor kids with cancer or something."

"We're poor kids," Matt said. "And we're out of beer. We are saving some kids."

"Barry was that kid with cancer. He died."

"Then he doesn't need the money, does he?"

"I need another beer," Katie said.

"Get her a fresh one, Bobby. We got enough."

Up the road, they pulled into the liquor store lot. "Bernie's here. We're golden. I'll be right back."

"I want Jäger," Katie said.

"No. We're just getting beer."

"Then you jerk-offs can just jerk off. I want Jäger. What do you want?"

Matt came back in just a couple of minutes, lugging a thirty-pack of Natty Lights. When he got into the car, he pulled a paper bag out of his coat and handed it to Katie.

"This is a little bottle."

"And you're a little ho. Drink it and shut up."

RONNY SAW WHERE MATT WAS HEADED AS SOON AS HE TURNED OFF the state highway—the old gravel pit, now an unofficial town dump. The Cherokee pitched and rolled as they headed down the dirt road that ended at the pit. His heart quickened a bit. He hoped that they had brought guns, though he wasn't sure that there was enough moonlight to really hit anything.

Katie fumbled the beer that Cabella passed over, and she bent over to pick it up off the floor.

"Don't open that," Matt said.

There was a woosh, and a few drops of spray hit Ronny, though most of it stayed in the front seat.

"Fuck," Matt said. "I told you not to open it."

Katie said nothing as she jammed her mouth over the opening in the top of the can, glugging the spray down as fast as she could.

"Beer can kill," she said, at last, gulping for air. "But not that way. Don't be pussies."

They came to the end of the road and parked over the gravel pit.

"We should have brought guns," Stablein said.

Shit, Ronny thought. This wasn't for shooting. This was for partying, partying with Katie. He began to feel apprehension closing around him. Stablein, Katie, then Matt got out of the Jeep. Cabella and Ronny stayed put in the backseat for a while, but when Bobby opened his door, Ronny opened his, too.

"Shit, it's cold out here," Katie said. "Get me another beer."

"Stiffening your nipples, Kates?"

Katie flipped the finger, then ran her hand over her left breast. "That part's working."

Ronny reached back into the Jeep and fished out another beer and handed it to her.

She pulled up her sweatshirt and bra in one motion and rolled the can across her breasts. She laughed. "Don't get close. These things can poke your eye out." She looked at Ronny and pulled her clothes back down.

"We need to build a fire," Stablein said. "Come on, Bobby, let's find some wood in this shit pile."

Ronny, Matt, and Katie stood in a loose group while Stablein and Cabella went down into the gravel pit.

"Shit, it's fucking cold here," Katie said. "Let's get back in the car, Matt." The three of them looked at one another.

"You and Virgie here can go back in the car if you want," Matt said. "I'm staying out here for a while."

Katie regarded Ronny with indifference. "Come on, Matt. I'm freezing my tits off."

"Don't do that. Ronny, take her back to the car. Warm her up."

"Come on," Ronny said. "You're right. It's fucking cold out here." He went back to the Jeep. Katie lingered outside with Matt, then shrugged and came over to the Jeep and slid in the backseat with Ronny.

"So, what's your plan, Virgie?"

"I, I didn't really make any."

"Well, see what you can come up with. It's not that warm in here, either."

Ronny reached over and cupped her breast in his hand and squeezed carefully.

"There's a thrill. Stop, stop. I think I'm going to come." Ronny pulled his hand back.

He could see, or at least thought he could see, Katie smirk.

"So, the 'virgie' part for real?"

"No," Ronny lied. "No, not at all."

"Didn't think so. You got real smooth moves. Like an old pro."

She reached down to his crotch, felt for his penis and squeezed. "What's the matter? This all too exciting for you?"

"No. It's just cold, that's all." He reached down to her crotch and began to rub. She scooted down in the seat a little and opened her legs some.

"Found it." She flipped her empty beer can behind the seat. He continued to rub her through her jeans.

"Hang on, Johnny Wadd. I need some Jäger." She turned over, leaned over the backseat, got the bottle, opened it, and took a long swallow. He ran his hand over her ass. He felt her jeans loosen, then start to slide down. He ran his hand down between her jeans and her buttocks, sliding between them and down, feeling the warmth of her crotch, and a lot of pimples.

She stayed that way for a minute, sliding her jeans down farther until her whole ass was available for his hand. "If you're done back there," she said, "I'd like to turn around. It's not real comfortable over this car seat." She turned over and slid down into the car seat again, tugging her jeans nearly to her knees.

He slid his hand over the fold of her belly, down past a small patch of pubic hair and around the stubble of her mons. His finger slid down into the slippery warmth of her vagina. She put her hand over his and pushed it farther into her.

He continued to slide his finger in and out, then around. He was aware of where her clitoris was supposed to be and knew it was important to find it and work on it, but he couldn't actually locate it. Outside the windshield, which was beginning to frost up, he saw the spark and flare of a fire being started.

"Is this working for you?" she said.

Disappointed, he stopped, and she pulled his hand out from between her legs and pushed him back and started unbuckling his belt. She undid his jeans and tugged them down as he lifted his hips for her. She reached into his underwear and took his slowly erecting penis in her hand. "I don't know why I always have to do all the work." She pulled at him a few times, then bent over and put her mouth over his penis.

He had a sudden, hard inhalation that come out as a gasp. He shut his eyes and leaned back as she moved her head up and down in his lap. Blow job, he thought. I'm getting a blow job, and kept repeating that to himself, trying to maintain his erection.

When he finally came, she kept working on him with her mouth until the sensation was so strong that it was almost, or something like, painful. He pushed her head away.

SHE TOOK ANOTHER LONG SWIG OF THE JÄGERMEISTER. "ALL RIGHT, scout. You're done." She climbed over him and crawled out of the Jeep, still adjusting her clothes. Ronny pulled up his jeans, buckled his belt, and started out after her. "Bring me a beer," she yelled.

They had a small, smoky fire going at the edge of the gravel pit. There was a small pile of wood, mostly broken-up furniture it looked like to Ronny, and Matt, Paul, and Bobby stood around it, staring into the fire and drinking beer. Katie moved into the group, standing next to Matt, leaning in toward him. Ronny followed, taking a place next to Bobby, as far away from Katie as he could get.

"You two have a good time?" Matt asked.

Katie just worked on her beer, so Ronny finally said, "Yeah. Great."

"Great," Katie said.

"This fire isn't giving off a lot of heat."

"That's because it's mostly paper and stuffing from a car seat. As soon as we get some real wood on it, it'll take off," Paul said.

Ronny looked at the pile of wood. Most of the busted-up furniture seemed to be particleboard with vinyl veneer. His father spent a lot of time bitching about that stuff. It was more glue and shit than wood. The fumes it gave off would be toxic, and they would drift his way in the slight breeze that was blowing. He thought of moving over toward Matt, but he wanted to keep his distance from Katie.

"That's not really wood. That's some bad shit, full of arsenic and other shit."

Matt regarded him. "So?"

"The smoke will be like poisonous."

Matt gestured down into the pit. "You don't like it, go down there and get what you want."

"There's not much light," Bobby said.

He didn't want to go down into the pit in the dark, but Ronny figured his old man had to be right about something. And since he was a carpenter, this would probably be it. "Come on," he said, nudging Bobby. "Let's go find some real wood."

"I've already been down there. Go by yourself."

He looked around. It seemed like everyone was smirking at him. He turned and trudged down into the pit.

There was junk everywhere. It had been totally cool when he was walking through it with a gun in his hand and another one tucked into the waistband of his jeans. Now it was just a jumble of shit no one wanted. He could barely make out the stuff he was seeing. He picked up a small branch that looked like it came from a bush someone had trimmed. He bent the branch. It was still green and wouldn't burn so much as smolder. He kicked at a couple of things he couldn't really identify. He listened. Aluminum.

Finally he found an old spindle-back chair. You couldn't make a chair like that out of anything but wood. He picked it up and put it behind him. He saw what looked like some two-by pine. He gave it a tug and it budged just a little. It was probably a wooden pallet from some business. He got both hands on it and yanked. He could hear a lot of stuff falling and resettling as he got it free.

He took the pallet in one hand and the chair in the other. The chair was easy. It weighed almost nothing. The pallet, however, was heavy, and though busted, it was still nailed together and awkward. He worked his way back up the dirt path, carrying the chair and dragging the pallet, jerking it through the dirt. The corner that was down kept snagging on rocks and tire ruts. He tried to right it so it would slide across the ground, but its off-balance weight kept the corner dragging on the ground. As he worked his way back up toward the fire, he heard them all laughing.

"Well, this piece of shit—" He swung it in front of him and flat onto the ground. "—is heavy. You try dragging it up the path."

They all looked at him as though he had said something that made no sense at all. Katie opened her mouth wide and stuck her tongue out all the way over her lower lip. She closed her mouth and spit. Everyone laughed again.

He kicked the chair, heard it crack as pieces of the back flew off it. He fumbled around in the low light, picking up pieces of the chair, and brought them back and threw them on the fire. The fire died down then blazed up again. "Now we're going to have a fire," he said.

"Come on," Katie said to Matt. "Let's go back to the car while these guys get a real fire going."

"Nah," Matt said. "I want to watch the fire."

"I'll go," Paul said.

Katie regarded him. "How much do you think you get for a few beers?"

Paul kicked dirt at the fire.

"Come on, Matt. Let's go," she said.

"No. I'm going to stay here."

"No. Let's go to the car. Fuck me, Matt. Giving your skinny friend a blow job didn't really do it for me."

"No. Not tonight."

"You afraid Vanessa Woodridge is going to find out you fucked me? Or do you only fuck her, now?"

"Drink your Jägermeister. It'll warm you up."

She held up the empty bottle. "It was a little bottle."

Matt frowned. "Why don't you go get us a couple of fresh beers?" Katie turned and stalked back to the Jeep.

Ronny and Bobby took turns jumping on the broken pallet, breaking more boards loose. Ronny stacked them on the fire as it continued to blaze and grow.

"There's a ton of burnable shit here," Paul said.

"Go down and get some," Matt said.

"Why? Why bring it up here?" He kicked the chair until he broke off one of the three remaining legs. He picked it up and set one end of it on the fire. He waited a minute, watching intently, then picked it up. The end that had been in the fire was burning brightly. "We can take the fire down there."

"This is good," Matt said.

"She wants to warm up. We'll take her down there. It'll be plenty hot."

"We're not going to set fire to the dump."

"Why not? It'll be cool."

"Because I said no. That's why."

"Shit, man. We'll have a huge fire. Way better than this pid-dling little piece of shit." He kicked some dirt onto the fire, knock-ing it down until it blazed up again. Ronny threw a couple more pieces of the pallet onto it.

"This is good," Matt repeated. "Fucking firebug."

"Pyromaniac," Bobby said. "That's what they call it. Fucking pyromaniac."

"So?" Paul said.

Katie came back with two beers and handed one to Matt. "Last of the beer."

"Shit," Matt said. "That was a fucking suitcase."

"I guess we're drunk," Katie said.

"You are. How many did you have?"

"Not enough. I'm drunk and still horny."

"Ronny. Take care of her."

"No. You," Katie insisted.

Matt shook his head and ignored her.

"That's right," Katie said. "You only fuck Vanessa Woodridge."

"Shut up."

"I want to go home."

"Fuck him." Matt pointed at Ronny. "He should be ready again."

"Or me," Paul said.

Katie looked at Ronny and Paul. "I want to go home. This sucks."

"You suck." Everyone laughed.

"We're out of beer. I don't want to stand around, watching some junk burn. It's cold. I'm freezing my ass off. Take me home."

Matt threw his beer can into the fire. They could hear the spilled beer sizzle into steam. "All right. Let's go. Everyone in the car."

Paul looked at the still-burning chair leg. He ran to the edge of the pit and threw it as hard as he could. They could see the burning end flare then subside, the glowing end turning circles in the air before it fell into the pit.

"Fucking Paul. What the fuck did you do that for?"

"It's not going to hurt anything. You saw it. It was out."

"It wasn't fucking out. That whole pile of shit is going to catch. Come on. Let's get out of here."

They got back into the Jeep and Matt wheeled it around and headed back down the dirt road, lights off. When they reached the top of the hill, he stopped. They looked back. There was a second glow beyond their fire. "God, fucking, damn it. There goes the best spot we ever had." He reached across Katie and tried to backhand Paul, but was blocked by Katie.

"Hey, watch my fucking boobs." She punched Matt in the arm. "That fucking hurt."

"Shit," Matt said. "Goddamn and fucking shit." He gunned the Jeep back toward the state highway.

By the time they got back to Lydell, Katie had fallen asleep between Ronny and Bobby Cabella. Matt turned the car off the highway and onto the frontage road, down a couple of miles, then stopped at Katie's house.

"You're home, Katie." Katie stirred, murmured something, and went back to sleep.

"Shit. She's out like a light. Get out and dump her," Matt said. "Fucking drunk whore."

"We can't just leave her."

"OK. Why don't you go up to the house, ring the bell, and ask her daddy to come out and get her?"

"Can't just leave her," Ronny repeated.

"You're getting to be a pain in the ass," Matt said. "Do what you want with her. You got two minutes. Then we're out of here."

"Come on," Ronny said to Bobby. "Let's get her up to her house."

"Her old man is going to come out here with a shotgun or something. Let's just leave her in the yard."

"We'll take her to the door. Leave her there."

"No. The yard."

"We'll just leave her by the door and get the hell out of here."

"One minute."

"OK. Let's go."

Ronny got her under her arms and pulled her out of the car. She stirred again and said something he couldn't make out. "Get her feet," he told Bobby.

He didn't give Bobby time to argue, but started backpedaling toward the door as fast as he could, forcing Bobby to keep up. When they got to the door, he let her down gradually, just as he heard the Jeep accelerate and pull out onto the dirt road. Ronny reached up, rang the doorbell, and then he and Bobby ran like hell down the road toward the taillights that were already receding ahead of them.

KATIE HAD DRIFTED OFF SOMEWHERE. NO ONE SEEMS TO KNOW OR care where or why. He wonders about her sometimes. About what happened to her. Is she still drinking, still a slut for attention? Is she still alive? Nobody ever mentions her. It's as if she never existed.

Except that he can't forget her or forgive himself for leaving her there, passed out at the front door of her house. It makes him sick and ashamed when he thinks back on it. Leaving her was Matt's idea, and he had done it because Matt told him to. But he had done it. He, not Matt.

It seems like he had no mind of his own back then. And then he turned on Matt to save himself after the gazebo fire. And he went on and found Gordy, and now he does what Gordy tells him to do. Has he changed, or has he just found a better person to follow? Did he actually push Matt Laferiere into the path of the white car? He wonders if getting Matt killed was just one last try to rid himself of Matt and the boy he had been.

HE WALKS BACK TO THE POND. THE TRAIL IS PRETTY CLEAR OF SNOW, except for patches that are shaded for most of the day. The ground is frozen, but barely. At several points, he can feel it give way under his boots. The pond has a thin layer of ice, but near the middle and around the edges there is water. At the edge of the pond he can see the tracks of deer and, probably, dog, though possibly coyote. No one would be tempted to try this ice. He watched a volunteer firefighter, two years ago, crawl out onto a pond wearing chest waders and pull out a Labrador after it fell through the ice. He had felt vaguely jealous that he was not the one who had accomplished the rescue, but glad enough to see the dog safely on the shore.

It's over twenty miles to Warrentown, but he thinks lunch will be more comfortable there where he isn't really known as he is at Edna's. The drive will eat up a bit more of the day, too.

At Applebee's, he sits at the bar because it seems too lonesome and stupid sitting at a booth or table by himself. He orders a twenty-ounce beer and turns his head, if not his attention, toward ESPN on the big screen next to the bar.

"You think Brady is the best quarterback in the NFL?" a guy two stools over asks him.

He doesn't really know all that much about football, but he knows the local area, which is close enough to New England that Patriots–Giants is a significant issue. "Yeah, probably," he says. "But the Mannings are good, both of them, and Aaron Rodgers is pretty close to Brady."

"No question," the guy answers. "No question at all." Ronny isn't sure what there's no question about.

"But you got to look around them," the guy goes on. "I mean a quarterback is only a quarterback. He can do only so much. A lot of what makes a quarterback is who he's got around him. Brady, he doesn't have the team around him that he used to have. But he's still good. Is he as good as he used to be? You tell me. And Rodgers, he's got a real good team around him. Does that make him better than Brady, or Brady better than him? You got to ask these types of questions. I'm telling you. I really think about this stuff."

"I can tell."

"You know, you sit on your fat ass all day, just watching football, engaging nothing but your eyeballs, what good does that do anyone? Nothing. You're just watching your life get pissed away. You got to think about it. Even if it's only football, you've got to think. These guys here"—he waved a hand around the bar—"they aren't thinking. They aren't using their brains. They're just watching and throwing back beers. That's not good. I'm telling you. No matter what it is, you've got to engage with it."

"I can see your point."

"So, the Rodgers–Brady thing. I mean, it matters, though it doesn't seem like it should. Nothing in this world matters until someone thinks about it. It's like the stool in the dark. It isn't there until you trip over it. Then it's there, and it matters. You don't trip, it's not there.

"So maybe having a better team around him makes Rodgers a better quarterback than Brady. Obviously, it makes the team better and makes Rodgers look better, but what if he is actually better because of that team? I mean how much of any one guy belongs to himself and how much belongs to the team? I mean we're all free individuals, only we're not. We can't just do what we want. I mean, look, I can drive a hundred and ten down the wrong side of the road because I've got free will, no? No. Something of me belongs to the world or the country or the town or something. I mean I have to do what's best for it. I mean *have to*. I'm not a hundred percent free. And that part of myself that is free is that way because of the town or country or whatever. I could have been born a Roman galley slave a couple of thousand years ago rowing a fucking boat around the Mediterranean. Then what part of me belongs to me? None of me. I'm just another part of the boat. I'm just another fucking oarlock or something.

"But what if I fuck up? I mean, say I push when I should pull. Aren't I then not part of the boat, but some force outside of the machine? Am I not then a human being with free will? Maybe it's fucking up that makes you human, makes you *you*. Ever thought about that? So Brady is the Patriots until he throws an interception, then he's Tom Brady, human being. Maybe if you don't fuck up, you don't really exist."

"How are you guys doing over here?" the bartender asks. She's looking hard at both of them, trying to gauge their sobriety. Ronny gives her a small, tight smile and a little shrug. Innocent bystander to the guy's rant.

"Great," the guy says. "We're doing great. We're about to solve the whole free will problem as it relates to professional football. What are you doing?"

"Pouring beers."

"Right. So, who's doing great? We are."

"How about you?" she asks Ronny.

"I'm fine. Barely following the conversation, but fine. I would like a burger, though."

"Bourbon burger, Philly burger, Cowboy burger? You want a menu?"

"No, just a burger. A regular burger with fries."

"Cheese?"

"No, just mustard and ketchup."

"You got it."

"And another tall one." The talker pushes his glass forward.

"Afraid not, Lou. I think you're at your limit."

"How many have I had?"

"A few. Quite a few."

"Do I need a cab?"

"Wouldn't hurt, Lou."

"Call one, then. Young man, it's been a pleasure talking to you. You're a bright young fellow. I predict you'll have a lot of success in your life."

"Thank you."

"Cheryl, I'll be on the bench inside the front door. Tell the cabbie. I'm not going out in this weather."

"HE'S A CHARACTER," RONNY SAYS WHEN THE BARTENDER BRINGS HIS burger and fries.

"He's a sweet guy. Really. Talk your ear off?"

"He was talking. I couldn't really keep up with much of the conversation."

"He was a big shot over at Masters and McLellan. Practically ran the place. Then he made some sort of mistake and that was it.

He got fired. Then he got drunk. Practically lives here until we have to throw him out."

"He's a real cooperative drunk. I've never met anyone quite like that. He must be the best drunk around."

"He's sweet. But he's a drunk. A drunk's a drunk when it all comes down to it."

"I suppose, but I've known quite a few. None like that guy."

"Yeah," she says. "It could be worse. It could always be worse, and generally, it gets worse."

AFTER RONNY LEAVES THE STATION, GORDY PRINTS OUT THE REPORT and puts it in the new folder, 417 Hit and Run. They're three days from the December town council meeting. He needs to be writing his report, but as he thumbs through the folders—citations, arrests, investigations—he knows he can't do it.

"Going home?" Pete asks.

Gordy hasn't even thought about it. "No," he says. "I'm going to ride around for a bit, show my face and see if I can stop any incipient crime waves."

"I thought 'incipient crime waves' was John's job."

"Then I'll help him out. Be back in a bit."

"It'll be lonely without you."

HE REALLY HAS NO DESTINATION IN MIND. PARTLY, IT'S A GOOD IDEA to just cruise around and let people see him. He does a lot of smiling and waving as he goes. People enjoy feeling that they know the police chief on a personal basis. He drives north a bit, then swings onto what was once the main street. His first stop is at the Stewart's, where he considers ice cream, then buys a one-pound bag of Peanut M&M's. They're not frozen, but they'll do.

The town is decorated for Christmas and has been for a few weeks, though he hasn't been down this way since Bonita died. There are silver and red garlands strung up on the streetlights, most of which aren't working anymore. On the windows of the storefronts that are still occupied—the card shop, the Country Goose Gift Shop, Royce's Hardware, and two antiques shops that sell occasionally to lost tourists, but mostly sell furniture from one Lydell family to another—there are paintings on the shop windows, as there are every year, done by kids from the Warrentown Regional High School Art Club. Lots of snow scenes and holly branches, and the occasional Merry Christmas, scripted with lots of flourishes. Halfway down the block he can hear a scratchy recording of Mel Tormé singing his "Christmas Song" from speakers installed in the sixties.

Almost every storefront triggers a memory of some other store that failed years ago. By next Christmas, a third of these stores will be gone, replaced by something equally futile—a homemade art gallery, folk sculptures of painted plywood, and God knows what else.

Beyond the stores and up about a quarter mile is the biggest ghost of all, the webbing factory that closed in 1993, now in Mexico or India, or someplace like that. He takes a handful of M&M's from the bag he holds between his legs. He wonders if they're still made in the United States, or imported from overseas as well.

A few people on the street wave, and he waves back, mouthing *Merry Christmas* though just the idea of the holiday is painful. One of his friends, Marty, a widower, too, refers to Christmas as "an emotional mugging."

He swings north again, still eating the M&M's, until he gets to

417. He turns onto it. As long as he feels the pain, he might as well feel all of it. Less than a mile down the road, he passes the Einhorn house that burned down when a home meth lab exploded. Meth is not common around here, but he supposes that it will become so. It took this old building right to the foundation. He drives past the Citgo and then he is coming over the rise in the road at the accident scene. It's a terrible spot. Drivers going west are just starting to accelerate to sixty when they come over the rise with no sight line at all. As he crests the hill, he can see balloons and flowers piled around a utility pole a few feet from where Matt Laferiere died.

He has asked the town council several times to have the road regraded here so the hill is not so steep and oncoming drivers can see better what's ahead of them.

He stops at the utility pole, thinks to get out of the cruiser, then thinks better of it. Some hundred yards ahead, he can see something big at the side of the road.

He gets out, walks up to it, and sees that it's a deer, a good-sized one, a doe, crumpled next to the road. It looks like it's been there for a couple of days. He doesn't remember anyone calling this in. It's been hit by a car. Small animals, maybe opossums and raccoons, probably a coyote, have been eating from the anus inward. There are bits of a headlight and some chrome trim scattered just in front of the deer.

He shakes his head. This will complicate things just a bit. Someone's going to need body work, and it will probably be called in, and they will have to come out and verify that it's not the hit-and-run vehicle they're looking for. And it's just a plain mess. A deer carcass rotting at the side of the road. What other bad impressions can Lydell make on drivers coming through? He gets back in the car and calls it in to Sue.

"We got a call yesterday," Sue says. "I called Norbert, and he said he would get it out of there. Guess he hasn't yet."

"Call him again," Gordy says. "Tell him I want it gone now. Not tomorrow or the next day." The anger in his voice surprises him.

HE HAS JUST STOPPED AT THE STEWART'S FOR ICE CREAM WHEN HIS phone rings.

"Chief, Steve. I thought you'd want to know. We have a suicide."

Gordy stops and feels his body go cold. Ronny. It would have to be Ronny.

"It's Ben Beacham. He's hung himself in his garage. I know you were friends."

"When?"

"Call just came in. John's en route. Thought you might want to go since you know the family."

"Right. I'm not far." He pulls back out onto the road, heading for the Beachams'.

He pulls in to the curb, just beyond the driveway, as John pulls up to the front of the house. They meet at the front door.

"Steve call you?"

"Yeah."

"I can handle this. Steve insisted that he should call you, but I know you've got a lot on your mind. You don't have to do this."

"Yeah," Gordy says. "I do. I'm a friend. Kay will need to see a familiar face." He rings the doorbell. There's no answer. He tries the door, which swings open. Lydell has changed a lot in the last few years, but there are still people who don't lock their doors.

They walk through the house to the kitchen. They can hear the yelling from there and a steady bass beat. Through the door into the garage, from the warmth to the cold again, they stop and just watch. Ben Beacham hangs from a rafter in the uninsulated garage. His face is purple with trapped blood and his tongue protrudes. Kay stands next to him, a broken rake handle in her hands. She keeps swinging it, thumping it into the body, while she keeps up a steady stream of obscenities—"Bastard, Whore, Fuck, Cunt, Asshole, Shithead, Cocksucker."

Gordy times the swings of the rake handle, then as she launches in to the body once more, he jumps forward and grabs her with both arms, bringing her to him in a bear hug. "Kay, Kay. It's Gordy, Kay. You're all right. Just calm down. Take a deep breath."

"Dickhead. Son of a bitch. Shitlicker. Pussy."

He holds on to her and begins to rock her back and forth. "Kay, Kay, Kay. Ssshh. Come with me. Let's go into the house."

She's sobbing now as if all of the energy she had has been expelled. Gordy can feel the wobble in her knees as he guides her through the door and into the kitchen. He looks at John and then nods toward the body. "Handle this like a crime scene, until we get full confirmation it's not."

He gets her to the sofa in the living room and sits with her while she cries and while her breathing gets ragged as she tries to regain control. He keeps his arms around her, mumbling hollow reassurances into her hair. For a man who never had children, he has done far more consoling in his life than all the fathers he knows.

And then Kay cries herself to sleep. He puts an afghan over her and walks back out to the garage. Ben still hangs there. John is taking pictures of a knocked-over fruit crate and the top of a workbench. "Called for a bus. We'll let them take him down. How's the missus?"

"She fell asleep. I think she wore herself out beating on him and swearing. I've never seen anything quite like it. Though while I was sitting with her, listening to her sob, I wanted to walk out here and take a few swings at him myself."

"At least he didn't make a mess," John says.

"Not one you can see," Gordy agrees.

They hear the ambulance roll to a stop in the gravel between the yard and street. Gordy walks over and punches the door release button, then steps back as the door opener groans and lifts up the double door to the outside darkness.

The attendants open up the back of the ambulance and take the gurney out, shake the wheels down and locked, and come up the walkway and into the garage. "Oh, jeez," the first one says. "I know him. He was a nice guy. A real nice guy."

"Yeah," Gordy says. "He was. He was."

He watches them take the body, untying the knot that holds the rope to the rafter and slowly lowering Ben's body until one of the attendants can take it and lay it on the floor. Then they unfold and unzip the body bag and place it alongside Ben. Finally, they pick him up by shoulders and ankles and move him onto the body bag, which they gently arrange around him, then zip up.

"That's it," one of the attendants says. "Sorry for your loss."

Gordy starts to say that it isn't his loss, but thinks better of it. It's his loss, too, though dwarfed by Kay's. "Thanks," he says.

He goes back into the house. Kay's up and in the kitchen, at the sink, pouring a glass of water.

"They're taking Ben now," Gordy says.

Kay stares out the window, sipping on the water. She nods. "OK," she says, still looking out the window.

"There's nothing more that needs doing tonight. They'll take him to Warrentown, and he will be released back to you sometime tomorrow. The funeral home will take care of all that."

"OK."

"Is there somewhere you can go tonight?"

"I'll stay here."

"Can I call someone who can come over and stay with you?"

"I'll be all right."

"Would you like me to stay? I can sleep on the couch."

"No. Thanks, Gordy. I'll be all right. Gordy, how do we get along without them? I mean Bonita . . . How do you get through your day and everything?"

He walks over to her, puts his arm around her shoulder, and pulls her to him. "You do. You just do. It takes time, but you do. Someone should stay with you tonight. Do you have anyone you can call? Anyone who can come over for the night?"

"No."

"Then I'm staying. I don't have to be anywhere. I'll just bunk down on the couch. I'll be right here if you need me. Otherwise, you won't even know I'm here."

"Gordy, this isn't necessary."

"It is. I'll be here if you need me."

"I think I'm going to cry all night."

"That's fine. Believe me, I know how that goes. I won't bother you. I'll just be here if you need me."

Kay turns and shuffles out of the room, her slippers making soft noises along the floor.

He takes off his service belt, his boots, empties his pockets onto the coffee table, and unbuttons his shirt. He lies down on the sofa in his uniform pants and T-shirt, hearing the sound of her slippers again as she comes back into the room and hands him a pillow and a quilt. She leans down, gives him a hug and a quick kiss on the forehead. "This is not necessary," she says. "But thank you."

"You'll be all right."

She nods. "He's gone now, Gordy, but he had been leaving for a long time. I knew this was coming. I'll start getting used to it tonight."

"OK."

OH, BEN. BEN, YOU DUMB FUCK, HE THINKS. THEN HE IMMEDIATELY feels guilty and wants to take it back. He knows Ben struggled with the general failing of his health and from the effects of the alcohol that he used to try to forget it. He had somehow known that this was coming, not like Kay knew, but still, he knew. But it's a shock.

He feels his own life being stripped away from him. Bonita, now Ben, who may have once been his best friend. What an idea that is. Best friend. How do you choose? How do you decide? Then it comes to him that he doesn't have a best friend, hasn't had one since Bonita died. But maybe the line just moves up. Maybe Pete is his best friend now.

Snow is coming down in small light flakes that swirl in the porch light outside the window. Nothing substantial, he guesses. There's just a lot of it this early in the year. A lot of death, too. The snow of the dead.

Ben and Kay had been his and Bonita's closest friends in the nineties. They went out to dinner at least once a week and were generally at each other's houses on the weekend. They were both childless, and that gave them a certain bond, as well as considerable freedom. But the stronger bond was drinking. A typical get-together involved several cocktails and, later, a couple of bottles of wine with dinner, their voices getting louder and louder, their laughter more raucous.

That had begun to change when Gordy and Bonita stopped drinking, partly for health reasons, partly for Gordy's job. They still saw each other, but less often, less joyously. Gordy couldn't help feeling that Ben, on some level, took Gordy's sobriety as an accusation of his own lack of it. Finally, they met by chance in stores and restaurants, greeted each other heartily, agreed to get together soon, then didn't.

He had heard that Ben's health was failing, and he had meant to be in touch. But their relationship became one of meaning to, but not following through. Kay looks considerably older. She was always small, and feisty. He guesses, if he thinks about it, her attack on Ben's body is not all that surprising. She was always quick to laugh, quick to anger. Still, he hopes never to see anything like that again.

He listens for a while and hears her soft sobbing then, later, her snoring. He drifts into sleep.

Gordy wakes in the dark. He has to pee. He swings his legs off the sofa, and they crash into something. He feels his way in the dark. He reaches for the doorknob to the bathroom and touches a smooth sheet of glass. He spreads his fingers and runs his hand over the smooth surface that seems to go on forever. Where is he? What is this? He moves to his right to find the light switch, though he has never needed it before. He finds, instead, an armchair. He stops and tries to orient himself. There's small ambient light from various sources, including a digital clock that reads 1:47. "Bonita?" He moves to his left and crashes into a hassock or ottoman.

Suddenly the room is flooded with light. It's all unfamiliar until he sees Kay standing in the doorway. "Gordy? Gordy, are you all right?"

"I didn't know where I was."

"You're right here. You're all right. Do you need something?"

"I got up to use the bathroom."

"Behind you and to your right," Kay says.

He turns and sees the open door. He nods.

"You going to be all right?" she asks.

"Just woke up confused. Confused myself more. I'm fine."

She takes a step forward and hugs him to her. He puts his arms around her, and they stand for a bit, just holding each other. He hasn't seen her in ages, but here they are now, both partnerless and grieving. He pulls her tighter, then quickly lets her go. She takes a step back.

"The light switch is right here." She indicates with her index finger. "Leave the light on if you want."

"I'll turn it off when I'm done."

"Good night, Gordy."

"Good night. Sleep well. It's hard, I know. But you get through it, Kay. Believe me."

TWO WEEKS BEFORE THANKSGIVING, SUE THE DISPATCHER HAD COME into the office, white-faced. "Gordy, we just got an emergency call. It's your address. Something's happened to Bonita."

He didn't stop to think or wonder what had happened. He ran out of the office without his coat, got into the Explorer, and headed for home under lights and siren. He heard the other siren as he neared the fire station. He saw the rescue vehicle pull out onto the road and hit the lights. He fell in behind it as it rocked along the bumpy road, south toward his house.

He pulled up in front, letting the rescue park in the driveway where it would be able to move unimpeded. There were already a couple of cars parked on the road, volunteers from the fire department. He ran to the house, right behind the EMTs.

"What happened? What happened?"

"Woman down in the bathroom. Head trauma. Heavy bleeding."

"My God, my God," Gordy said. Bonita. Bonita had fallen.

The EMTs, both of them, went to the bathroom door and stopped. There were already two men in the bathroom. "Let us in," one of the EMTs said. The men rose up and stepped out of the bathroom so the EMTs could get in. Gordy crowded up to the door behind the EMTs. He could see Bonita's flowered housecoat and a lot of blood. Her wheelchair was overturned next to her.

"She's alive," one of the volunteers said. "Lots of blood, though."

"Let me in," Gordy said.

One of the EMTs said, "Stay back," then looked up and saw who it was. "Give us room to work here."

Gordy leaned inside the bathroom door, looking over the back of the EMT who was raising Bonita's head from the floor. There was blood everywhere, especially on her face. She looked unresponsive.

Someone tugged at his sleeve. He waved his arm to be left alone.

"Gordy, it's Lois. I found her. She's hit her head."

He turned. Lois Schlemmer, in jeans, heavy boots, and a snowflake-patterned sweater under a barn coat, leaned against the wall, trying to keep out of the way of the paramedics. She took Gordy's arm and pulled him next to her. "I came over to check on her, and she didn't answer. I found her on the floor like that. It looks like she had been on the toilet and tried to pull herself up. But she slipped and hit her head on the sink. I don't know how long she was on the floor."

"I need to talk to her," Gordy said.

Lois again pulled him by the arm. "She can't talk. I tried to wake her up, but she would go right back out. Let the paramedics do their job. It's the best we can do right now. Just let them work."

"I should have been here," Gordy said.

"Oh, no. Don't you start blaming yourself. You have to work. You can't work and stay home both."

"I should have stayed home."

"Gordy, stop it. You have a very important job. Don't blame yourself for what you can't control." She reached down and put her hand on his. He realized that he had been wringing them. "They're working on her now. She'll be OK."

He nodded dumbly.

"Excuse us. Coming through." Two more EMTs were pulling a gurney up to the bathroom door. "Make way. Please. Let us through." They stopped at the bathroom door. "OK. Everyone out of the hallway. We need room here. Please, into the other room." A couple of people pushed past him, and he looked through the door and got his first good look at her, lying on her back now, her head swathed in gauze. Her eyes were closed, and she was absolutely white. She looked terrible. Lois pulled him by the arm, but he pulled away and moved toward the bathroom door. "Bonita. Bonita?"

"Chief," one of the EMTs said. "Please. She's ready for transport. We have to get her out of here." Lois pulled his arm again, and they stepped into the living room.

He heard the count and the grunt, then the clicks as the gurney was lifted and unfolded. They were sounds he had heard hundreds of times, and from the living room he could see in his mind's eye exactly what was going on. He had never felt quite so helpless.

Then the EMTs were maneuvering the gurney out of the hallway and through the door to the living room. Once in the clear, they moved faster. As they came past him, Bonita's eyelids fluttered, then closed again.

Lois grabbed his arm and pulled her to him. "I flushed the toilet," she said. "And pulled up her underpants. She didn't have time. I know you're not supposed to touch things in emergencies, but the poor dear. She would be so embarrassed. I'm sorry if that was wrong."

"No," Gordy said. "You did right. It's not a crime scene. It's an accident. Thank you, Lois. You're a good neighbor and friend."

"Gordy," Stan Maynard said. "We're taking her to Warrentown. They'll be able to stabilize her there. They'll decide if she needs to go somewhere else. You want to follow us?"

"How is she?"

"Hard to tell right now. We got the bleeding stopped, and she goes in and out of consciousness, but she's not responsive. She lost some blood, but it's a head wound, and they're bleeders. They'll be able to tell more in Warrentown. I don't think it's all that bad, but you never know. A little worried about the lack of response. You want to ride with her?"

He turned and followed the gurney back out, waited as they loaded her, then stepped into the back of the bus next to her. An EMT he knew only as Sherry was setting up an IV of Ringer's. She smiled at Gordy and motioned for him to sit on the box at the back door. "Try not to fret, Chief."

"We're in an ambulance."

"We're taking care of her," Sherry said.

Bonita's eyes came open as the ambulance lurched forward and the driver switched on the siren. She looked around her, saw Gordy. Her eyes widened a bit, then closed as she went back to sleep.

It was a forty-minute ride to Warrentown. In the back of the bus, with no windows except two small ones, he couldn't judge their progress. He looked out the windows a couple of times, but he could see only the bare tops of trees.

When it seemed they were long past time to get to Warrentown, he felt the bus slow, turn, and finally come to a gliding stop. Sherry moved to Bonita's head and motioned him to get against the wall. The doors came open, someone reached in and unlocked the gurney and pulled. Sherry got on the front end, pushed, and the gurney went out the doors, the wheels came down, and she went through the glass doors and into the emergency room.

The emergency room was worse. He was relegated to the hallway as doctors, nurses, orderlies came and went. Each time the door opened he searched for her in the line of curtained cubicles, but he could never see her.

He called the station to talk to Pete, but Ronny Forbert answered the phone. "Pete's out. I'll have him call you back. How is she?"

"Don't know," Gordy said. "I think she's all right, but I don't know. We won't know for a while."

"I hope she's OK, Gordy. We're all worried. I'll have Pete call you."

"No, that's all right. He doesn't need to. I just wanted to check in. I'll need a ride back to the house later on."

"We'll get you. Everything's cool here. Nothing really going on."

"Great. I'll talk to you later."

"Cool. Good luck, Chief. Call when you're ready."

HOURS LATER, ONE OF THE DOCTORS CAME OUT TO SEE HIM. HE WAS calm, matter-of-fact, and bloody.

"Did you get her stitched up?" Gordy asked.

"Yeah. Minor cut. We stitched her and stopped the bleeding. That was all pretty minor. But that's not all. In fact, it's not even a significant part of what's going on, more effect than cause." The doctor paused, shook his head, and started again. "She's had a stroke. A big one. Right now, it's full paralysis. Whether it's going to stay that way or not, it's too early to tell. She was a long time without help. I understand a neighbor found her. You have any idea how long she was down?"

Gordy shook his head. "I left the house at seven. She was fine. Lois, our neighbor, found her just before noon. I don't know how long she had been lying there."

"That's a crucial element in stroke, how soon the patient gets treatment. This is frankly not a good scenario. We've treated her with thrombolytic, but the effectiveness of that correlates to the time between the cascade and administering the drug. This may have been a long while or it may well be within the framework of the drug's effectiveness. It'll be a couple of weeks before we know much. Recovery is always slow." He reached out and touched Gordy's shoulder. "We're going to do everything we can."

"That's it? Wait and see?"

"Wait and see," the doctor said. "Wish I had something better to tell you, but it's what we have."

He stayed with her until evening when Ronny Forbert drove to Warrentown to pick Gordy up. Gordy leaned over and kissed her cheek. "You're going to be all right. You'll be home for Thanksgiving. Just wait and see."

Three days later, she died without ever regaining consciousness.

CHAPTER 5

ROUGH NIGHT?" PETE ASKS WHEN GORDY FINALLY MAKES IT IN.

"The worst. I spent the night on Kay Beacham's sofa."

"How's she doing?"

"About like you'd expect. She's going to have to deal with the details for a couple of days. That should help, actually. It will keep her mind occupied. No time for random thoughts. Those come later."

"Well, yeah. I have some news for you, though."

"What do you have?"

"Tox screen on Laferiere is .21."

Gordy whistles softly. "Blasted."

"Even more. Positive for THC."

"That will be some good news for Ronny."

"Substantiates his story. You want me to call him and let him know?"

"I'll do it. He probably thinks I'm ignoring him."

"Worrywart," Pete says.

"Yeah. Take a bit of the load off him."

"There's more. We got a call last night. Abandoned white sedan in the woods off 417. Front-end damage."

"You got someone on that?"

"Not yet. Thought I'd wait for you on that. Call came from Pam Garrity."

A slight shock goes through Gordy. Pam Garrity. The Goat Lady.

"I didn't even want to try to call this one. It's your decision." Years earlier Gordy and Pam Garrity had become "involved." It had lasted several months, and the news of it moved slowly through Lydell, as such information always moves through a small town. Gordy and Bonita had barely survived it, but they had, and Gordy and Pam had no more dealings with each other beyond a nod and hello if they ran into each other at the market, though he never saw her or heard her name without the same shock he had just felt.

"Where's Steve?"

"He's checking on another barn break-in. Farm equipment missing. The usual. He'll check out Glendenning, but he won't find anything."

"Did it happen before or after Laferiere got killed?"

"Noticed it this morning. Hard to tell if it went missing last night or a couple of days ago. Martin would know. Should I pay him a call, just to aggravate him?"

"Let's keep on the Laferiere case. We won't find the stolen equipment." Ronny Forbert had implicated Matt Laferiere, as well as himself, in the disappearance of farm equipment, but they had never been able to track it down. It was pretty common knowledge that Martin Glendenning was paying Laferiere and his crew of misfits to steal the equipment, but they had never been able to find it, despite several searches of Martin's property, which only increased the tension between Gordy and Martin. Ronny had told Gordy about helping Matt Laferiere steal a small disk harrow from a farm some ten miles out of town.

"THOUGHT YOU WEREN'T COMING, MAN." MATT OPENED THE DOOR, let the other two in then climbed in himself, closing the door after him. There were four of them. Matt, Paul, Bobby, and Ronny.

"It took my old man a while to get into the Heaven Hill."

"You weren't a little scared?"

"No," he lied. "He just stayed up longer than he usually does."

"Then we go. Just head west on 417." It was crowded with all four packed on one seat. Bobby Cabella had a twelve-pack. "Don't drink that in the truck," Ronny said.

"You're shitting me. What are you? My mother?"

"He can't know we have the truck. He finds out, and I never get it again."

"Don't worry your pretty little head. We'll clean it up when we're done. Just go down 417. About ten miles."

"You got directions?"

"No. I'm psychic. Hell yes, I got directions. Let's go."

"Ain't going to catch the midnight rider," Bobby began to sing.

"Does he have to sing that?"

"Yes. He does. Have a beer, then shut up and drive where I tell you."

They went out 417, then cut down Birch Pole Road and headed north. In about a mile Matt said, "Slow down. Cut your lights."

They came onto a small house just off the road, only a porch light burning. "Real slow, now." It was a dirt road, and the ladder racks on the truck rattled at every bounce. They crept past the house. It stayed dark.

"Keep it slow. There's a turn up here," Matt said.

"Can I turn on the lights?"

"No. It's got to be dark from here on until we get back to the main road. Just keep it slow. Look for the gap in the fence."

They went through the gap in the fence and they were on a tractor road, heading between two fields. "OK. It's up here about another two hundred yards. OK. Stop here. Don't shut it off, just take it out of gear and keep it running. Bobby, get out and get the license plates."

"You're taking the license plates off?"

"Unless you want someone with a flashlight to be able to tell the police exactly who was here, yeah. It's a precaution. Just a precaution."

They all got out of the truck. Bobby Cabella went to the front end with a screwdriver. Matt Laferiere said, "Come on. It's right over there."

"Where? It's dark."

"Dark is good. That's why we do this at night when there's not a lot of moon."

"Don't you have a flashlight?"

"A flashlight will be seen for a long way on a night like this. We'll find it. Your eyes will adjust. You'll see it."

They moved across the field, three of them abreast ten yards apart. No one said anything. They walked slowly. Ronny could see little, and he walked slowly, afraid he would trip over whatever it was they were looking for. They had walked fifty yards when Matt came up to him and pointed to the left. He could make out the outline of Matt, but not his features.

He saw it just to his left, about five yards away. He grabbed Laferiere's arm and pointed.

"Yeah. That's it."

"What is it?"

"A disk harrow." They were speaking just above a whisper. "Go get the truck. Leave the lights off."

He maneuvered the truck off the tractor path and into the field, which was furrowed, the ground still soft. He kept it moving slowly, afraid it was going to get stuck in the soft dirt. As he got to where he thought the harrow was, he slowed further until he saw Matt waving at him, giving him signals to get the truck into position. Matt held up both arms for him to stop.

Ronny got out of the truck and went to where Matt, Bobby, and Paul stood around the harrow. "This field is all plowed up, all loose dirt."

"It's just been harrowed, man." Matt motioned to the piece of equipment on the ground. Matt moved to the truck and lowered the tailgate, then gathered them together. "Everyone take a corner. Take a good grip. Lift it straight up, then we walk it to the truck and lift it in. Not slide it. Lift it. Once the front of it is on the truck the guys in the front climb into the truck and lift it, the ones in the back lift and push. It should go right in."

Ronny got on the back end of the harrow with Paul Stablein. There was a frame of angle iron that was cold against his hands.

"OK. One, two, three. Lift."

Ronny felt the frame of the harrow move under his hands, but he could lift it only a little, not enough to free it from the ground. It slipped from his hands and back down again.

"Hang on to it, damn it."

"How heavy is this thing?"

"Heavy. Now come on. Lift."

This time it came free of the earth and moved up. He got it up to waist-high and was then pulled forward as Matt and Bobby pulled it toward the gate. He stumbled slightly but held on. He could feel that his corner was lower than the rest, but he moved slowly ahead. Already his arms were burning with the exertion.

"OK. Paul, Ronny. You guys hang on for a second. When I say 'lift,' lift it high. It's got to clear this tailgate. Move slow. Don't knock us down. Lift."

He tried pulling his arms up, but it did little good. He bent his knees and moved his elbows out so he could get his shoulders under it. The harrow moved forward a little.

"Hold it. Hold it. You guys just hold it for a second. We've got to move over to the side. Don't let go. Just another couple of feet." His arms were wavering now and his shoulders had joined in the burn.

"Lift."

He moved it up another couple of inches and pushed forward. He lost footing in the loose soil and fell forward, the harrow coming down with a bang in the bed of the truck, his corner catching him hard on the shoulder, but the harrow stayed up, resting in the truck bed.

"Fuck. Forbert. You just about crushed my foot. Now lift."

He got his body under it one more time and lifted and pushed it another foot into the truck.

"Good. Good. We're good. Gentlemen, the prize is ours."

He looked back to where the house was, waiting for the lights to come on. The noise the harrow made coming down into the truck was horrific, but the house stayed dark. He and Bobby Cabella and

Matt got into the truck. "OK," Matt said. "Back this thing out. Go slow. Paul will guide you. Keep your foot off the brake. We don't want any brake lights."

His arms were shaking. He turned and looked out the rear window where he could just make out Paul Stablein waving him back. He put the truck in reverse and started out. He could feel the wheels sinking into the ground.

"Give it gas," Matt said. "But not too much."

They moved back, slowly, unevenly, the weight of the truck pushing deeper into the furrowed ground. Finally, they made it back to the tractor path, then back another couple hundred yards to the road.

"Now. Slowly, lights off until we get well past the house."

It was one of the hardest things he had ever done, moving the truck slowly down the road. The bumps in the road caused the harrow to rattle and bang in the bed. He just wanted to get the hell out of there, and he fought the impulse to floor it and be gone.

They came up toward the intersection of the main road, and Matt told Bobby to get out and put the plates back on.

"Fuck."

"What?"

"I left the plates on the bumper."

"You fucking moron. Get out there and see if they're still there."

Bobby jumped out and went to the front of the truck. He held up a plate. "One. I got one."

"Shit," Ronny said. "What will we do?"

"We need to get out of here. We can come back tomorrow and find the other plate."

"No. We got to get back onto 417. If a cop sees us, we're pulled over for sure, and then they find the harrow in the back. We're really, totally, and completely screwed."

"You're going to have to drive us back."

"I don't want to drive past that house again."

"We could walk back. It's not that far."

"I need to get this truck home before the old man wakes up and finds it gone."

"We got three choices. Walk back, drive back, or try to make it home with one plate."

"What kinds of choices are those?"

"Ours."

"I say we walk back."

Ronny said, "No. That will take forever."

"Then we drive back, or we go on without a plate."

"No. We can't do that, either. We'll get caught for sure, or my old man will see it first thing in the morning. We have to get those plates."

"Then we drive."

Ronny looked back at the still-dark house. He could feel the odds starting to stack against him. "All right."

"Wait," Stablein said. "If one of the plates was still on the truck, where did the other one fall off? If we're driving, we'll never see it without lights. We have to walk."

"Oh, fuck."

"No. He's right. We walk."

They started back up the road, walking four abreast. "No talking," Matt said. "No smoking. No light."

They moved past the house for the third time, the crunching of gravel on the road sounding as loud as a car's engine. They all kept their eyes on the road but kept sneaking glances at the house, waiting for a light to come on in one of the windows. Just in front of the turnoff to the tractor road, Bobby Cabella said, "Got it. Stepped on it." He held it up for them all to see.

They turned and started back toward the truck. Ronny felt the tension grow as they got closer to the house. When they got up even with it, Paul Stablein bolted. "Fuck," someone said. A window in the far corner of the house lit up. "Go."

They ran back to the truck and piled in.

"Let's get the fuck out of here."

"The plates aren't on."

"Fuck it. Go. We got to go now."

Ronny put the lights on just before they hit 417, sliding from Birch Pole Road onto the main road, cutting off a car that blared its horn at them.

"Just keep going. Don't slow down." They were heading west on 417, no plates, speeding, with a pissed-off driver behind them who could call the police. They kept going until they saw a sign for a side road. Ronny slowed, took the side road, and drove down it a quarter mile until he pulled over to the side of the road. Bobby Cabella jumped out and started screwing the plates back on.

Ronny saw the car lights behind them before the others did. There was nowhere to go, nothing to do. The car pulled up even with them, and the driver rolled down his window. "You all right? Need help?"

Ronny shook his head and waved his hand, signaling that they had everything under control, though he was barely keeping his bowels under control.

"We're good, man," Matt yelled, holding up a beer can. "Everything's good."

The driver leaned over, closer to the door. "Then get out of here."

"We just have a little repair here. As soon as we get this fixed, we'll be on our way," Ronny said.

"People live on this street, and we have to pick up your god-damned beer cans and bottles, and God knows what else every damned weekend. You get out of here. I'm coming back in a few minutes, and if you're still here, I'm calling the police. You got that?"

"Yessir. Soon as we get this little thing fixed, we're gone."

"And I don't want to see a bunch of beer cans here, either."

"You won't. No problem. I promise."

"Ten minutes. You got ten minutes to get out of here."

"We'll be gone," Ronny assured him. Then, as the car drove on, he turned to Matt. "What did you do that for?"

"What?"

"Wave that beer can around. Were you trying to piss him off?"

"No, man. Just some kids out partying. And if something should go wrong, we got a witness that we were here. You got to think, man." Then he threw his beer can into the road.

When everyone got back in the truck, Ronny turned it around and headed back to 417.

"West, another couple of miles. I'll tell you where to turn."

"What? Are we getting something else?"

"No, man. We're dropping the harrow off. Unless you'd rather just leave it in the truck and let your old man drop it off for us."

In three miles he pulled the truck onto a side road and then down another tractor path into a field.

"This is good. Right here."

"Is he meeting us here?"

"No. We drop it off. He knows where it is. I'll get the money from him tomorrow."

"Is this his land?"

"We're just going to drop it off here. You don't need to know the rest. I'll take care of all that."

The harrow came out of the truck easier than it went in. But it was still an effort, and Ronny felt a huge sense of relief when they turned the empty truck around and headed back toward the IGA to drop off the guys. It was well past midnight, now, and he still had to get the truck home.

"When do we get our money?" The thought had come to him unbidden.

"When he calls me."

"Who is he?"

"You don't need to know that."

"You'll collect the money and split it up?"

"Mostly I'll just collect the money. We all make the money and we'll all use the money. We'll have gas, beer, weed, and, yes, ammunition for the next month or so."

"But I provided the truck."

"We'll gas it up. Do you know how much you had when you took it?"

"No," Ronny said. He had forgotten to check that.

"Then we won't gas it up. Everyone is used to having less gas than they thought. They never have more gas. Better to leave it down a little than to fill it up. Trust me on this."

"YOU GO CALL ON MARTIN," GORDY SAYS. "MAYBE YOU'LL LUCK OUT. I'll check out the car."

Pete just nods.

"GOAT LADY" WAS AND WASN'T A GOOD DESCRIPTION OF PAM GARRITY. It was what most of the town called her because she lived as far from anyone else as she could with a small herd of goats. She sold milk, cheese, and goat's-milk soap in a lot of the stores in the area and at farmer's markets. She lived by herself, alone with the goats and no one to help her except a distant neighbor woman who delivered her products a couple of times a week. Pam was an attractive woman, small and slight, though well-muscled, and her red hair was glorious.

Gordy turns down River Rock Road and immediately slows. The road is barely graded, rutted and badly eroded, and it gets worse the farther down it you go. To get to Pam's place, you have to want to pretty badly.

Often enough, he had wanted to very badly. They met when he was just a patrolman investigating a call from her that dogs were getting over her fences and attacking the goats. One of her goats had been killed, another badly mauled. She had shot one of the dogs inside the pen. Not much had happened. The dog's owner was located, allegations were exchanged, then everything just quieted down.

Except that Gordy continued to come back. He liked her fiery red hair and temper. She was one of those women who looked you in the eye, a look that was demanding. There was not a lot of art to it. He made several trips to her house, and he was sure he was welcome.

He pulls into her driveway, negotiating the erosion at the side of the road, where it crosses a small ditch. Little has changed. Her house is small, the smallest building on the property, kept up, but plain. She has made no attempt to prettify or gussy it up. It's the house of someone who lives alone, happy living that way.

He finds her in the barn, mucking out the milking stalls, still small, though a few pounds heavier. She wears canvas pants, a canvas coat, and muck boots, nearly to her knees. Her red hair, streaked with gray now, spills out from under her John Deere cap.

"Hello, Pam."

She stops shoveling and turns to face him. "Gordy Hawkins. As I live and breathe." She shifts her weight, stands hip-shot, and stares him down with the slightest trace of a smile. "You get demoted? They send you out this far?"

"Sent myself out," he says. "How are you, Pam?"

"Good, Gordy. Just me and the goats. It seems to suit me better than me and people. How about yourself?"

"Not so bad. I got a job, no goats."

"Two bad decisions there, Gordy."

"Probably. Yes. Heard you found a car."

"Out there." She nods vaguely to the northwest. "Don't know if it's what you're looking for, but it might be. Hasn't been there very long. Come on. I'll show you." She looks at his shoes. "That the best you got for shoes?"

"Do I need boots?"

"Not if you're willing to ruin your shoes. There's a lot of wet out there. Not all of it's frozen. Got some muck boots if you want them."

"It's all right. Probably need new shoes anyway. Let's take a look."

They move around the barn, past the goat pens. The goats run over at the first sight of them, doing little dances of anticipation. He finds goats creepy. He isn't crazy about herbivores in general, just because of what he perceives as their lack of intelligence. But goats have those eyes. Devil eyes.

"I was sorry to hear about Bonita, Gordy. I truly am sorry." She stops and turns to face him. Her face is starting to line quite a bit, but she's a good-looking woman. It's strange how a woman with mud and goatshit on her face can still be an attractive woman.

"Thanks, Pam. We all have our struggles. All of us."

Pam nods, turns, and walks through the pens, toward a small path into the woods.

The ground seems solid enough for a few steps, then a pile of leaves gives way under his foot, which gets sucked into the mud.

"You can go back and get those boots. We're still a couple of weeks from a real solid freeze on the ground."

He shrugs. "I've made my choice, Pam. I'll live with it."

"We all do, eventually. One choice doesn't necessarily mean you're stuck with it for life, though. Hate to see you ruin a good pair of shoes."

"So, I'll look like a working cop instead of a desk-sitting cop. Go ahead on."

The car sits amid a copse of birches, a white Lexus, old, already going to rust. He guesses it's early nineties, '92 or '93. The plates and inspection sticker have been removed.

"Don't know how it got here," Pam says. "Pretty sure it wasn't here last week, though I don't know if I was out this way last week. Anyway, it hasn't been here long."

Gordy looks at the front end. The right front headlight is broken and the bezel smashed. The right front fender is crumpled and turned toward the grille, which is badly bent, the bumper cover heavily dented. He looks for traces of blood. There's rust and, maybe, some blood. "How did it get here?"

Pam points to the northwest. "There's an old logging road that goes out to Rattail Road. Mostly overgrown, but kids still use it." She runs her boot through the leaves and sticks on the ground, uncovering flattened beer cans and rotted condoms. "The usual kid stuff—beer cans, cigarette packs, empty bottles of shitty alcohol, used party hats. Pretty much all over the place."

Gordy walks behind the car and back along the path it must have taken to get here. He feels frozen wheel ruts under his shoes. "That would be it, I think. I'm going to call the state police to come in here and take a look at this. They need to go over the car for evidence and rummage around for any ID that might have been left behind. It's hard to say, but I'd put money on this for our car."

"State police, huh?"

"Yeah. Hope you don't mind a bunch of cops out back here."

It's clear that she does mind. "That's a horrible thing, to just hit someone and drive off. Send them out. I'll bring them back here. Have them call first. Cops usually don't do that."

"Yeah. Sorry. I was anxious to get here and see this. I got an officer who's pretty busted up over this. I'd like to clear this as fast as I can."

She pushes the John Deere cap back on her head. More of the red hair spills onto her face, and she brushes it back behind her ears. "You seen enough of this?"

"Yeah. I think we have what we're looking for here."

Pam turns and heads back toward the house. Gordy follows. He tries not to notice, but she's still trim in the legs and backside. Pretty good for a woman close to sixty.

"You want some tea or something? I don't keep coffee."

"I better not." He starts to explain, then just leaves it. "I ought to get back to work."

"You're welcome to come in."

"Reports and stuff. Got to call the Staties."

She turns and faces him. "Do what you need to do."

"I really appreciate this, Pam. Thanks for calling it in." He isn't sure what to do. He starts to stick out his hand to shake, then drops it. He wants to hug her, but that isn't right, either. He's standing close enough to her that he can smell her, even in the cold air. It's a good smell altogether, sweat and dirt, maybe a whiff of goat here and there. She doesn't back off.

"You're welcome. I mean, you're welcome to come in. If not now, another time. I mean, situations being what they are and all. You're welcome here. You know the way."

He reaches out and touches her shoulder, and that draws her in, though he isn't sure that's what he wants. She puts her arms around his waist, and he puts his arms around her shoulders. They stand like that for a few seconds, unsure of the next step, if there is a next step.

"I do know the way." He drops his arms from around her and steps back, breaking free of her grasp.

She nods, turns, and walks back toward the house.

"Pam. Thanks again."

She waves her hand without turning around and goes on.

HE SETS OFF BACK DOWN THE TRAIL HE HAD JUST WALKED AND COMES back to the car. He looks inside. Pretty clean. No doubt the VIN numbers are gone. He looks at the broken brush behind it, pushing some aside and walking what he assumes is the path of the car. It's harder going than he thought it would be. Because of the semi-frozen ground there are no tracks. Only the broken brush shows the path the car traveled. He keeps walking, looking ahead of him for more signs that the car came this way. He feels it first with his feet, as his left foot slips and then his right. There was a hump here that indicates the tracks of trucks and wagons. It's now just a matter of walking out. The nervousness about finding the old logging road gives over to the question of whether this is the car they want or not. If it is, will it exonerate Ronny?

But there's more troubling him. Even though they live in the same small town, it has been years since he has seen Pam, and even more years since he has talked to her. And it has all come rushing back, not just the memory of their time together, but the jumble of feelings he's always had trouble sorting out.

His time with Pam had been full of turmoil. He was drinking a lot, and trying to convince himself that he wasn't. He had moved to Lydell a few years before, taking the job of patrolman after his job in Salem had dead-ended. The small, fiery goat woman had caught his attention early on, first as a novelty, then as a woman who seemed to be everything Bonita wasn't.

Pam was fiercely independent, living deep in the woods with her goats, selling their milk and cheese at the local stores, surviving, but not much more, yet happy and proud that she was surviving. She seemed to him a hippie holdover, an exotic creature from an exotic time. She was an artifact from a time of powerful emotions, many of them sexual.

And Pam was unabashedly sexual. He had been investigating the ownership of dogs that were attacking Pam's goats. It was exactly the kind of odd thing that had pulled him to small-town police work. He had not even realized the depth of his attraction to her much beyond the simple acknowledgment that she was a good-looking woman, despite the smell of goat and stale sweat that seemed always on her.

And then he reported a settlement offer from the dogs' owners, who seemed to have no real interest in restraining their animals until he explained that he had the authority to have them picked up and, after a hearing, put down. He found himself looking at her for a response to their offer to restrain the dogs and pay damages, and then seamlessly moving in to her for a kiss that would jumble his new life in Lydell.

They had been lovers for several months, if *lovers* was the correct word for it. Pam seemed entirely accommodating, receptive to him whenever he made his way back to River Rock Road to her little farm. He was thrilled by her openness and aggressiveness, her desire that seemed unalloyed. She wanted sex and took it. There was no talk of love, no need of it. He had been tempted many times to tell her he loved her, but didn't for fear that she would dismiss him from what seemed a perfect relationship. He was fascinated with her body, smaller than Bonita's but densely packed with muscle. So packed that at the peak of passion, her ferocity brought him close to fear that she would hurt him, despite their differences in size.

They went on for weeks into months of sex and drinking and talking that went so far beyond the mundane chatter he shared with Bonita, he found himself falling more and more deeply in love with her, and when he realized it would never be reciprocated, he grew resentful. He had begun to think how he might leave Bonita and begin a new life with Pam, and then had to deal with the realization that he was living with a fantasy. Pam had no real interest in a life with him, and he felt betrayed in a way he never thought possible.

The irony of their reversal of the conventional didn't escape him. The thrill of protecting, even possessing in courtship, turned against him as he became the vulnerable one, kept. When, on rare occasion, he made love to both Pam and Bonita in the same day, he began to despair that Pam didn't care what he did when he wasn't around her. He took refuge where he could, in drinking.

Did the affair lead to the drinking, or the drinking to the affair? He'd never been able to decide, knowing just that it was a time of being lost, walking in circles, trying to find a way out among an infinity of ways that led nowhere. And it was only when Pam cut him loose, tired of the drinking and moping, that he was able to right himself, quit drinking, and work his way back to something that seemed, to him, normal.

And considering this now—the feeling of being lost, the inability to choose any particular direction—Gordy realizes that he's lost. Not metaphorically, but literally lost. He has wandered from the ruts and into some smaller trail, likely a deer trail that is beginning to get smaller and smaller.

The only thing to do is to go back and walk carefully, feeling the way with his feet until he hits the ruts of the old logging road again, and then head either out or back to Pam's and his cruiser. The logging road isn't far. He comes on it in a matter of only a few minutes. But once back to the logging road, he has to decide whether he needs to turn right or left to make it out to Town Pound Road. There's not enough sunlight through the solid gray clouds to indicate direction. He curses himself for not paying more attention as he came down the road. To wander off a logging road is pretty hard to do, and to lose one's direction is just plain stupid, but he has, and now he has to make a decision. Only he doesn't. If he turns the correct way, he will walk on to Town Pound Road. If he goes the wrong way, he will be back at Pam's and his cruiser. He turns left and starts walking, and he walks until he comes up to the broken brush that lead to the white Lexus, and, beyond that, to Pam's little farm.

"You forget something?" she asks as he walks back between the goat pens.

"No, not really."

"Got lost, huh?"

"Yeah. I guess I did."

"It's all right. The logging road comes out just a quarter mile beyond Bird Creek. Can't really miss it if you're paying attention."

"And why didn't you tell me this earlier?"

"You seemed set on a walk through the woods. I wasn't going to spoil that for you."

"Well, thanks for that. I think I'll just get in the cruiser and head back to the station. We'll have someone out here to get the car off the property."

"Gordy, when you get to the end of River Rock Road, turn left."

"I haven't forgotten."

"Could have fooled me."

RONNY FORBERT STAYS IN BED AFTER HE WAKES. HE GOES BACK OVER the whole scene in his mind. Why didn't he give Matt Laferiere a field sobriety test? He tried, but Matt refused. Is that right? Is that true? Did he try? He thinks he did. He's pretty sure of it. He got Laferiere into position, legs spread, hands on top of car.

He took one hand down. Right? Left? Right. Cuffed it. Pulled the other hand down. That's when it all started. Laferiere spun to his left and tried to grab him by the back. He spun around himself, grabbing Laferiere by the front of his jacket. They spun together and Laferiere slipped. Or did he slip? He slipped. Laferiere came across his body and thumped against Ronny's leg. He went down and sprawled into the road, which lit up with the headlights of the car. Did he put his leg out to trip Laferiere? No. Yes? He can't remember.

He gets up, starts the coffee, goes back into the bedroom, and gets down on the floor. He stretches his hamstrings, quads, and lats. He does one hundred crunches, a hundred reverse crunches, then forty push-ups. He struggles with the last four or five of the push-ups. How long has it been since he's been in the gym? He had better get in there today. He is starting to feel the deterioration already.

While he showers, he goes through it all in his mind again. The leg. That's what really bothers him. His leg. Did he deliberately try to trip Matt? Did he do it accidentally? Did he do it at all? He feels the thump of Matt's leg against his just as Matt lurches out onto the road. But this is new. He didn't remember that earlier. Is it coming clear in his mind, or is he making this up?

Out of the shower and dressed, he calls Nessa, and this time she picks up.

"Hi. You have time to get some breakfast, before class?" he asks.

"No. I'm afraid not. I have a final this morning at eleven. I don't feel at all prepared for it. I need to study."

"How about after? Lunch? Dinner?"

"No. I'm so sorry. Tomorrow I have two more finals. I'm going to be studying for those right up to the last minute. And one more the next day. Then I'm done. No more. I can do whatever I want, and I want to be with you. Is that OK? I know this is a really bad time for you. I know you need some company and some talk, and that I'm letting you down. I feel bad. This really makes me feel awful. Can you hang in there?"

"Yeah," he says. "I can hang in. You hang in, too. I remember what finals are like. But I need to see you. Soon. It's kind of a rough time."

"I know it is. I'll see you soon. Very soon. Promise. Call me whenever you want."

"It's OK. It really is. I'm OK." He hangs up and sighs. He's trying to be understanding. He really is, but he's finding it difficult. He remembers finals in college. It was a bad time, and he always tries to give her plenty of room to take care of her studies, even though it probably means losing her sometime after graduation to a job in some other place. What will happen then, he doesn't know. In the meantime, he's going to respect her plans. He isn't the fool that Matt Laferiere was.

But it's the isolation that gets to him. He's been alone most of his life, but he has never felt so alone as he does now. He's living inside his head, and he needs to get out of it. The whole thing just keeps replaying and replaying, and he can't stop it.

He needs to get out of his apartment, but he has nowhere to go. He can't go to the station, and he can't see Nessa.

And that bothers him. It's as if he and Matt Laferiere are in a battle for Nessa, and he's losing to a dead guy. He's never been able to completely believe that Nessa is his girlfriend. Somehow, somewhere he has always sensed Matt's presence in his relationship with her, as if one or the other of them has never quite let go of Matt, though both of them should have, and they both claim to have let go long ago.

He wonders sometimes if Nessa is with him just to spite Matt Laferiere for the many slights he gave her. And in the past few days, he has started to wonder if he is with Nessa to get back at Matt for turning his back on him after the fire. Now Matt is dead, but he doesn't seem to want to stay dead, mocking him, even when Ronny wins, even when Matt is dead.

He's always had the feeling that he has lucked into his relationship with Vanessa Woodridge. Looked at from nearly any angle, it would seem that she is out of his league. She's attractive and self-possessed, as if nothing in Lydell actually sticks to her. She is, by his standards, rich, though she denies it. Her mother teaches and her father is a lawyer, albeit a small-town one, one who has served on the town council and now represents the town in legal matters. She was popular in high school, though not of cheerleader caliber, and smart, though she has chosen to go to community college in Warrentown, rather than one of the universities.

And Ronny is neither rich nor popular, and though smart enough, he's never been ambitious enough to push that. He has gone to the same college Vanessa attends, but in criminal justice while working as a patrolman. They seem to have little in common, except Lydell and Matt Laferiere.

HE HAD BEEN A PROBATIONARY PATROLMAN, GETTING READY TO GO through the academy, on the first assignment of his career—directing traffic around a construction site on Route 78. It was late June, and he wore a fluorescent-yellow nylon safety vest over his summer white shirt and dark pants. The shirt was already soaked with sweat, and his pants were beginning to chafe.

One hundred yards up the road was Vanessa Woodridge, who had been Matt Laferiere's girl up until six months ago. The argument had seemed to be over Vanessa's decision to go to college after graduation from high school. Ronny wasn't sure about that, but Matt seemed plenty pissed off that she was set on doing it. It didn't seem to Ronny that it was the sort of thing you broke up over, but then he had never had a real girlfriend, only hookups and fumblings in the dark. The whole thing seemed odd to him.

Vanessa was the construction company's official director of traffic. She carried an orange stop sign on a short stick. She wore a yellow safety vest, too, but underneath she wore a white T-shirt and cutoff jeans rolled up, and heavy work boots on her feet. It was a pretty good look, Ronny thought. Her hair was tucked under a yellow hard hat, but it was already coming down in long, sweated strands. He had never seen her this way, sweated and wearing cut-offs. The clothes surprised him and made her seem more complicated and mysterious than she had ever seemed before.

A giant Caterpillar excavator was tearing chunks of pavement out of Route 78. It would roll onto the highway, the bucket would come down, the huge teeth on the bucket tearing, buckling, then breaking the asphalt, and pulling up the dirt and gravel under it. Then the bucket would rise, and the excavator would back up, turn, drop the load into a pile in a dump truck, and come back into the road.

When the excavator came onto the pavement, Vanessa would stop the traffic until the excavator had bitten again and taken its load away. Then she would let the traffic through, one lane at a time. Ronny stood by cruiser four, the worst heap of a car he had ever driven, to take the other direction if they needed to stop traffic in both lanes, and as a backup in case some impatient driver tried to do something stupid and ignore the woman with the sign.

He checked his watch. It was two fourteen. The work crew was on until four thirty, and so was he. He heard Vanessa yell. He looked up and saw the excavator lumbering toward a blue Camry in its path. Vanessa was waving the stop sign in front of the Camry, which stopped and backed up. Crisis avoided. There was nothing interesting here.

Then the driver of the excavator, a guy he barely knew from school a few years earlier, leaned out of his cab and yelled something at Vanessa that Ronny couldn't hear. She shook her head and raised her hands up in bewilderment. The car was out of the way, Vanessa was back off the road, and the excavator came the rest of the way forward, took its chunk of pavement, and backed off. Vanessa reversed the sign for the Camry from Stop to Slow.

And then it happened again. The excavator, still fully loaded, jerked forward and came toward the Camry. Vanessa yelled and the excavator stopped, inched forward again, then stopped and backed up. Vanessa watched as the excavator backed up farther, then waved the Camry through. The excavator lurched forward, stopped, then backed up again.

Ronny walked over to Vanessa, who was turning her head rapidly from the Camry to the excavator, which had now turned in preparation for dumping his load into the truck. "What's going on?" he asked Vanessa.

"I don't know. He's being an asshole. He's not paying attention to me, like he can't read the signals. I don't know what's going on. Ask him." She turned away in obvious disgust.

Ronny nodded like he knew a cop should, then turned and walked back to where the excavator was dropping the rest of its load. He walked up to the side of it and knocked on the window glass. "Is there a problem?"

"Hey, man," the driver said. "No problem. No problem at all."

"You scared the hell out of the guy in the Camry. Her, too."

The driver smiled. "It's all good, man."

"You two need to be in better sync."

"I'd like to sync with her. That's a sweet little ass there. Think she's going to pee her pants?"

"I think you guys better get back to work and quit fucking around."

The driver grinned again and saluted.

THE NEXT TRIP TO THE ROAD WAS UNEVENTFUL, BUT ON THE ONE after that, the excavator started to back off then lurched forward toward a white F-150 that had just started to cross the site. Again, Vanessa yelled. Ronny moved forward and pointed back, telling the driver to get the excavator out of the way. He could see the driver grinning at him.

Fifteen minutes later it happened again. This time the excavator went right at Vanessa, causing her to turn and run. Ronny ran back to the site. "I saw that," he said.

"Me, too. Love it when she turns around, though her front isn't bad, either."

"Quit fucking around," Ronny said. "Get back and do your job. Leave her alone."

"I'm just fucking with her. No harm. Just playing. This job is boring as shit."

You should try my job, Ronny thought. "Quit fucking with her. Quit fucking with me. Quit fucking with the traffic. Now. I'm telling you."

"Or what?"

He hesitated. He remembered this guy from high school, though he was older than Ronny. He had something of the reputation of a badass back then. A slight tremor of fear rose from his memory. "Or you're going to jail. Public endangerment."

"Oh, fuck. Get real. Stop being a hard-ass. It's just a little fun on a hot afternoon."

"I mean it. You do it again, and you're going to jail."

"Yeah? What then? The job gets shut down, everyone loses money, and it's all your fault."

"No, not my fault. Your fault. You've been warned. That's all you get. One warning. I want this stopped right now."

The driver scowled and put the excavator into reverse. It lurched backward.

Ronny didn't think he really had the authority to arrest the guy and shut down the job. And the driver was probably right about the consequences. Still, he had made the threat.

On the next trip, the excavator came forward and suddenly dropped the bucket down to about four feet from the ground and swung the bucket toward Vanessa. She yelled, turned, threw the stop sign at the excavator, slipped on a pile of dirt, and fell. Ronny took his radio and called for backup. Then he ran to the excavator, holding his hand up, and turned it counterclockwise—turn off the machine.

The driver lifted the bucket all the way up and drove the excavator into the one open lane of traffic. He shut the machine off, jumped out, and threw the keys to Ronny, who missed the catch. The keys landed somewhere behind him.

"Fuck you," the driver said, now enraged.

"No. You're fucked. You're going to jail. You're under arrest."

"Bogus. Completely fucking bogus. I am not going to jail." The driver climbed back into the cab.

Ronny walked over and tapped on the glass again. "Get out."

"I know who you are," the driver shouted.

"Good. Get out."

The driver crossed his arms and leaned back in the chair, uncrossed his arms, gave Ronny the finger, and then recrossed them.

Less than a minute later Ronny saw the cruiser coming, lit up. It stopped next to his cruiser. Pete Mancuso got out. Thank God for Pete. No one was going to fuck with Pete. In the meantime, the foreman of the construction company came up in a hurry, asking what was going on.

Ronny held up his hand to the foreman and walked back to where Pete was coming toward them.

"What's going on?" Pete asked.

"This idiot was charging cars and the sign girl with his excavator. Really dangerous. I warned him, but he kept doing it." He turned to where Vanessa was brushing herself off.

"He hit her with the excavator?"

"No. Chased her. She fell trying to get out of the way. I warned him."

"That all you did? Warn him?"

"No. I arrested him."

"For what?"

"Reckless endangerment. He was going to hurt someone."

"Why isn't he in cuffs?"

"He ran back to the excavator and shut himself in."

"What was he doing? I mean, is he drunk? High? Sunstroke?"

"I think he was showing off for her." He pointed to Vanessa. "Shit."

Pete walked over to the cab of the excavator. "Get out," he told the driver.

The driver wasn't so sure now. It was one thing to have the kid cop threaten him with arrest, but this big cop seemed another matter. He stayed in the cab.

"Now I told you to get out. You get out. There's no other option for you. If you don't get out, I'm going to snatch your skinny white ass out of that seat and haul you out. I promise, you won't like that."

"What the hell is going on?" the foreman asked.

"That's what we're finding out," Pete said. "Now you go stand back over there somewhere."

"I've got deadlines."

"Then move over there faster. You," Pete said to the driver. "You coming out, or am I coming in after you?"

Slowly, the driver opened the cab and crawled out. "I didn't do anything."

"Then this will work out OK for you. Do you understand that you are under arrest?"

"I didn't do anything."

"He was being a complete asshole," Vanessa said.

"Tell you what. Turn around and put your hands behind you. I'm going to cuff you for your own safety. Once you understand that you are under arrest, we'll talk about what you did or didn't do."

"What are you doing to my driver?"

"You stay back. You and I will talk later." Pete turned again to the driver. "You have any weapons on you? Guns? Knives? Brass knuckles? Bazookas or bombs? Anything sharp I might stick myself with?"

"Pocketknife. Front right pocket."

Pete fished out the knife and cuffed the driver, then took his shoulder and turned him around. "OK. Now, what didn't you do?"

"Anything. I didn't do anything."

"Miss? You all right?"

Vanessa smeared some blood from her scuffed knee. "Yeah. I'm all right."

"That young lady is bleeding. That look like you didn't do anything?"

"She tripped."

Pete looked up and down the road. "Patrolman Forbert, get this traffic moving out of here."

Vanessa hopped up from the dirt pile she was sitting on. "That's my job. I'll do it."

"There's a first-aid kit under the dash of my car. You'll want to clean up that knee."

Pete moved the driver back so he could lean against the excavator. "My officer says you were grab-assing and fucking around with that young lady and menacing traffic doing it. He wrong about that?"

"I was just joking."

"That's what I thought. Tell me. Just how stupid are you? How you figure that charging people and cars with twelve tons of equipment is just joking?"

"It was. It's all that it was."

"Fool. You're going to jail. You were warned to stop by an officer of the law, and you didn't. How damned foolish is that? You're going to jail for being a nitwit. Come on." Pete walked the driver back to his cruiser and put him in the backseat. "Going to be hot in there. Another price for stupidity. Think the young lady likes you better now? Fool." He slammed the door.

"Where are you taking my driver?" the foreman asked.

"Jail."

"Who's going to finish this job?"

"You know how to operate this thing?"

"Of course I do."

Pete shrugged. "Problem solved."

"I'm the foreman here."

"And a damned fine job you did, letting your driver fool around and jackass himself right into jail in the middle of a job."

"Shit. Where are the keys?"

Ronny pointed to where he had been standing. "I don't know. In the dirt where he threw them."

"Officer. Officer," the foreman yelled. Pete turned. "When you take him to jail, tell him he's fired, too."

Pete smiled and shook his head. "It would be a pleasure. But I only do my job, no one else's."

Ronny walked back to where Vanessa was standing by the road. "Are you sure you're OK?"

She looked down at her knee where the blood was coagulating. "Yeah."

"That guy was a class A jerk."

She nodded. "Yeah." She walked over and picked up her sign. "Let's get back to work."

THEY BROKE AT FOUR THIRTY WITH THE FOREMAN HANDLING THE EX-cavator and supervising the cleanup for the night. Forbert arranged traffic cones and signs around the dug-up section of the road. It would be another two days, he figured, to get the work done and the road repaved. He headed back to the station. The holding cell was empty.

"Where's the prisoner?" he asked.

"Probably in a bar somewhere. Don't know, don't care. We let him go half an hour ago."

"Aren't we charging him?"

"Gave him a summons. Let the court sort it out. But you and I, Patrolman Forbert, need to have a little talk. Get a couple of things straightened out. I will get your back. I always will. But I don't want to be hauled out of an air-conditioned office for this kind of foolishness ever again."

"I needed help. He wasn't going to cooperate."

"But he did, didn't he? He cooperated with me just fine. It's part of your job to make him want to cooperate."

"What was I supposed to do? Draw my weapon?"

"Did I draw mine? Hell, no. You played your biggest card first, and you left yourself with no alternatives. Understand?

"You tell someone you're going to arrest them, you better be prepared to arrest them. Got that? But don't just jump right into that. Talk to the guy. Don't put him on the defensive. Try to reason with him some. Give him a chance to back down, gracefully. Try not to arrest people. It saves us a lot of time and aggravation. Next time you call for backup, you better be in danger. You weren't in any danger at all here. You just had an uncooperative jerk." He leaned toward Ronny and lowered his voice. "When you called me, you lost points with that fine young lady out there. You think about that? Bad move, son."

"I wasn't trying to impress her."

"What? Are you blind? She's fine. Way fine. Hell, I was trying to impress her. She's fine, and not all inked up. I, myself, prefer women with sensible skin."

"I know her."

"And you want to know her better, don't you?"

FOR THE NEXT TWO DAYS, HE KEPT HIS EYES ON VANESSA AS SHE moved the traffic through the construction zone. The jerk driver had returned the following day and behaved himself.

"I thought he was fired," Ronny said to the foreman.

The foreman shrugged. "He's good at what he does. He's on notice, though. He won't give you trouble."

Ronny nodded and went back to his post next to his cruiser. Everyone, it seemed, knew more about handling people than he did. He supposed that he would have to learn that. He held himself straight and tried not to look like the kid just out of community college that he knew he was.

He watched Vanessa. Even she seemed to understand things that he didn't, and she was a few years younger than him. But to him, she was a hot, rich girl. She lived in the world he looked at from the outside. As least, that's what he had always thought. She had a nice house, and her father, formerly a town councilman, drove a new Accord.

She was going to the community college, not the university, and her job was worse than his. He had been surprised that she even had a job. He supposed that her father just gave her money for whatever she needed. And now it was he who was on a career path. He was a cop, and he intended to rise through the ranks and, someday, be the police chief, like Gordy.

It bothered him that she had been Matt Laferiere's girlfriend. He couldn't make sense of that. Laferiere was a loser. He seemed like a very cool guy in high school, and maybe he still was. But he was going nowhere. He would end up broke and drunk, maybe even in jail. Matt Laferiere didn't have much to offer someone like Vanessa Woodridge.

He guessed she kind of liked bad guys. A lot of girls did. He thought of her as the kind of woman who would marry well. Have a good job. Maybe a couple of kids. Drive a good car and live in a nice house. Maybe belong to a country club. Laferiere would never be able to give her any of that. But, he thought, maybe Patrolman Ronald Forbert could swing it. Matt Laferiere was something she just had to get through.

He had seen her house a couple of times. It was a raised ranch with a split-rail fence and a mowed lawn and flowers and bushes and trees that had actually been planted, not just ones that came up. He had never been inside, but he imagined they had nice furniture, not old beat-up couches like his, but good ones, ones you could sit in and be comfortable. Probably even wall-to-wall carpeting, maybe air-conditioning. He wanted to have a house like that someday, a house where he could live with someone like Vanessa and raise a family that wouldn't fall apart like his had.

And Vanessa herself. She was, as Pete said, "Fine." And maybe Pete was wrong about the tattoos. Maybe she had some. Some you couldn't see, ones just for the special guy. And, maybe, that could be him.

He really wanted to talk to her, to ask her out. But she seemed like she was from a different world than his. But she had gone out with Matt Laferiere, and Matt was no better than he was. Definitely worse. He lived in a trashed-out house surrounded by junk cars and farm equipment. Ronny was going to be someone. He was going to be Officer Ronald Forbert, Lydell Police Department.

AT THREE FORTY-FIVE THE FOREMAN CAME TO HIM. "WE'VE GOT ANother two and a half, three hours before we're done here. I just talked to the office. They want us to finish tonight. They're willing to pay the overtime to get us out of here and on to another job. We're going to need you or another cop until around seven, plus cleanup. Can you get clearance to stay?"

"I don't know. I want to knock off. Get dinner."

"What? Are you fucking kidding me? She'll stay, too. Maybe you can make up your mind about her."

"What do you mean?"

"You've been watching her like she was the last quarter of the

Super Bowl. She'll be gone tomorrow. You'll have a couple more hours to figure it all out if you stay."

Ronny reddened and frowned.

"I mean it, man. Tomorrow, she's fifty miles from here. You can make your move tonight, if you're ever going to. You really want her to slip through your fingers?" He nodded at Vanessa. "And I'm buying dinner."

"I can't force you to do it," Gordy said when Ronny called him. "I mean I can't order you to take an overtime shift, if you really don't want to do it. But I'd like them out of here tonight. It'll put a couple extra bucks in your next paycheck. And I would appreciate it. I don't want to have to call in another officer for a couple of hours of standing beside the road. If you can swing it, I would like you to do it."

"Chief says OK," Ronny told the foreman.

"Outstanding. I'd like to tell you we might be done early, but once they go on the double bubble, they slow down. But we should be done by seven. I'll go up to that place on 417 and get dinner. You want anything special?"

"Get me the turkey dinner plate."

An hour later the foreman was back with several bags. He sorted through them and started handing them out. "Eat while you work," he said as he passed out the Styrofoam go-boxes.

Ronny walked over to the foreman's truck.

"Here you go. Turkey dinner plate. Grab some utensils and napkins from the other bag. And here. She wanted a salad. Take it to her. Ask her if she'd like a better dinner later on. It might work. Not a terrible move."

He walked the box over to Vanessa. "Dinnertime. Boss says eat while you work." He watched while she stopped a car heading west and waved an eastbound through. She came back and opened up her Styrofoam box. It was all lettuce, tomato, and chicken with a clear plastic cup of dressing on the side. He took the plastic bag with the napkin and utensils from his pocket. "Silverware?"

She opened the cup of dressing and drizzled less than half of it over her salad. Then she got the fork out of the back and poked a piece of lettuce with it. "Fuck," she said and ran out to stop a westbound pickup and wave a Honda through. He stood and watched her. He felt stupid just standing there watching her work, but he fought the impulse to turn around and walk back to the cruiser and his own dinner.

"Thanks," she said when she came back. "For the dinner."

"No problem." Then, "I thought maybe you'd like a better dinner. I mean some other time. A real dinner."

She forked more lettuce into her mouth and gave him a quizzical look. "You're asking me out?"

"Yeah. You know. Dinner. In a real restaurant. Plates and silverware."

She squinted as if to get him into focus. "You still hang out with Matt Laferiere?"

"No. Not anymore. That was a long time ago."

"Yeah." She regarded him as though he were a used car in questionable shape. "Me, too. Yeah. I guess we could do that."

"Great. This weekend? Saturday?"

She took more lettuce and shook her head. "No. Can't Saturday."

"Sunday?"

She shook her head again. "This whole weekend is no good. Next?"

"Sure. Next Saturday?"

She took her phone from her back pocket. "What's your number?" She punched the numbers into her phone and in a second, his phone rang. "OK. You've got my number. Call me."

"I will. For sure. Next Saturday."

"Cool. Oh, shit." She put down her salad, picked up her sign, and ran out to slow a speeding Ford Escort. He followed her and made a down motion with both hands to the driver, who slowed, then smiled weakly as she eased through the construction.

"I'll call you next week."

"Right."

HE CALLED HER THE FOLLOWING WEEK. THEY WENT TO AN ITALIAN restaurant just outside Warrentown, Pete's recommendation. He watched what he drank, trying to relax and get comfortable, but fearing letting his guard down. They endured an overly attentive waiter and began telling their lives from the present forward.

"Right now I'm just general ed," she said. "To start with. I'm going to transfer to the university when I graduate at the community college. I'm thinking business administration."

"Wow. Cool." He could think of nothing more to say.

"I don't know if it's cool. There should be some money in it and the chance to get out of Lydell and move up in some company."

"Cool." He nodded. "Why didn't you just start at the university, rather than the community college?"

"Money." She shrugged.

"Money? But you're rich."

Vanessa laughed. "Rich? Far from it. You think I'd be out working on road crews if I were rich? I mean, yeah, I'm getting a great tan, but it's pretty nasty work out there on the road every day."

"Hmmm." Her answer stymied him a little. He was poor, or had been poor. He understood that. But what was Vanessa if she wasn't rich? Middle class? Wasn't that a form of rich? Or was it just another shading of poor? "I'm going to college, too. I mean, kind of. Taking courses at night."

"What are you majoring in?"

"Criminal justice. I've already taken a couple of classes. I'm only able to take a course or two because I have to do it on my own time. But Gordy has agreed that he'll schedule me around my classes. It'll take a long time. I know that. But I have a good job, and I know that when I graduate, I'll be able to get a better job."

"Like what?"

"Not sure. Maybe stay with Lydell and work my way up—sergeant, maybe even chief. Gordy's getting kind of old. Or move over to state police. There's a lot more room there to work your way up. I may even decide to go on to law school." He stopped himself. He wanted to tell her that he felt like a rat in a maze, helplessly lost until he had suddenly turned a corner and seen a way out he hadn't seen before. And once he was out of the maze, there were an infinite number of ways he could go. He would be free, and he could be a success, something he had never even considered possible before Gordy put him on the force.

Vanessa lifted her glass again. "To future successes." They clinked glasses.

"So," he said. "You think you'll get out of Lydell?"

"Why not?" she asked. "What's in Lydell? It's dying. I mean, it's dead. It just doesn't know it yet."

"I don't know. I don't think that's true. I mean, things are bad. No question about that. But they can get better."

She shook her head. "In some ways, I really love Lydell. It was a good place to grow up in. But it hasn't stayed a good place. There's really no future in Lydell that I can see. Lots of past, but no future. The mills aren't going to reopen. The farms are all dead. If you look around the edges of town, it's all starting to get overgrown. Each year the forest gets closer in. One of these days, it's going to just take over, and there won't be a town anymore, just some deserted buildings in the middle of a forest. It's too bad, but that's what I think is happening."

"So, after college, you're getting out."

"I'm already out. My body's just stuck there for a while. You know, when I broke up with Matt, I think I broke up with the town, too. He's just like the town. He's got no future. He's just hanging out, waiting for the inevitable end, doing what he's always done, hanging on, getting by, never changing, not even to save himself. One day I looked at him and realized that the guy I thought was so cool was just sad. The forest is going to take him over, too. I mean it already has. He's doing what guys in Lydell do. He's cutting fire-wood now. And that's not a life. I want a life."

"Me, too. And I know what you mean. I thought Matt was the coolest guy there was. I wanted to be like him. Him and Bobby and Paul. They're still riding around in the Cherokee, getting high and hanging out. It was fun while it was new, but, man, that got old fast."

She smiled. "And you got out of that trap. Maybe you're getting out of Lydell, too."

"I don't know about that. Part of me really wants to stay. Take over Gordy's job when he's ready to retire. Another part keeps telling me that there's more future somewhere else."

"Anywhere else."

"I don't know about anywhere else, but somewhere else. I don't know. I don't think I'd like to go down south. All rednecks and humidity."

"You got both of those, right here, just not so many, I think. You know what place I think about? You're going to think this is silly."

"No. No I won't."

"Dallas. I think about Dallas. It seems like a really cool place to me. People think about Dallas, and they think about cattle."

"And cheerleaders."

She gave him a fake frown. "But it's not like that. I mean, I've never been there, but I've seen pictures. It's this big, beautiful city, with tall buildings. There's this one that's outlined in green lights at night. It's just amazing. It's a big city, and it's getting bigger. There are lots of jobs there. I think if I get to Dallas, I will have put Lydell completely behind me. I'd come back, of course. Sometimes. I think my parents are going to stay here, though maybe not. I think if they had grandkids somewhere, they'd move to be near them."

"You want kids?"

"Of course. Not right away. I want to get myself settled and into a good job, a career, but, eventually, I want kids. Yeah. How about you?"

"Well, I guess I'd need a wife first."

"Not absolutely necessary, but helpful, certainly."

"No. I want a wife. I know that. And kids, too. I could give a kid the things I never had."

"Like what?"

"Like a nice home. And parents. I mean I had parents, have parents. But neither of them is much in the way of parenting. My mother left us when I was twelve. My dad tried, but he didn't do a real good job. I think having a kid got in the way of his drinking.

Not that he didn't have time to do plenty of it." He pointed to her wineglass. "You want another glass?"

"Uh, sure. I'm having a good time."

"Me, too."

He called the waiter over and ordered another glass of the Chardonnay.

"You're not having another?"

He smiled. "You know how embarrassing it would be if I got pulled over for DUI? I'd, like, never live it down. Even if it didn't cost me my job."

She smiled at him, nodded, and regarded him silently for a minute. He felt like he was being studied, and thought, maybe, he was doing all right.

AFTER DINNER THEY WENT TO A MOVIE IN WARRENTOWN. HE HADN'T known what movie to suggest. Action adventure seemed wrong, as did a horror film and an animated feature aimed at kids. That left the romantic comedy. The perfect choice. A chick flick. She wouldn't think of him as the macho cop. The seating was awkward and rife with high school conflicts. Put his arm around her, hold her hand? It all seemed way too obvious and gawky. So they sat quietly next to each other, occasionally sharing the popcorn.

On the way out of the theater, he guided her through the door and she quickly stepped away from his hand at the small of her back.

"What did you think?" he asked.

"Cute. No chemistry, though."

That seemed clearly to be a comment on the movie, but it could have been more.

When they got to her apartment, they sat for a minute in the truck.

"This was nice," she said. "You're nice." Then she put her finger to his lips before he could respond. "No coffee or drink," she said. "Sleep. Alone."

He nodded. "Can I call you?"

She leaned over and kissed him. It was a good kiss, probably the best kiss he had ever had. It wasn't eager and sloppy, but still forceful enough that he felt a shudder go through his body. She leaned back, smiled a tight smile. "Yeah," she said. "You can call me."

WITHIN THREE WEEKS, RONNY FORBERT WAS AS HAPPY AS HE HAD been in his life. The vague dreams that he had barely allowed himself to dream had suddenly come true. He had a job that he liked, an apartment of his own, and he had a girlfriend. It was far too early to admit it to anyone, even himself, but he was in love, and he thought there was a chance, at least a possibility, that Vanessa was as well. The life that he had thought so distant, one of a kind of general prosperity and respectability, seemed to be right in front of him.

Not that he was prosperous. His pay was, he understood now, not very much. He wished that he had bought a cheaper truck, maybe even a used one. Dating itself was expensive. Dinner at Applebee's and a movie after was not so bad, but he had to keep buying clothes. Each date seemed to require a new shirt until he could build up a rotation of them. Once he had done that, he thought he would be able to stop shopping every midweek, though summer was coming to an end, and he would likely need sweaters and such. Vanessa was not demanding and didn't seem much concerned by what he wore, but she dressed well, and he didn't want to become an embarrassment to her.

He had credit cards, and as long as he could keep making the payments on the cards, he would be all right. And things looked better just ahead of him. In another six weeks, he would advance from probationary status to full patrolman. That would mean a raise in salary. And there were rent-a-cop opportunities that Pete knew about and was willing to share. Construction sites and events needed off-duty police for hourly or daily work. And the money was pretty good.

And Vanessa was helpful. Often enough, she insisted on paying her own way—splitting the dinner check or alternating paying, and paying her own way into the movies. And they had gone straight from dinner last week to her apartment, made love, and then gone to sleep. And Sunday they had lounged at her place, luxuriating in each other's bodies and presence, and then gone grocery shopping and ate dinner in. It was the best weekend of his life, and seemed like a template for much of the rest of their lives.

CHAPTER 6

PETE HANGS UP THE PHONE AND WALKS INTO GORDY'S OFFICE. "The Staties have a registration on the Lexus. Whoever stripped it missed a VIN number."

Gordy looks up. "Great. Is it our car?"

Pete nods. "Looks like it. They found some cloth in the grille. Looks like denim. They're trying to match it to Laferiere's jeans. Even better, there's blood, human blood. Car's registered to a Marie Caplette in Waynesville. I have an address. You want me to check it out?"

"A woman," Gordy says.

"A drunk," Pete says. "Don't imagine gender has anything to do with it."

"Do you want to ride to Warrentown?"

Pete shrugs. "It's OK by me. Your call."

"Why don't I do it, then. I get itchy waiting to hear."

"Fine. Don't forget you have a town council meeting in a couple of days."

"I'll do the reports when I get back. No big deal. I'll go play cop, you can play chief."

"You're the boss."

THE WARRENTOWN POLICE DEPARTMENT MOVED SOME YEARS AGO from the older part of town to one of the newer sections on the north end. It's a modern building, all brick and glass, certainly much better equipped than the Lydell department, but, Gordy thinks, lacking in some of the charm. Gordy checks in at the station, lets them know he's in town and prepared to question a resident, then drives south to the old section of town.

In some ways Waynesville, the old section of Warrentown, is as bad as most of Lydell. Waynesville had been the main mill town and the largest mill, the shoddy mill, operating through most of the nineteenth century and into the twentieth until it shut down at the end of the First World War as recycling old cloth gave way to new materials.

Shoddy was a type of cheap cloth, made by shredding old, used cloth and scraps from the textile mills that dotted the area. The new cloth that was woven from the scraps was low-quality cloth, mainly used for packing and insulation. It was picked and sorted, shredded by machine, then, depending on the quality, woven or felted into new cloth. Sometimes new wool was added to the shoddy to make a better-quality cloth called mungo, which was used in blankets, rugs, and coating.

The mills once supported whole towns, from the ragpickers,

who bought used cloth from factories and homes, to the sorters in the mill, machine operators, weavers, and felters. A good deal of shoddy and mungo was surreptitiously sold as higher-quality cloth. Because of the deception, shoddy gained a bad reputation, and laws were enacted against the sale of the material, and eventually, the industry faltered and fell.

Gordy thinks it odd that an age that embraced recycling had come around nearly a hundred years after shoddy had been done away with and existed in the language only as a word for something poorly made. Companies now spent millions of dollars on advertisements that crowed their use or manufacture of such material. The shoddy mills that had thrived in this countryside were mostly ruins, and the town they left behind existed more in name than in actuality.

THE RUINS OF THE MILL ARE MOSTLY OVERGROWN, MUCH OF IT TORN down for someone to retrieve the bricks and timbers for the construction of new buildings they wanted to look old. There's a scattering of small businesses, garages and antiques stores, a Cumberland Farm, a drugstore, craft shops, head shops, and a storefront computer repair shop. He passes one small grocery store clearly on its last legs.

Marie Caplette's house must have been one of the finer buildings in Waynesville, though it's now falling down and, perhaps, beyond repair. He parks in front, goes through a rickety gate and up an overgrown stone walkway to the small portico with its crooked roof and rotting posts. Boxes of bottles and stacks of newspapers litter what is left of the portico.

His knock on the door is answered by a small woman, in her

eighties, he guesses. She's dressed in a heavy coat over a sweater, and her thin white hair peeks out from under a red knitted cap. "Ms. Caplette? I'm Gordon Hawkins. Chief of police in Lydell." She steps back from the door so he can come in.

The inside of the house is worse than the outside. There are newspapers and cardboard boxes stacked everywhere. There's a strong odor of cat urine, and the carpet is threadbare where it covers a worn linoleum floor. "Sit," she says, taking a seat in an upholstered rocking chair covered with an antimacassar. He looks around. There's a sofa, also stacked with newspapers and magazines. There's a small color television with a digital converter box resting on a metal stand, turned so it faces the rocker. "Did you want to watch the television?"

"No, ma'am. I've come to ask about your car."

"I don't have a car."

"But there is one registered to you. A 1993 Lexus."

"My grandson," she says. "Sean. That's his car. I gave it to him."

"Oh. All right. But it is registered to you, and the registration is current."

"He doesn't have a lot of money. He's out of work. It's hard to find work. Even in the best of times."

"Yes. Yes it is."

"And this isn't one of those."

"What's that?"

"A best time. This is not a best time."

"No. No, it certainly isn't. So you pay the registration on the car, but he drives it."

"I haven't driven in years."

"So you weren't driving it this week."

"Of course not. Why are you interested in Sean's car?"

"Well, we think it was involved in an accident a few days ago. In Lydell, where I'm from."

"Oh, dear. I hope he wasn't hurt."

"Me, too. I hope so, too. Have you heard from him?"

A look came over her face that he couldn't quite read— confusion, regret, despair?

"He's a quiet boy. He doesn't talk a lot. And he's very busy."

"Yes," he says. "People are very busy these days."

"I don't know what it is they do. They have all of those things now. Things we never had."

"It's an electronic world. Cell phones, iPods, computers. I don't understand a lot of it myself, but they do. It's their world now."

"Would you like a cup of coffee?"

It's terrible coffee, old and reheated, bitter as regret. He tries not to look at the cup, which feels greasy. He takes a couple of sips to be polite and then sets it down on a stack of magazines on what appears to be an end table. "Do you have an address for Sean or a phone number?"

"No. I think he lives in Falls Village. With some other boys. Louise would know. She's his mother."

"Would you have her number or address? I'd like to talk to him. She could put me in touch with him."

"I do. It's in my phone book. Let me get it for you. He wasn't hurt?"

"No. No, we don't think so, but I would like to find out to be sure. I'm afraid the car is pretty badly damaged."

"Oh, dear. Let me find my phone book."

The phone book is an old metal case from the fifties or sixties, one that had a lever that went to the letter of the alphabet, then popped the case open to the page of addresses and phone numbers. He and Bonita had one like it years ago.

"I haven't seen one of those for a while."

"I've probably had it too long. Lots of scratch-outs and erasures. Here it is." She hands him the address book and points. "Louise Texiera. She married a Portuguese man," she says in something just louder than a whisper, as if she's afraid someone will overhear.

"And is that his name, too? Sean Texiera?"

"Oh, no. No. He's a Gross. She's been remarried."

"I see. Sean Gross."

"Yes. I hope he's not hurt or in trouble."

"Right now, I just need to talk with him a little. Find out what happened."

He leaves, depressed. It's a tough world for older people. The world keeps spinning faster and faster, and they can't keep up with it. They're frequently confused, living alone, surrounded by memories they can't hold on to. He thinks about Bonita in her last years. But that's stuff that he doesn't want to think about.

He's not sure about calling the mother. Or dropping by. If he calls the mother, she will likely call Sean, and he might rabbit. Or maybe bring himself in. But this case isn't moving forward, and he has a cop dangling by a thread while nothing happens. It's worth taking the chance that the kid would rabbit on him. At least he's moving forward with this.

The mother's house is a little north of the grandmother's. That makes it a little more upscale. When he gets there, there's a car parked in the middle of the front lawn, minus hood and engine, and the shingled house is in need of paint or stain, but the porch isn't buckled. It's what passes for upscale in these parts.

When he knocks on the door, a woman in green sweatpants and a blue Giants sweatshirt comes to the door.

"Mrs. Texiera?"

"Yeah."

"Gordon Hawkins. Chief of police, Lydell. Is Sean Gross here?"

"Oh, God. What did he do?"

"I don't know. Maybe nothing. I just need to talk to him. Is he here?"

"He doesn't really live here. He just uses this as his address. You can leave a message and I'll have him call you when I see him, though I don't really see him that often."

"Does he work? Is there a place I might likely find him? This is only to ask him a few questions."

"I don't know if he's working or not. It's tough to find a job right now, you know? But he and some friends hang out at a house on Walton Avenue. He might be there."

"You have an address?"

SHE TURNS AND LEAVES HIM THERE, FEELING THE HEAT OF THE house. It feels like the house is heated to eighty or ninety degrees. Where do these people get the money to burn through oil like that? She comes back then and hands him a slip of paper: 74 Walton Avenue.

"Thank you, Mrs. Texiera. I need to ask you just one more favor. Don't call him, please. Let me speak to him."

"Why would I call him? He doesn't call me."

Seventy-Four Walton Avenue. He already passed Walton Avenue on the way over from the grandmother's house. He figures he has about five minutes to get there. It will be a race to get there before he rabbits after getting his mother's call, which Gordy's sure she is making right now.

He makes it in less than five minutes, driving the cruiser across the driveway to block two cars parked there. The house breaks the north–south paradigm for Waynesville—poor south, richer north. It's north of the grandmother's place, but in far worse condition. He goes up to the door and knocks.

A man in his early twenties, jeans, hoodie, no shoes, opens the door.

"Sean Gross?"

"No, man." The guy tries to push the door closed. Gordy gets a shoulder on it and holds it open, not exactly pushing his way in, but keeping his body in front of the door so that he can't close it.

"No. Seriously," Gordy says. "Sean Gross. Where is he?"

"He's not here."

"Well, when will he be back, do you think?"

"I don't know, man. Sometimes he's gone a long time."

"Well, I need to talk to him. Can you get a message to him?"

"I can try."

Gordy hears a door squeak open at the side of the house. "Hold on," Gordy says. "I think I hear him now." Gordy pushes off from the door and runs around the side of the house, clomping as well as he can through the crusted snow that gives way with each footfall. He sees another kid, dressed in jeans and hoodie, huffing through the snow, toward the back fence of the house. Oh, damn, he thinks. Not over the fence.

"Sean Gross," he says. "Lydell Police. Stop. I need to ask you some questions."

The kid turns and looks at him, then takes off again for the fence, stepping into a drift of hardened snow, and goes down. Gordy, running as hard as he can, lifting his knees high, goes after him. The kid struggles, gets upright, leaving one of his boots stuck in the snow, and heads for the fence again.

"Stop," Gordy says. "Stop. Police. Don't go over the goddamned fence." He's gaining on the kid, slowly, keeping his knees up high, struggling to stay upright in the snow. He has a small advantage now, since the kid has on only one boot. But he's already breathing really hard, and he's running out of gas fast. Briefly, he wishes he had left a few of the M&M's in the store.

He has almost caught up to the fleeing kid, when the kid catches ahold of the chain-link fence and pulls himself up and pushes off, going headfirst over the fence, into another snowdrift on the other side. Gordy reaches the fence right after him, nearly going over, too, just from his own momentum. The kid is struggling to get himself out of the snowdrift when Gordy sees that the kid's jeans are snagged on the fence top. He grabs the kid's leg and holds it as tightly as he can, wrapping it up in both arms. He takes his cuffs, gets one around the kid's ankle, and locks the other one to the fence. The kid is still thrashing around in the snow, trying to get his head free.

"Let me go."

Gordy leans against the fence, struggling to get his breath back. He looks back toward the house. All in all, he must have run twenty yards. It was through snow, but twenty yards? Jeez. He ought to be able to do more than twenty yards without being completely gassed.

"Let me up."

"In a minute. I got to catch my breath. You Sean Gross?"

"Let me up."

"You Sean Gross?"

"Let me go. I didn't do anything."

"No. I'm not going to let you go until you talk to me. You made me run through all that snow. I want you to feel as miserable as I do, now. Tell me."

"Yeah."

"Yeah, what?"

"I'm Sean Gross."

"Thank you, Sean. Let me put a couple of things straight for you here. We found your car."

"I don't have a car."

"I know that, too. We found your grandmother's car. The car you've been driving. The car you were driving the night you hit Matthew Laferiere on Route 417."

"I don't know what you're talking about."

"Oh, yeah, you do. Car's at the state lab right now. They're tying you to that car so many ways you'll never get away. You're going to be dragging that beater Lexus to your grave. I won't lie to you, and I would appreciate it if you didn't lie to me. You're in a lot of trouble. There's no question about that. And if you keep lying to me, you're going to be in even more trouble. Right now, I need answers, and I'll do what I can for you if you give them to me."

The kid put his face down in the snow. Gordy could see his shoulders start to heave. "I know you didn't mean to hit him. That was an accident, wasn't it?"

The kid tries to nod in the snow, then turns his face, slick with tears that are already starting to freeze, and says, "Yeah. An accident."

Gross pushes at his face with the sleeve of his sweatshirt, trying to dry it. "Will you let me up?"

"Will you run?"

"No," the kid says. "There's nowhere to go."

"Give me your hand. Other hand." Gordy takes Gross's hand, unlocks the cuff from the fence and puts it around his wrist, so that he is held, hand-to-foot. "This will get better. Be patient." He helps

Gross get to his feet, then unlocks the cuff from his ankle and locks it on his own wrist. "OK. Come back over the fence."

They do a complicated dance with Gordy pulling Sean by his belt and sweatshirt as the kid struggles to get back over the fence without cutting himself up on the twisted wire at the top. Clothing gets snagged and torn, including the sleeve of Gordy's jacket. "Are you all right?" he asks when the kid has made it over the fence and back on solid ground.

Sean Gross nods, and Gordy plucks at his jacket sleeve, which is already starting to disgorge white filling. "Shit," he says. "These things cost three hundred bucks."

The kid looks at the sleeve and says, in complete seriousness, "You can stitch that back up. It's not bad."

Gordy walks Gross back to the cruiser. "You're not under arrest," he tells him again. "I just need to ask you some questions. We're going to the car because it's warm in there and out of the way of traffic. You understand that?"

The kid nods. He's starting to shiver.

Gordy gets Gross into the backseat, then sits in the front seat, passenger's side, so he can turn to face him.

"Why'd you run when I came to the door?"

"Can I have a cigarette?"

"I don't have any. Can't smoke in the car anyway."

"I have some in my pocket. We could open the door."

"Which pocket?" Gross turns his head and looks at his front shirt pocket. Gordy reaches back, unbuttons the pocket, and takes out a box of Newports. "You got matches? A lighter?" The kid pushes himself up from the backseat and holds himself horizontal. "Right front pocket." Gordy looks at the kid for a minute, shakes his head, and asks, "Anything sharp in there? Anything going to hurt me?" The kid shakes his head, and Gordy reaches two fingers into his pants pocket until he finds the lighter and takes it out.

He opens the box of cigarettes, takes one out, and puts it up to the kid's lips, then lights it. "Thanks," Gross says. "You can have one if you want it."

Gordy starts to say no, then shakes another out of the box and lights it. "If I uncuff you, you going to try anything stupid?"

The kid shakes his head.

"Turn your back to me." When he does, Gordy unlocks one of the cuffs. "Bring your hands to the front." When Gross does, Gordy recuffs his hands in front of him. "Again. You're not under arrest. You're cuffed for purposes of safety. Why'd you run?"

"I was scared." Gross reaches up, takes the cigarette from his mouth, and exhales.

"Of what?"

"You. Of what you'd do to me."

"Why are you afraid of me?"

"Because I hit that kid. Killed him."

"All right. Now you're under arrest." Gordy reads him his rights. "Do you understand? Everything you say can and will be used against you."

Gross nods.

"Do you want a lawyer?"

"I guess so."

"Do you have a lawyer?"

"No. I want one, though."

Gordy exhales the smoke from the cigarette. He's already starting to feel light-headed. It has been, many, many years since he has smoked. It isn't very good, and the Newport is much stronger than he remembers cigarettes being.

"OK. Finish your cigarette. Then I'm going to recuff you behind your back, and we're going up to the police station in Warrentown and check in, then I'm taking you back to Lydell. Anything you tell me before we get you a lawyer is admissible in court. Remember that."

"I didn't mean to do it. It was an accident."

"Yeah," Gordy says. "I kind of figured. It was leaving the scene that has gotten you into all this trouble, and you are in trouble."

"That wasn't an accident. I had to do that."

"Hit him?"

"No. Run."

"What do you mean, you 'had to do it.'"

"I went into a skid. I mean I hit something, and the car spun on me. I was trying to stay on the road."

"You hit something?"

"Yeah. Something."

"You didn't know you had hit someone?"

"No, man. I saw a guy. I mean I didn't see him, then I did. Then I didn't. I kept going. Later, I saw the busted headlight and all that. Like the next day some guy told me a guy got hit on 417. I still didn't know I had hit the guy."

"You hit a guy, and you didn't know it?"

"Not until later. I figured it out. Then I knew I was in a lot of trouble. I was scared. I ditched the car."

RONNY STICKS HIS HEAD INSIDE THE DOOR OF THE POLICE STATION. He catches Pete's eye and raises his eyebrows, a question. Is Gordy here? Pete shakes his head. Ronny steps into the office and shuts the door behind him. "What's going on, Pete?"

"What are you doing here?"

"Bored. There's nothing to do all day and all night."

"Where's your girlfriend?"

"Studying. Taking tests. She's busy."

"That's too bad. She ought to be some good entertainment."

Ronny starts to say something then thinks better of it. Then, "What's going on here?"

"I can't tell you. I can't tell you that we think we found the vehicle. A white Lexus. A beater. Busted-up front end. That sound right to you?"

"Maybe. I thought Camry, but Lexus could be right. You find the driver?"

"Can't tell you. Can't tell you and I don't know. I got to hit the crapper and Sue is off on an Edna's run. Come on in and sit at the desk for a bit. Gordy's off to Warrentown. You'll be safe for a bit. Don't answer the phone."

Ronny sits down at Pete's desk, not even wanting to look at his own desk. The chair's nice and warm. Pete is like a furnace, pumping out heat at a steady rate. The office has begun to look good to him again. When he first signed on as a probationary patrolman, the office had been strange, exotic and wonderful, and it was a new world, and it was his. It's starting to look that way again. In two more days he will be back to work, and he promises himself to never again wish he weren't working.

Pete keeps the day-watch desk neat and orderly, not like he and John do. It's almost bare except for the blotter and a couple of pens. And in the blotter is a pink memo. He reads it. "Working on truck at Baxter's Garage, evenings 12/16–12/24, with owner permission—P. Stablein, B. Cabella, two others. Out by midnight."

He reads it over twice. Ronny guesses that Stablein and Cabella are trying to get Stablein's truck on the road, no doubt. So they're still at it. Matt's gone, but Stablein and Cabella are going to keep on cruising. The truck has never run in the time he has known those guys. It's always been something in the background, like the mythical job or girlfriend.

The phone rings and he reaches for it, thinks better of it and lets it ring. It goes to the answering machine, and he hears Gordy's voice.

"Pete, I got the driver, Caplette's grandson. I'm on my way back. ETA about forty-five minutes."

"Gordy just called," he tells Pete when he comes back. "He's got the driver. Things are looking up."

"Maybe," Pete says. "You never know. You better get on out of here before Gordy gets back."

"Forty-five minutes. But this is good. He's got the driver."

"Don't go out celebrating. We've got a long way to go. Make yourself scarce."

GORDY COMES BACK TO THE OFFICE USHERING SEAN GROSS THROUGH the door. "Pete, we need to book this young man. Leaving the scene of a fatal accident."

"That's the charge? Leaving the scene?"

"For now. We'll let the prosecutor figure out the rest."

"I want a lawyer."

"And we'll need to provide him with an attorney."

"I'll call the county prosecutor. She can get the attorney."

"Just put him in the holding cell until she gets here. Sean, you need something to eat?"

Sean Gross shakes his head.

PETE MOTIONS GROSS TO THE EMPTY CHAIR NEXT TO HIS DESK, THEN takes a pink message slip from the desk and hands it to Gordy.

"Renee Lawson, Channel Eight. And the phone number."

"What does she want?" Gordy asks.

"You. Wouldn't talk to me. She wants you to call her."

"Don't have anything for her." Gordy wads up the message and drops it in the wastebasket.

"She'll just call you back."

"Then she'll call me back. I still won't have anything for her. I'm going to lunch."

EDNA'S IS STILL PRETTY FULL WHEN GORDY GETS THERE. IT'S JUST after one, still part of the lunchtime rush. He grabs an empty stool at the counter. Diane comes up to take his order. "Gordy. What'll you have, hon?"

He wants a burger, loaded, lots of good fries. But he restrains himself and orders the diet plate—hamburger patty, cottage cheese, and a small house salad. He can feel eyes on him, and he leans on the counter, shoulders hunched in an almost protective pose. Guys on either side of him nod, but no one speaks. He gets up and goes to the end of the counter and picks up a couple of pieces of the paper. He can still feel the eyes on him, and then he sees Roger Laferiere sitting at a table with a couple of other men he recognizes but can't name. He starts to turn back, then turns again and walks over to Roger, who is stirring a nearly empty cup of coffee.

"Roger." Laferiere looks up at him and nods grimly. "Roger. I want you to know that we have made an arrest in your son's death. We found the car and traced it back to a kid in Warrentown. He's over at the jail now."

Roger keeps staring at his coffee cup.

"I just wanted you to know. We're working the case hard. We got the driver."

He waits for Roger to answer or at least look up. "Like I said. Just wanted you to know." Gordy turns to go back to the counter.

"He was murdered," Roger says. "He was murdered by Ronny Forbert."

Gordy comes back to the table. "No, Roger. He wasn't. He was hit by a hit-and-run driver, and we have him under arrest. It was an accident, Roger. An accident."

"The wife and I don't see it that way," Roger says. "It wasn't no accident. Gayle's talked to a lawyer. He don't see it that way, either. It wasn't no accident. Ronny Forbert threw our son out into that road to kill him. And he did." One of the other men at the table nods in agreement.

"Roger, I lost my wife a little over a month ago. I know how hard this all is, but it wasn't what you think. I know you want to put an explanation on this. To blame someone for all the pain they've caused you, but you have it wrong. It was an accident."

"It doesn't look like it from here," the guy who nodded says. "It doesn't look like an accident. It wasn't no accident."

"Sorry you feel that way, but you're wrong. We have quite a bit of evidence, and it all points the same way." Gordy's tempted to say that Matt was highly intoxicated and under the influence of drugs, but he stops himself. "You're wrong. I'm sorry."

"Cops," a guy in a Citgo cap says. "Cops always stick together. They'll lie their asses off to protect one of their own. It's like a game they play—Cover your ass, and then cover everyone else's."

Gordy can think of nothing to respond to this, except to shake his head. He goes back to his seat at the counter. His salad and diet plate are waiting for him. He picks at the salad, then he eats half of the burger patty and a couple forkfuls of the cottage cheese. He pushes the plate away.

"Lose your appetite?" Diane asks.

"Pretty much. Take this away and bring me a slice of the apple pie. With ice cream."

"You sure, Gordy?"

He nods and says nothing.

RONNY'S DRIVING TO WARRENTOWN. HE'S GOING TO HAVE TO GAS UP the truck again. He's just burning up gas this week, spending money when he can least afford to, but he wants a workout, partly to burn off some of his excess energy, mostly to burn up a part of another day. All of the towns have an agreement that lets them use the state police academy facilities, a well-stocked gym, an indoor range, a pool, and a quarter-mile outdoor track.

He is driving west on 417 when he spots it. He hasn't confronted it yet. Though he has passed by it a couple of times already, he looked the other way or just let his eyes glaze over until he was past the impromptu memorial on 417. He drives a few hundred yards past it now, then hits the brakes, pulls the truck off the road, and backs up.

It's anchored by a cross of one-by-two pine: Rest in Peace, Matt. There's the usual array of cut flowers wrapped in cellophane, Mylar balloons tied to the cross with fading ribbons, burned-down candles in glass containers, and several chrysanthemum plants, already frozen in their plastic pots. A worn Red Sox cap is wired to the top of the cross.

Scattered among the flowers and candles are photos of Matt

Laferiere and letters, handwritten and inserted into plastic sleeves. He picks up one of the letters.

"Matt, you were a good kid, and you could always make me laugh. I will never forget you. Ever. Stacy." He tries to remember who Stacy might be, but he can't. There are a couple of cans of Natty Light, unopened, and one empty. Did someone place the empty beer can there, or did some other visitor open and drink it? Both seem, somehow, appropriate.

There are photographs, some in plastic, some already sodden with rain and snow. Matt sitting on the hood of the Cherokee, Matt with Paul and Bobby, Matt as a kid. Maybe junior high. But in the middle of all of them, a framed eight-by-ten photo of Matt in a tuxedo, his arm around Nessa. A prom picture. He picks it up. Matt looks completely out of place in a gray tuxedo that looks tight on him. His hair is too long and he has a goofy grin. Nessa is in a high-cut shiny green dress. Her hair is up, and there is a corsage on her wrist. She looks twenty-five, but she must have been only seventeen or eighteen when this was taken. Did someone bring it from Matt's house, or did Nessa leave it? The picture shocks him as if he had never seen Matt and Nessa together. He places it back where it was.

Who put this here? There is only one obvious answer. Nessa. No one else would have a framed prom picture of the two of them. Only Nessa. He picks the photo up again. She hasn't had time to see him except that once. But she has found time to come to this site and leave the photo. It is, he guesses, her way of saying good-bye. He starts to put it back again, but pulls it back. He studies the way Matt's arm is around Nessa. It's casual and relaxed, as though that was where it was supposed to be.

He has taken Nessa from Matt but, he realizes, not entirely.

The photo must be four years old, maybe five. But there is an immediacy to it that bothers him, as if it shows that Matt never has, never will let go of her. Or she of him. The look on her face is one he hasn't seen before. It's a look of complete and utter happiness. He stands up and, underhanded, spins it back into the woods as if it were a Frisbee.

HE WALKS INTO THE GYM AND THROUGH THE WEIGHT ROOM TO GET to the locker room. The weight room is just about empty except for the guy in the squat rack, exhaling hard with every rep, squatting a bar stacked with fifty-pound plates. He knows who it is. The guy is a monster who spends most of his free time lifting. The guy is six four, six five, absolutely ripped, strutting around the weight room in shorts and a sleeveless T-shirt that shows off his massive arms.

Ronny changes into his workout clothes and walks back into the gym. The big guy is done with the squat cage and moves over to the bench. He begins unloading the bar in the cage and begins stacking the plates onto the bar on the bench. Ronny guesses 240 pounds. The guy rips off a quick five reps and then racks the bar.

"You done with that?" he asks.

"For a bit. You want it? You want me to strip the bar for you?"

"I'll take off a couple of plates. It's OK."

"It's a lot of weight."

"I know. I'll take some off."

Ronny's not the skinny kid he was a few years ago, but he's not a big-time lifter, either. He strips off fifty pounds, then gets down on the bench. He gets his hands on the bar, feet flat on the floor, and starts to push the bar up. It's almost two hundred pounds, more than he's ever used before. He gets one rep down and up, goes for another, struggles and gets his arms fully extended. One more, he tells himself. One more.

He gets the bar down, slowly, until it just contacts his chest. He pushes it up a third of the way, struggles, pushes harder and gets it up about halfway. But the bar is starting to jiggle as his arms twitch with fatigue. He tries to go up, but the bar pushes his arms down and the weight comes slowly to his chest. He adjusts his feet on the floor and tries again to push it up. He can get it up a couple of inches but no more.

Defeated, he says, "A little help."

But the big guy isn't there. He lets the bar back down until he's supporting it with his arms and chest. "A little help," he repeats. His arms are shaking and he's taking more of the weight on his chest.

"I got you," someone says. "Come on up. I got it."

He's still struggling, but the bar is coming up. He sees someone above him, pulling, and he struggles with the bar, and then the weight slips back and settles onto the rack. He lets go of the bar and slides out from under it. "Thanks," he says.

"No problem, man. You should have a spotter with that much weight on."

He sits up. It's not the big guy, but it's a face he recognizes but can't place.

"I thought I did."

"You mean that guy?" His savior nods with his head. "He doesn't care about you. Or me. Or anyone but him." He leans into Ronny. "His biggest muscle is in his head. Jim Purcell. We were in the academy together."

"Oh, right. Right. Well, I'm glad you came along. Ronny Forbert."

"Yeah. I remember you. Day off?"

"Yeah. I'm working in Lydell."

"No shit. Big fucking mess over there, right? I mean that guy getting hit by the car."

"Yeah. Big fucking mess."

"You're not the cop in that, are you?"

"Afraid so."

"What did they do? Suspend you?"

"A few days. Didn't call for backup."

"That's not so bad. Glad you're OK. You want another crack at that press? Maybe a few less pounds. I'll spot you."

"No. I think I'm done with this."

"OK. What is it over in Lydell? A lot of politics?"

"Lots of politics. My chief is standing by me, though. It's going to be OK."

"That's good," Purcell says. "You got a good chief, you're all right."

"Gordy Hawkins. He's the best."

Purcell extends his hands. Thumbs up. "So many of these police chiefs are so afraid of losing their jobs, they just cover their own asses. Mine's pretty cool. Seifert over in Glendale. But no one told us how fucking political this job is, did they? Or did I sleep through that?"

The big guy comes back. "You going to use that?"

Ronny gets up and waves to the bench rack. "All yours."

The big guy grunts and goes over to the racked plates, pulls off two twenty-five-pound plates, and slides them onto the bar next to Ronny's weights.

"Where are you in your workout?" Purcell asks. "You just starting?"

"Maybe I'm done. I don't know."

"Got a minute? I have something I want to show you."

Purcell turns and goes toward the locker room. Ronny follows. Behind them they can hear the big guy grunting as he starts moving the weights.

In the locker room, Purcell goes to his locker and unlocks it. "I was thinking about going over to the range. Want to shoot some?"

"I was just going to work out. I didn't bring my weapon."

"This is your lucky day. I got you covered. Come on. Let's get dressed and head for the range. I got an extra in my car."

Ronny walks over to the range, checks in. Purcell comes back with a holstered Glock and an aluminum case. He puts the case up on the shelf and starts to unlatch it. "This is what I wanted to show you. You're going to like this."

When the case is open, Ronny looks in. "Wow."

" 'Wow' is right, my man. Desert Eagle Mark VII, .357 Magnum, automatic, laser sight. Pick it up, man."

"Three fifty-seven auto?"

"A piece of work, man. The gun Dirty Harry wishes he had. Let's load it up and you can see for yourself what it can do."

It's the biggest gun Ronny has ever held. He's seen pictures of it, but never actually put one in his hand. Purcell hands him glasses and hearing protectors. "You're going to need these."

Ronny has a little trouble holding the gun steady, its weight fighting him as he brings it into firing position. He bangs off two shots. "Jeez."

"Hell of a weapon, isn't it? Here." Purcell takes the gun and switches on the laser sight. "Now give it a try."

A bright red spot appears on the target. Ronny pulls the trigger. A hole appears right under where the red spot was.

"It takes a little getting used to, especially if you've been using one of these." Purcell takes out his Glock. "But once you get the feel for it, you're going to love it."

Ronny fires two more rounds. "I pretty much love it now."

Purcell has a big grin on his face. "I knew you would. It's for sale."

"Really."

"Yeah. Breaks my heart. I love that thing. The power is awesome. But Christmas is coming up, and I need some bucks. I'll sell it cheap."

"Oh. I don't know. I'm kind of strapped right now. Suspension without pay."

"Fifteen hundred bucks. You can search high and low, and you'll never find a deal like that. Laser sight goes, too. And I'll throw in the case. You just can't beat a deal like that."

"I like it. But like I said. I'm strapped."

"Me, too. You got kids? I do. I got to buy Christmas presents. I wouldn't give this up if it wasn't for that. I love this thing."

Ronny looks at the gun. Desert Eagle Mark VII. He wants it. But he has Christmas presents to buy, too. Or at least one. He hasn't found anything for Nessa yet. He's thinking jewelry, but he knows nothing about jewelry. Only that it's expensive. "It's a good price, man. I know that. Just not sure I can swing it. Fifteen hundred."

"I can't let it go for less. That's way under what I paid for it."

"It's a great deal."

"Can you put something down and make payments? I'll trust you. One cop to another. A Christmas present, for yourself. Where you going to get another for that?"

Ronny does some quick calculations. He'll be back to work next week. Maybe he can get an advance or a loan from someone. And he still needs to buy something nice for Nessa. Other than that, he's in the clear. The gun has an emotional pull on him that seems stronger, more urgent than even the desire he felt when he went to get his truck. "I got eight hundred. I can get you the rest in a week or so."

"Eight hundred would help me out a lot. I don't want to have to go back to the gym and try to sell it to the ape there." Purcell extends his hand.

Ronny shakes Purcell's hand. He can't afford this, but he really wants it, and Purcell has a point. He'll never get another chance at one this cheap. "We'll have to go to the ATM."

"I got the time, if you've got the money, honey."

At the ATM, Ronny taps in a withdrawal of eight hundred dollars. The machine whirs and clicks, then reads Withdrawal Limit Exceeded. He goes back to Purcell, who's waiting in his car. "The ATM won't let me take out eight hundred."

"Do you have that much in your account?"

"Yeah, I'm pretty sure."

"We can go to the bank. They'll let you withdraw it inside."

So they drive another two miles, and Ronny goes inside the bank and fills out a withdrawal slip. Eight hundred dollars. The teller takes the slip, checks his ID, and begins to count out eight hundred-dollar bills. He takes the bills and looks at his receipt. He's got about $170 left in his account. He can buy Nessa something with the card. When Purcell drives off, Ronny takes the gun back to his truck and puts it on the passenger's seat. Halfway home, he puts his hand on the aluminum case and leaves it there, driving one-handed.

A FEW MONTHS AFTER HE HAD STARTED HANGING WITH THE LAFE-riere bunch, because it was Matt's group, no question about that,

Bobby stopped him in the hall. "Don't be late today, dude. We got some major shit. This is going to be one major day."

He got out to the Cherokee after his last class. Laferiere and Cabella were already there. Stablein hadn't showed yet. "You like guns, dude?" Cabella asked.

"Yeah, I guess. I don't have one."

"Show him, Matt."

"Not yet. Wait until we get out of here."

When Stablein showed up, they all got into the Cherokee, pulled out of the school parking lot, and headed north, up into the big woods. "Now?" Cabella asked. "Can I show him now?"

Stablein passed a bundle in folded cloth. Cabella carefully unfolded the cloth. There were two guns, a revolver and an automatic. "What do you think of this?"

"Very cool."

"And ammo. We have plenty of ammo." Stablein held up two boxes of bullets.

"Can I touch them?"

"Hell, yes, dude. We're going to do some damage with these."

Ronny picked up the revolver, blued steel with walnut grips. He was surprised by the weight of the thing.

"We got a Smith and Wesson .357 Magnum here and a genuine, I mean genuine, Colt .45 1911 model. One's my dad's, the Colt was my grandfather's. It was in World War One."

"Your dad lets you use these?"

"He doesn't know. I take them every once in a while. He doesn't even know that I know where he keeps them."

"They're beautiful," Ronny said.

"You better believe that."

He had never held a gun before, a real gun. It was heavier than he had expected, but it felt wonderful in his hand, the heft, the wood of the grips.

"That's not loaded," Bobby said. "But it's a good idea to check it. Always check a gun before you handle it."

"How do I do that?"

Bobby took the gun from him, unlocked the cylinder, and flicked his wrist to open it. There were six clean holes in the cylinder waiting to be filled with bullets. He handed the gun back to Ronny. He clicked the safety on. "Don't dry-fire it. It's bad for it."

"If you're going to pull the trigger, blow something away. No sense in wasting a trigger squeeze on nothing."

They drove up the state highway, then off on an unmarked side road and through the woods until they came to a dirt road, barely more than a couple of wheel ruts. At the end of the road, they came to a fence posted No Trespassing.

The sign had been riddled with bullets and was held together by little more than rust.

The fence had once been chained and locked, but the chain hung from the fence, the lock nearly touching the ground. "Open the gate," Matt told him, and Ronny got out, pulled the chain through a link in the fence, then pushed the gate open as Matt drove the Cherokee through. He was still holding the Magnum.

They drove farther down the two-track road until the woods opened up to what seemed to be an abandoned gravel pit. The road skirted the pit and went on into the woods. A couple of piles of gravel and dirt remained, but mostly it was bare ground scraped out to a depth of twenty or thirty feet. The pit was full of old machinery, trucks, appliances, and other trash someone had hauled out here. Ronny had lived in Lydell all his life, but he had never seen this.

"What's down the other road?" he asked.

"Nothing. Trees. Nothing important. Most people don't know this place is here, except the ones who dump their shit here. It's a cool place. The cops don't even come out here. Come on. Let's rock. Ronny, give me the gun and get the beer. Get the empties, too. Lock and load, men. Lock and load."

Paul Stablein broke open the boxes of ammunition on the hood of the Cherokee and started loading the guns. Ronny watched in fascination as he filled first the cylinder of the revolver, then the magazine of the automatic with bright, brassy rounds.

Matt took two beers and handed one to Ronny. "I think our virgie ought to get the first shots. Stabes, give him the Colt."

"What should I shoot?"

"No sense shooting at the empties. You couldn't hit them anyway. Just walk down into the pit and shoot the first haji you see."

Ronny took the Colt, which was heavier than the Magnum, picked up his beer with his left hand, and started down into the pit. He was looking for a big bottle or can to shoot, and he came to a refrigerator, door still on, leaning toward him.

"There. On your right. Get him, man."

Ronny spun to his right, leveled the .45 at the refrigerator, and pulled the trigger. Nothing.

"Pull the slide back. You got to cock it, dude."

Yeah. He remembered that from the movies. He set the beer down and reached across his body and pulled the slide back with his left hand, re-leveled the big Colt, and pulled the trigger.

The recoil knocked him back, sending his right hand back over his shoulder. Behind him he heard their laughter.

"Kicks like a bastard, don't it?"

Ronny looked at the refrigerator. There was a clean hole in the front right side of the door and a big gash on the side where the bullet had come out. He had never felt anything like that before. The noise was amazing, and the jagged gash on the side of the box was a beautiful thing.

"Got him, man. But you're going to dislocate your shoulder if you keep trying to shoot like a guy on TV."

He was aware then of the pain in his shoulder, elbow, and wrist from the gun's recoil. "Wow," he said.

"Here," Matt said. "Give me the gun. Let me show you how it's done."

Matt set down his beer and took the gun from Ronny. He took a couple of steps back, motioning Ronny to get behind him. Matt held the Colt out in front of him, centered on his body, holding it with both hands, arms extended. He fired off four quick rounds, knocking the refrigerator back a bit until it wobbled and fell.

"Dead," Matt said. "I shot that fucker dead."

He gave the gun back to Ronny. "Two hands, my man. Two hands. Quick. Get that chair."

Ronny turned to where Matt pointed. It was an old chrome dining room chair with a torn vinyl back and seat. He pointed the gun at it and aimed it the way he had seen Matt aim and fired off two shots in quick succession. Neither of them hit.

"Slow, dude. Slow. And lock your wrists. That second shot was three feet over it."

Ronny pointed the gun at the back of the chair, braced his upper arms against his chest, locked his wrists, aimed, and fired. This time the chair slammed backward, flipped up in the air, and crashed down a foot away

"Whoa," Matt said. "A killah. My man Ronny is a stone killah."

"That thing really has a kick to it," Ronny said, as if he had been shooting guns his whole life and just encountered this kind of recoil for the first time.

"Nothing. Stabes, give him the Magnum. This thing is empty anyway."

The sharp crack of the pistol jolted him, and the recoil was much harder than the Colt's. "Wow," he said. "You could stop anything with that."

"No man. The .45's better for stopping shit. It flat lays things down."

"It doesn't matter," Ronny said. "It doesn't matter. They're great. Both of them. Just fantastic." He sighted at a car door standing against some lumber. He fired three shots, trying to hold the Magnum steady. It was really hard. He fired three more, resighting after each shot. The door filled with deeply punched holes that knocked off the paint and rust in a neat circle around it. "Fantastic," he said. "Just fantastic."

"Here's what we're going to do," Matt said. "We're each going to take both guns, one at a time, fully loaded. Fourteen shots. Walk through the dump and every time you even think there's a haji, blast him. I'm going to reload these with hollow points. Keep that in mind. We'll take turns."

Ronny gave the gun reluctantly to Stablein. He walked over to the cooler, took a beer, closed the cooler lid, and sat on it as he watched Stablein reload the guns, then move through the pit in a semi-crouch, arms extended and locked in front of him. Matt nudged his arm. "Watch this. See about ten feet in front of him to the right? You can barely see it, but he's going to see it as soon as he comes around the bend there."

Ronny looked where Matt pointed, didn't see, then did. It was the white tank of an old toilet. Almost immediately, Stablein went into a full crouch, whirled around, and fired, missing it. He reset himself.

"No, dude," Matt yelled. "No good. Everyone gets one shot at the crapper. That's it. One shot. Go on." Laferiere turned back to Ronny. That's the prize, man. Hit the shitter. That thing is really going to blow."

When Stablein came back, they reloaded both guns and gave them to Bobby Cabella. Cabella made his way through the junk standing straight up, walking with an exaggerated swagger. He turned alternately right and left, snapping off shots with the Magnum, hitting various piles of garbage. It was impossible to tell if he was hitting targets, because any bit of the garbage could have been a target or not.

"He's a pretty good shot," Ronny said.

"He's better than Stabes, here, but he's not the best."

"That's you?"

"Just wait and see," Matt said.

Cabella was continuing to move right and left as he rounded the small turn that brought him into position for the toilet. He took careful aim and pulled the trigger. Nothing.

"Dude," Laferiere laughed. "You forgot to count. You forgot to count, you stupid douche." Cabella took the .45 Colt from his belt and replaced it with the empty Magnum.

"No, man. You don't get another shot at it. You only get one try. No. You forgot to count. You're through, man."

"The fuck I am."

"The fuck you are," Laferiere yelled. "I'm not kidding here. You're done. You pull that fucking trigger, and you're going to be shit when you get back here."

Cabella turned and faced them, bringing the .45 around in front of him until it was aimed at Laferiere, who took a drink with his left hand and gave Cabella the finger with his right. Ronny was frozen at the sight of the .45 aimed in his direction, but he, too, brought up a finger in defiance of Cabella.

Suddenly Cabella whirled and fired wildly past the toilet. Laferiere began a laugh that was nearly a howl. "And then he misses it. The dumb fuck takes another shot and misses it. You see that? He's a good shot, too. But he fucking missed." Laferiere was laughing so hard the beer was coming out his nose. Caught up, Ronny couldn't stop laughing, either.

Cabella shot seven more times at various objects and then started the climb back out of the pit and up to where Ronny and Laferiere stood.

"You can go next," Matt said, still laughing.

"No. It's OK. You go."

"Rock, paper, scissors, man."

On three, Ronny held his hand out flat to Matt's fist. "Paper covers rock."

"Load him up," Laferiere said to Cabella. "He's next."

"You load him up, then go fuck yourself," Bobby said.

Laferiere laughed and took the guns, loading the Magnum first and handing it to Ronny. Then he took the clip out of the .45 and began pushing bullets into it. When he filled it and slid it back home, he turned to Bobby Cabella and kicked him hard in the back of the leg. Cabella went down with a yelp and Laferiere climbed on top of him and held the .45 at the side of Bobby's nose.

"You want me to blow your fucking nose off? That what you want, little man?

"Because you know I will. You made two mistakes out there.

You took a shot I told you not to, and you missed. You're shit, man. I ought to kill you just for that." He stood up then, still holding the .45 on Cabella, made a small motion with his arm, and said, "Pow." Then he handed the gun to Ronny.

"Go to it, my man. You're not going to hit the crapper, you know. You think you are, but you're not. It's mine, man." Laferiere reached a hand down to Bobby, who took Matt's hand and pulled himself upright. Ronny looked on, bewildered. "He knows I was fucking with him. He knows that. Don't you, Bobby?"

"That's all you do, is fuck with me."

Laferiere gave a laugh and swung his arm around Bobby's shoulder, pulled him toward him, and kissed his forehead. Then to Ronny, "OK. Let's see what you got."

Ronny started down the path through the garbage, slowly and cautiously. He carried the .45 in his right hand and the Magnum stuck down the back of his jeans like he had seen on TV. He wanted to shoot at the toilet with the .45 because it was easier to control. He shot at a gallon paint can and missed, then at a chunk of red plastic from a car taillight. He hit the edge of that. He was keeping careful count of his shots. When he got to shot six, he thought about the chance that Matt had short-loaded the .45. There was no way to look and see. He fired the sixth at the back of an old wooden chair that fell back in a shower of splinters when he hit it. The next shot was the seventh. He took a couple of extra steps, stopped, sighted the toilet tank, and pulled the trigger.

It was a beautiful thing. The toilet tank did not just break, it exploded in a corona of white porcelain and dirty rain water flying through the air. Behind him he could hear cheering and laughter. He took a step back and threw his arms in the air. It was, probably, the coolest thing he had ever seen. All that was left of the tank was a few jagged pieces of porcelain. He looked back to where the guys stood. Cabella and Stablein were high fiving. Matt Laferiere stood with his arms crossed in front of his chest.

For a moment, he didn't know what to do. He had six more bullets in the Magnum and one more in the .45. He wanted to keep shooting, but there seemed to be nothing worth shooting now. He took the Magnum from behind his back and fired off all six rounds into the air, relishing the sound and smell of it. Then he aimed the .45 at the bowl of the toilet and pulled the trigger. Nothing. The slide was fully retracted. The magazine was empty. Matt had loaded seven bullets, not eight.

He walked back to where they stood together. Bobby Cabella reached out and gave him a high five. Paul Stablein gave him a small punch in the shoulder.

"Nice shooting," Matt said. "Why'd you go for it with your seventh shot?"

Ronny shrugged. "It seemed like time."

"You weren't planning on taking another shot at it, were you?"

"No. No, just the one."

"Because normally you'd wait until your last shot, not the next to the last."

"Turns out, there was no next shot. That was the last one."

"No, man. I loaded it myself."

Ronny shook his head. "I think you lost count."

Matt grabbed him by the front of his shirt. "You lost count. I didn't lose count. That was your eighth shot, dude."

"You just said it was my seventh." He looked over at Stablein and Cabella. Stablein looked away and Cabella shrugged.

"It was your eighth. Gun holds eight."

He started to say something. He wanted to insist that he had kept his count. It was his seventh shot. There was no eighth bullet. "Well, it doesn't matter. I got it."

"It matters. Are you saying I short-loaded you?"

Ronny was confused now. How had this changed so fast? Just a minute ago, everything was cool. It was fun. Now Matt was clearly mad, ready to fight. He thought about Laferiere holding the gun to Cabella's nose. Would he really have pulled the trigger? Why would you hold a loaded gun to your friend's head? What would make you that mad? He didn't know, and now he was starting to be scared.

"I'm not saying anything, man. Nothing. Can I have another beer?"

The simple question seemed to knock Laferiere off his stance a little. "Hell, yes. It's why we're here. Have another. Get me one, too."

"You going to shoot, Matt?" Cabella asked.

Laferiere shook his head. "No. No more shooting. Buffalo Bill here took the prize. It's beer time."

They grabbed beers from the cooler. The atmosphere had cleared like the sky after a storm. "Buffalo Bill," Stablein said.

"Wild Bill," Cabella said.

"Ronny Earp."

"Annie Oakley."

At that, everyone started to laugh. Laferiere caught Ronny around the shoulder with his arm and pulled Ronny to him, dripping a small stream of beer on his head. "Annie Oakley, dude. Not Virgie, anymore. Annie Oakley, for sure."

WHEN HE GETS HOME FROM SCHOOL, SAMMY SEES HIS FATHER'S Camry in the driveway. Shit, he thinks. What did I do now?

When he gets inside the house, his father is sitting at the kitchen table. Across from him is Martin Glendenning.

"Here he is," his father says. "How was school, Samuel?"

Sammy shrugs. "I don't know. Like always."

His father nods. "I guess that's good, huh?"

"Yeah," Sammy says. "I guess so."

"You know Mr. Glendenning." Sam nods at Martin.

"Yeah."

Martin Glendenning gets up from the table and walks over to Sammy, extending his hand. "Good to see you, Samuel. Are you doing all right? Recovering from the accident the other night?"

Sammy doesn't even know what that means. Recovering? "I guess so. I'm OK."

"I'm glad to hear that, Samuel. Glad to hear that you weren't injured. It was a horrible thing. A real tragedy. A tragedy for all concerned. I'm glad you're all right. I hear you have been talking about what happened. In school, I mean."

"Everybody wants to know."

"I'm sure. Nothing like this has ever happened in Lydell before. Everybody wants answers. I wonder if you would mind telling me what you remember about that night?"

"He can do that. Can't you, Sammy?" his father says.

"It's still kind of fuzzy. It happened really fast."

"I'm sure it did, I'm sure it did. It would be very helpful if you could go over this with me," Martin says. "It's vitally important to the town."

Sammy nods, takes a deep breath and begins with the pull-over, the arguing between Matt and Ronny Forbert, the struggle, then the car coming over the hill and Matt flying through the air. Then Matt lying dead.

"That's very good," Martin says. "You have a good memory, and you're very observant. You would make a good witness. Very credible. Lots of details."

"Witness for what?"

"Well, for whatever. We have lots of questions. Everybody does. I don't know if there will be an inquiry into this, but if there is, you will be very helpful to everyone. One of the things we're most interested in, of course, is the actions of Officer Forbert that night. We're going to need to know, for example, if we have a bad officer on our police force. You can help us with that. You can help the whole town."

"I told you what I remember."

"Yes, yes you did. And you did it very well." Martin leans forward and puts his chin in his hands. "How did Matthew Laferiere end up in the road?"

"I'm not sure. Sometimes I think one thing, then sometimes I think something else." Sammy stops and exhales hard and fast. Then he is crying.

"Oh, I know this is hard," Martin says. "Take your time. No one's blaming you for anything. And we can be done with this in just a minute or two. Let me ask you. Did Officer Forbert throw Matt Laferiere into the path of the car that hit him?"

Sammy shakes his head, then nods. "Maybe. Maybe he did."

"Again, Samuel. I don't want this to be hard on you, and I'm really sorry I have to make you go through all of this, but I think we have an officer who may be a danger to other people. I'm pretty sure you don't want anyone else to go through what you did, do you? Can you be a little more definite?"

No, Sammy shakes his head. No. He doesn't want anyone else to go through this.

"Did he throw Matthew into the road, Samuel?"

Sammy nods. "Yeah. I think he did. I think so."

"Martin. Maybe he's had enough," Sam Colvington says.

"Of course," Martin says. "Again, I apologize. You're a very brave young man, Samuel. And you're doing a service to your community. I need you to stay brave. Maybe you'll even save someone else's life. I wonder if you could help me out? Help all of us out?"

WHEN RONNY GETS BACK TO THE APARTMENT, HE SEES THE CHANNEL Eight truck parked up the road. He pulls into his driveway, parks the truck and picks up the aluminum case with the Desert Eagle and goes into the apartment. He puts the case on the kitchen counter, unlatches it, and takes out the gun. He holds it in his hand, flicks on the laser sight, and moves the red dot around the outside of his refrigerator.

It's an ungainly thing, and the red dot still wobbles as he moves it across the refrigerator door. He shouldn't have bought this. It can't be his service weapon, and he has entered into an illegal, unregistered gun sale. It was a foolish thing to do.

But, still, he feels an attraction to the gun that he can't quite explain to himself. It goes beyond wanting and feels like need.

There's a knock on his door, then another. He puts the gun back in the case, puts the case on the floor next to the kitchen counter, and goes back into the living room.

It must be Nessa, but he's not sure he wants to see her right now. He keeps picturing her with Matt Laferiere's arm around her shoulder.

Another knock on the door, and then, "Mr. Forbert. Mr. Forbert. Renee Lawson, Channel Eight News. Can I have a word with you?"

He parts the living room curtain just a bit and peeks out. Renee Lawson, in a parka, stands at the door. Behind her is an older guy with a camera on his shoulder.

"Mr. Forbert. We have some questions for you."

"I have nothing to say," he yells.

"Mr. Forbert. We have new information on the hit and run you were involved in. Just give me a minute or two of your time."

"No. Go away."

"Mr. Forbert, we have an eyewitness who will testify that he saw you throw Matthew Laferiere into the path of the oncoming car. Will you comment on that?"

"No."

"Mr. Forbert, did you throw Mathew Laferiere into the road that night?"

He can feel his heart beginning to pound. He steps back away from the window and says nothing.

"Mr. Forbert, did you kill Mathew Laferiere?" She pounds on the door. "We need a comment from you, Mr. Forbert."

He slowly walks backward out of the living room and into his bedroom.

"Mr. Forbert. Did you kill Mathew Laferiere? Mr. Forbert. Are you a murderer?"

He stays in the bedroom while Renee Lawson continues to pound on the door, and then when the pounding stops, he sits down on the edge of his bed. A murderer, he thinks. They think I'm a murderer?

PETE KNOCKS AT GORDY'S DOOR AND THEN OPENS IT. "PROSECUTOR'S here."

Gordy looks up from his reports, takes the open bag of M&M's off his desk, rolls the bag shut, and shoves it into his desk drawer. "Send him in."

"Channel Eight called again."

"I don't have anything for them. Maybe tomorrow, maybe the next day."

Pete motions to the outer office and then backs up a step. A large woman in a long down coat comes in, dragging a wheeled briefcase behind her. She sticks out her hand as she comes through the door. "Chief Hawkins, Julie Summersby, County Attorney's Office."

"Oh. I was expecting Kent." He extends his hand, and she takes it.

"Kent will be involved in this, I'm sure, but I'm here to get the preliminary information. God, it's cold out there." She unzips her down coat and pulls it off.

"There's a coatrack," Gordy says.

She throws the coat over a chair. "This will be fine. You have a suspect in your hit and run. Is that right?"

"Sean Gross. He admits he was the driver."

"You Mirandized him?"

"Yeah," Gordy says. "He admitted it before and then again afterward. He's requested a lawyer."

"Got one," she says. "Rob Weingarten. He owes some pro bono. He's going to meet us here in a little while. I wanted to get together with you before he arrives. Just to get our facts right."

"Sean Gross. Like I said. From Waynesville. He was driving his grandmother's car. Car's in state impound. Says it was an accident. Ran because he was scared."

Julie Summersby pulls out a yellow legal pad and a pen from her briefcase. "And he said this after he had been Mirandized?"

Gordy nods.

"Did he put it in writing?"

"No. He's waiting for his lawyer."

She takes a small digital recorder from her briefcase and puts it on the desk. "Just in case I miss something," she says.

"Of course."

"So, you're sure you have the right guy?"

"No question. He was the driver. He was alone."

"That's good. Why don't you just give me a quick rundown of what happened."

"All right. Sure. It was Sunday night, about midnight. My officer pulled over a Jeep Cherokee heading west, clocked at sixty-eight miles an hour, one headlight out. Matthew Laferiere was the driver, and there were three other boys with him. They'd been drinking and smoking grass."

"Drunk?"

"All four of them. We have Breathalyzers on three of them, blood alcohol on Matthew Laferiere. All over the limit."

"I'll need paper on all of that. And so your officer . . ."

"Patrolman Ronald Forbert."

"And so Patrolman Forbert pulls them over."

"For excessive speed. Sixty-eight in a fifty-mile zone."

"And he placed them under arrest?"

"One of them. Matthew Laferiere."

"The victim."

"Of the hit and run, yes."

"Go on."

"The three passengers were cooperative. They got out of the

car. But the driver, Laferiere, was uncooperative. I should say, at this point, that there was history."

"With the patrolman?"

"He used to hang out with Laferiere in high school. And there was some trouble from a few years back when the kids, including Forbert, burned down the gazebo in Henry Stuhl Park."

"And they were charged on that?"

"No. We settled that. The boys rebuilt the gazebo."

"So no charges were brought?"

"No. They confessed and agreed to rebuild the gazebo, but Laferiere didn't want to confess that. I have their confessions. Forbert confessed first and the others followed. Laferiere was unhappy about that."

"So the kid who burned down the gazebo is now the arresting officer?"

"Yeah. He was a good kid. It was kid stuff. And he's been a good officer. Not a single write-up before this."

"You wrote him up for the accident?"

"He neglected to call for backup. I gave him five days' suspension."

"I don't really like this."

"There's more. Patrolman Forbert is dating Laferiere's ex-girlfriend."

"Messy."

"A little. Like I said. There was history."

"OK. So Patrolman Forbert puts the Laferiere guy under arrest."

"Yeah, but there's a struggle when Ronny—Forbert—tried to cuff Laferiere. There's some pushing and shoving. Laferiere slips on the ice at the side of the road, goes into the road, and gets hit by the oncoming car. Dead at the scene."

"And do you have corroboration on this?"

"More or less. The three others were off to the side of the road. They didn't really see the whole thing. The Jeep Cherokee blocked their view. But they've all agreed that's pretty much what happened."

"Be nice if we had a clear eyewitness."

"Yeah. It would. But we don't."

"And the officer is on suspension?"

"Right. Five days. He's got two more to go."

"And you have no reason to doubt his account of what happened?"

"No. None."

Julie Summersby leans heavily back in her chair and exhales hard. "Can the driver, what's his name, corroborate the officer's account?"

"I think so. It sounded like that's pretty much what he saw."

"We'll need him to corroborate. If he does, this looks pretty clean. And you have details on the driver?"

"No. He's admitted striking Laferiere and leaving the scene."

"Speed? Alcohol?"

"We don't have anything on that. He had to have been going pretty fast. There was black ice on the road. Nothing verifiable on skid marks. The impact threw Laferiere into the back of his Jeep Cherokee. That's what killed him, we think."

"You have confirmation of cause of death?"

"No. We're waiting for the autopsy results. I don't expect any surprises. Laferiere's injuries seem consistent with hitting the Cherokee headfirst. It was a bad mess."

"You have pictures?"

"Pete can give you those. They're pretty awful."

"All right. We can question the driver—Gross?—when Rob gets

here. I'll need to see the reports, the photos, whatever you have."

Gordy gets up. "I'll get Pete to give you all we have. It's well documented."

"And the Gross guy. He have any paper?"

"Not that we know of. We're checking with Warrentown and the state on that. No outstanding warrants. He's pretty scared."

"He should be. How did you charge him?"

"Leaving the scene. I thought we'd leave the rest up to you."

"Maybe vehicular homicide."

"That would be your call."

"Kent's, actually. OK. Let me have the material. Is there a place I can go over all of this?"

"Use my desk. You can shut the door."

GORDY GOES BACK TO THE OUTER OFFICE AND ASKS PETE TO GIVE Summersby the files. He looks at Sean Gross, who's sitting in the holding cell, head down, arms on his knees. "Your lawyer will be here shortly," Gordy tells him. Gross nods without looking up.

RONNY IS TRAPPED. HE STAYS IN THE BEDROOM. HE WOULD LIKE TO go out, but he's afraid that the Chanel Eight reporter and photographer are out there someplace, waiting for him. "A murderer?" Is he a murderer? He didn't kill Matt Laferiere. The hit-and-run driver killed Matt. He was just there, doing his job. He didn't throw Matt into the road. Matt went onto the road on his own. He slipped on the ice. How can they call him a murderer?

He calls the police department and asks for Gordy. Pete tells him that Gordy's with the prosecutor and can't be interrupted.

"Channel Eight was here. They told me a witness saw me throw Matt into the road. They called me a murderer."

"That's bullshit," Pete says. "We have the driver. He's confessed. And we've got him. Gordy's talking with the prosecutor right now. He killed Matt Laferiere. I don't know what the fuck they're talking about. You want me to have Gordy call you when he's done?"

"Yeah," Ronny says. "I need to talk with Gordy."

As soon as he hangs up, he calls Nessa. Her phone goes immediately to voice mail. She's taking a final, he thinks. Then he looks at the clock next to the bed. It's three twenty. Matt Laferiere's funeral is going on right now. Is Nessa at the funeral? Would she go to the funeral? He goes back into the living room and peeks through the curtains. There's no one there. Still, they could be waiting for him downstairs, by his truck. How could they call him a murderer?

"I SAW THEM WHEN I CAME OVER THE HILL," SEAN GROSS SAYS. "THERE was this guy in the road. I don't know. I hit the brakes, but suddenly he was in front of me, and I hit him. I couldn't stop. I couldn't swerve around him. He was just there, and I hit him. And I saw the other guy on the side of the road. The cop. It was like something was going on. I don't know. My car went into a spin. I was scared. Scared as hell. Scared shitless."

"What do you mean, 'something was going on'?" Julie Summersby asks.

"I don't know. A guy in the road. And a cop at the side of the road. It was like something was happening, and suddenly I was in the middle of it. It was really fast. It happened really fast."

"Were you speeding? Were you drunk?"

"He doesn't have to answer those questions. He's telling you what he saw. That's all he's going to talk about. What he saw," Rob Weingarten says.

"You tried to avoid him?"

"Yeah. But I couldn't. He was just right there in front of me."

Julie asks. "Was he standing up? Running? Walking?"

"I saw him straighten up. Like he was trying to stand up. Like he had fallen and was getting back up. That's when I felt the car hit him."

"Why didn't you stop? Didn't you know you had to stop?" Julie asks.

"I was scared. Really, really scared."

"He hit him," Rob Weingarten says. "That's it. There was no time to stop, no time to avoid hitting him. Matt Laferiere was in the road, right in front of him."

"How fast were you going?" Julie asks.

"No. He can't answer that," Weingarten says.

"Not that fast," Sean Gross says. "I don't know. Fifty? Sixty? I don't know."

"OK. That's it. No more questions. Are you going to charge him?"

"Chief Hawkins has already charged him with leaving the scene. We have a fatality, though. That looks like vehicular manslaughter to me."

"But you have no proof of that. My client wasn't drunk or speeding. The fatality was an accident. You can't win that one."

"I think we can. We have a death here. Juries don't like to leave that hanging. I think we can get a conviction."

"I think you're bluffing."

"Maybe, maybe not."

"Can I say something?" Gordy asks.

Julie Summersby raises her hand to stop him, but Gordy pushes on. "I have an officer that some people think is responsible for Matthew Laferiere's death. He isn't, but I'm getting a lot of pressure on this. I would like to get my officer cleared. Mr. Gross's testimony could clear him of that."

"My client can't testify to that. He didn't see enough to do that."

"He saw that there was a struggle. That corroborates his story," Gordy says.

"But he didn't see a struggle, only the aftermath."

"He said that it looked like Matthew Laferiere slipped and fell. He could testify to that."

"Not if there's a charge of vehicular manslaughter he couldn't."

"If manslaughter's off the table, he would testify?"

"He could do that."

"And plead to leaving the scene?"

"Would you agree to that?" Weingarten asks Sean Gross.

"I don't want to go to jail."

"I can't guarantee that," Julie says.

"What can you do?"

"I think we can ask for the minimum if he testifies in any action, criminal or civil, and pleads."

Weingarten looks to Sean Gross. "I'll go to jail?" Gross asks.

"For a year or two. Maybe less. We wouldn't argue against a reduced sentence."

"I don't think you're going to get a better deal," Weingarten tells him.

"It wasn't my fault."

"Maybe killing Matthew Laferiere wasn't your fault, but leaving the scene of the accident most certainly was. You're going to have to answer for that."

"Can I confer with my client on this? In private?"
Julie nods and she and Gordy leave the room.

"I DON'T WANT ANY TAINT OF SUSPICION ON MY OFFICER," GORDY
tells Julie. "He should have called for backup. No question. But he
did everything else right."
"They'll take the deal," Julie says. "Your officer is in the clear."

ROB WEINGARTEN COMES OUT INTO THE OFFICE. "HE'LL PLEAD AND
testify. The manslaughter charge goes away, and you recommend
leniency."
Julie nods. "I can't guarantee this. It's Kent Blythe's call. But I'll
recommend the deal."
"OK. But those are our terms. No manslaughter, leniency."
"I think that will fly," Julie says. "That will be my recommendation to Kent."

WHEN THE LAWYERS ARE GONE, GORDY GOES BACK INTO HIS OFFICE.
The town council meeting is tomorrow night. He will give a report
on the last month. There will be discussion of the Matt Laferiere
incident, but he feels like the weight is off. Martin Glendenning
and his crew will scream, but he and Ronny will be all right. By the
weekend, everything will be back to normal. He picks up the folder
Pete has prepared for the departmental report to the council. He
starts to read the reports, closes the folder, puts it in his briefcase,
and leaves the office.
"We're good," he tells Pete. "And thanks for doing the report for me."

"What's the story on our friend here?" Pete nods toward Sean Gross.

"He's pleading to leaving the scene. And he will testify in any civil case that Laferiere was struggling with Ronny. He'll back up Ronny's account." Sean Gross looks up, then returns to staring at the wall.

"We'll keep him here until Kent Blythe agrees to the deal, then we can move him over to Warrentown for arraignment.

"Works for me," Pete says.

"Works for all of us," Gordy agrees. He walks over to the holding cell. "I know you wanted to walk on all of this, but this is a good deal for you. You're going to be OK."

Gross looks up and nods, glumly.

FOR THE FIRST TIME IN MONTHS, GORDY'S GLAD TO BE HOME, EMPTY as it is. He's cooked himself a dinner tonight, watched a little TV, and he feels like things are starting to return to normal, as if life without Bonita could ever be normal. He also feels something else. It's a tiny bit of happiness. He senses he can be happy again. It won't be for quite a while yet, he knows, but it now seems possible that he will someday.

Before he gets ready for bed, he sits on the sofa and takes out the report and begins to read over it. Then he gets up and turns on the TV. He's not halfway through the report when he becomes conscious of what's being said on the television.

"We have a breaking development in the hit-and-run accident in Lydell that we first reported a few days ago. Renee Lawson has the story."

"Thanks, Larry. A major development in the Lydell hit-and-run story. Matthew Laferiere of Lydell was struck and killed Sunday night during a routine stop by Lydell police. Mr. Laferiere was being detained by Officer Ronald Forbert when a scuffle took place and Mr. Laferiere ended up on Route 417, where he was struck by a hit-and-run driver. Now a witness has come forward with a shocking account of what really happened that night. The witness wishes not to be identified, and we have altered his voice to conceal his identity. You can hear for yourself what he says he saw that night."

The picture switches to a shot of Renee Lawson seated in a darkened room. The picture is shot from over the shoulder of a figure seen from the back. The lighting is dim.

"Can you tell us what you saw during the traffic stop?"

"I saw the cop throw Matt Laferiere into the road," the figure says in a gravelly voice.

"Can you give us your account of what happened?"

"Officer Forbert was putting Matt under arrest. He had one cuff on him when they began to struggle. Matt was complaining about being handcuffed, and the cop, the officer, pushed him up against the Jeep and pulled his arm down hard. Matt yelled and turned back toward the officer."

"And they struggled?"

"Yeah."

"And then?"

"The officer had a hold of Matt's arm and he pulled him real hard and threw him by the arm onto the road. The car came over a hill and hit Matt while he was in the road."

"Did Mr. Laferiere slip on the ice as the Lydell police have reported?"

"No. The officer threw him."

"And you saw this as it happened?"

"Yes."

THE PICTURE RETURNS TO A SHOT OF RENEE LAWSON. "LARRY, WE tried to get the Lydell police to comment on this allegation, but the police department would not return our calls, and the officer in question, Ronald Forbert, refused to comment."

It switches to a tape of Renee Lawson at Ronny's door, holding a microphone to the door. A voice, Ronny's voice, behind the door says, "Go away." Then Renee Lawson again. "Mr. Forbert, are you a murderer?"

Back to Renee Lawson standing in the snow outside Ronny's apartment. "And, Larry, there's more. A group of Lydell citizens, led by the victim's parents, is asking for the town to disband the police department. I talked with the parents earlier today." They switch to a shot of Roger and Gayle Laferiere. "Mr. Laferiere," Renee asks, "is it true you want the town of Lydell to disband the police department?"

"The officer, Forbert, he killed my son. Over a broken headlight. A headlight, and he killed Matt."

"And the police are protecting him," Gayle Laferiere says. "In cold blood. Ronny Forbert killed my son, and the police department is trying to cover it up. They can't get away with this. I want justice for my son."

Back to Renee Lawson. "I talked today with town council president Martin Glendenning." They switch to a shot of Martin Glendenning standing in front of his house. "Mr. Glendenning, can you comment on this citizens' drive to disband the police department?"

"Renee, we've suffered a great tragedy here in Lydell. And emotions are running high. People are very upset that something like this could happen in Lydell."

"Are you considering disbanding the police department?"

"That would seem premature. There is an investigation going on. The police are investigating the actions of their own officer. I don't know that there is any cover-up by the police. We'll have to see what they come up with. I don't want to take any sides on this. I just want the truth. When I get that, we will decide what to do."

"If you disbanded the police department, who would protect Lydell?"

"Who's protecting us now? But if it came to that, to disbanding the department, we would come under the jurisdiction of the state police. A number of small towns have taken that route. But I want to stress that it's still too early to consider such a move. We're waiting for all the facts to come out."

"Larry, I attempted to talk with Lydell chief of police Gordon Hawkins, but as of yet, he has not returned our calls. We're going to keep working this breaking story, a very complicated one, and as soon as we have any new information, we will be back with it. Renee Lawson, Channel Eight News."

Back to Larry. "Thanks, Renee. That is a stunning allegation. Good work on bringing us this significant story from Lydell. Next up, there's more snow on the way. Details after this."

GORDY FEELS HIS STOMACH TIGHTEN. "SHIT," HE SAYS. "SHIT." HE WONders if Ronny has seen this, and then remembers that he was supposed to call him. He guesses that Ronny knew this was coming and wanted his advice. When he dials, the phone goes right to voice mail. "Ronny, this is Gordy. I don't know if you've seen the news. Either way, call me back as soon as you can. I'm at home, or call my cell."

LONG AFTER THE NEWS STORY IS OVER, RONNY REMAINS SITTING IN the living room. He has thrown the remote across the room and smashed it beyond repair. He has to get up and push the button on the side of the TV to turn it off.

He has lots of questions. Why did they do this to him? Why do they have it in for him? Why does everyone think he killed Matt Laferiere? But he keeps coming back to: Who was the witness? Maybe the hit-and-run driver. More likely one of the passengers. He can imagine either Stablein or Cabella turning on him like that. They were both loyal to Matt, and loyal for years against his months. He figures it could be the Colvington kid, but he hadn't been riding with Matt that long. Someone's got a hard-on for him, but he doesn't know who.

He has gone over the whole accident scene in his mind, hundreds of times. He didn't do anything he shouldn't have. He just did his job. Maybe he tripped Matt as he lurched past him, but that was all. And he wasn't sure he had done that. And what had he done to the people of Lydell to make them think the worst? How do you lose the respect of the town to a loser like Matt Laferiere? Ronny knows he's not a hero, but how did Matt Laferiere become one?

He's still worried about losing his job, though Gordy has assured him that that's not going to happen. But Gordy and Martin Glendenning hate each other. And Martin is the major political force in the town. He will lose his job. He will lose his truck. He will lose Nessa. He will lose everything he has managed to gain in the last few years. He will end up working with his dad as a carpenter. And with his dad, he will become a drunk, living from job to job.

CHAPTER 7

(DAY FOUR)

RONNY GETS UP, UNSURE HE HAS SLEPT ANY AT ALL. MOSTLY, HE lay awake thinking, trying to work it all out in his head. After coffee and a slice of bread, he calls Nessa. This time she picks up.

"Where were you?" he asks. This comes out much stronger than he meant it to. And he has a waver in his voice.

"I was out. I didn't have my phone with me. Are you all right?"

"No. I'm not all right. They think I killed Matt. They think I'm a murderer."

"No," she says. "No one thinks that."

"It was on the news. I murdered Matt. They said it. They have a witness. They're going to arrest me for murder."

"No, Ronny. No. You're overreacting. I was just at Matt's funeral. No one said anything about you."

"You went to Matt's funeral?"

There's a long silence, then, "Shit. Yes. I went to Matt's funeral. It was kind of an impulse."

"How could you go to Matt's funeral?"

"I told you. It was an impulse. I thought I needed some closure."

"Closure on what?"

"Matt. We were together a long time."

"But you needed closure? You're with me. Isn't that closure?"

"Ronny. You're upset. I don't think we should be having this conversation."

"I do. I think we have to have this conversation. I'm sitting home, being accused of murder, going to lose my job, everything, and you're getting closure with Matt?"

"Please, Ronny. Calm down."

"Calm down so everyone in the town can fuck me over?"

"I don't know what they said on the news. I don't know why they said anything on the news. But I know, and everyone I know knows, you didn't kill Matt. He died in an accident. I know that, you know that, and Gordy knows that."

"Then why are they on the news saying I killed him? And why are you at his funeral?"

"I told you. I need closure."

"You're still in love with him. You're only with me because you were trying to make him jealous."

"Ronny. I'm sorry. But that's really stupid."

"I'm not stupid. You thought I was, but I'm not."

"Do you want me to come over there? Will you calm down if I come over there?"

"I don't want you here."

"Ronny. You have to calm down. I don't know how much of this I can take. Let me come over there and we can talk. You'll feel better."

"You're still in love with Matt Laferiere."

"I'm not in love with Matt Laferiere. I was once, and there's still a little part of that in me. I loved Matt and I love what he could have been. But I'm not in love with Matt. That's long over. I told you that months ago."

"You're not in love with me."

"Ten minutes ago, maybe I could have said I was in love with you. But you're making this very difficult. You want me to love you? Stop acting like Matt. Stop acting like a big angry baby."

"Don't call me names."

"Ronny, we shouldn't be having this conversation right now. You're upset, I'm upset. Let's just drop this. Right now. We can talk things through when we're feeling better. Please."

"I want to drop every goddamned thing that's happened in the last week. Everyone thinks I killed Matt. I didn't. I just did my job."

"I know that, Ronny. I know you didn't kill him. I know who you are. I trust you."

"I don't think you do." He doesn't say good-bye. He doesn't hang up. He throws the phone against the wall where he just threw the remote control. He lies down, faceup on the sofa. How did things go so wrong? How has his life come completely unraveled? How has Matt Laferiere ruined him, just like he said he would?

AS SOON AS GORDY GETS INTO THE OFFICE, GORDY CALLS CHANNEL Eight in Warrentown. "I'd like to speak to Renee Lawson. Right now. This is Gordon Hawkins, chief of police in Lydell. This is urgent. I need to talk to her."

"I'm sorry. Renee isn't here. Can you leave a callback number?"

"I know she's there. I need to speak with her."

"Sir. She's not here."

"Then let me speak to the station manager."

"I'll connect you with Don Flemming. Hold on."

He waits as the music, some tune he knows, but can't place, whines in his ear. He is shaking with anger.

"Don Flemming. Can I help you?"

"Are you the station manager?"

"No. I'm the news director. Can I help you?"

"This is Gordon Hawkins, chief of police in Lydell. I'm calling about the report you aired last night with Renee Lawson about the hit and run here in Lydell."

"All right."

"How the hell do you air a piece like that, accusing my officer of a crime in the middle of a police investigation?"

"I understand you're upset, Chief Hawkins. We vetted that story very thoroughly. We're confident of its veracity."

"Thoroughly," Gordy scoffs. "Why wasn't I consulted about this? I want a retraction. Now."

"It's my understanding that Renee tried to contact you. Several times. We're not going to retract it. We're confident of our source. We can give you airtime if you want to challenge it."

"Who's your source?"

"I can't tell you that. We promised confidentiality on that. It's a solid source."

"I'll get a court order."

"Well, you can do that. I don't think it would help. Renee's adamant that she's not going to reveal the source."

"We'll see about that. You're destroying my officer with some bogus accusations. This is completely irresponsible."

"Chief, I don't think it is. If you want to get a court order to try and force Renee to reveal the source, you're welcome to, of course. But I don't think Renee is going to back down on this, and the station will stand behind her. As I said, if you want airtime, we will certainly give you that. We made several attempts to get you to comment before we went to air."

"You shouldn't have aired this without consulting me."

"We tried, Mr. Hawkins. We tried."

"I'll see you in court."

WHEN HE HANGS UP, HE IMMEDIATELY CALLS RONNY, BUT IT GOES TO voice mail. "Ronny, this is Gordy. Call me as soon as you get this message. I'm at home. I'll be waiting for your call."

The day passes slowly. Pete takes Sean Gross to Warrentown to await his arraignment, then takes the rest of the day off. Gordy checks and rechecks Pete's report for the town council meeting for lack of anything better to do. All in all, things are coming together, and, despite the news report last night, the hit-and-run case is as good as closed.

GORDY NEEDS SOME DINNER, BUT HE DOESN'T WANT TO STOP AT Edna's or even the Market Basket where he will be fair game for anyone with an opinion on the whole business, and that seems to him like everyone. So he stops at the Citgo, gets a loaf of bread and a can of tuna fish, a diet Pepsi and a one-pound bag of Peanut M&M's, figuring he will need the energy from the sugar, and if not, he will need the comfort of eating something he really likes. He doesn't really need a drink, but he could use an AA meeting.

He drives his cruiser to the town meeting hall and parks it

across the street, not in the police department lot where people might come to find him, but on the roadside. His plan is to make himself a poor tuna sandwich, but he doesn't have a can opener for the tuna. He could walk to the office, where there is one, but he stays in the cruiser. He opens the bag of M&M's and takes a handful and pops it in his mouth, a few at a time. He has eaten so many frozen M&M's that he feels there is something lacking in this new, unfrozen bag.

He tries Ronny again, but it goes directly to voice mail. He wants to tell Ronny not to come to the meeting, fearing that Ronny will become a magnet for the Glendenning crowd. If most of the people in town have not heard the Channel Eight report, they will have at least heard of it. He wants to control the meeting, turn the discussion, when it comes, to the arrest of Sean Gross. He grabs another handful of M&M's.

A crowd is starting to build around the meeting hall, tight clusters of party faithful, more Republicans than Democrats, he notices, and looser clusters of neighbors and families, some couples and singles, just standing and waiting for the doors to open. Mostly, they huddle in their parkas and overcoats, stomping their feet on the frozen ground. He looks around for Martin Glendenning, but doesn't see him. About five people have keys to the meeting hall, and Gordy is one of them. He looks for someone else—Lois, the town clerk, Sam Peterson, the director of public works—but he sees none of them.

He shuts down the cruiser and gets out, walks across the street, and begins making his way through the crowd. A couple of people say hello, call his name, and someone pats him on the back. The rest just watch him and step back as he makes his way to the door. He unlocks the door and pulls it open. A wave of hot air pushes out. At least someone has come in earlier and turned up the heat. People start streaming in. Some acknowledge him, some ignore him. He guesses it's pretty easy to tell where he stands right now. He feels sacrificial.

"You trying to take my job?" Martin Glendenning asks, putting his arm around Gordy's shoulder and patting him on the back.

"I wouldn't have your job for anything, Martin."

"Take my job. Please." He laughs heartily at his own wit. Gordy smiles a tight smile. Martin holds out his hand. "Hope things go well for both of us, tonight, or at least for the town."

People continue to file in, in a steady stream. He's never seen this many people at a town council meeting. Pete comes in and takes Gordy by the arm and leads him to the back of the room. "Where'd the bitch on TV get that witness?" Pete asks.

"Don't know. I called the station this morning, but they're keeping it to themselves. It's got to be one of the passengers, but the station isn't talking."

"People in here are going to talk. I stopped in the office. Steve says we've had more than thirty calls so far demanding that we arrest Ronny, or at least fire him."

"What can you say?"

"Thanks for your concern."

"Does your mastery of irony ever feel ironic to you?"

"All the time, Gordy. All the time. Son of a bitch."

"What?"

"Back door."

Gordy turns and looks and sees Ronny Forbert sidling in. "Son of a bitch."

Pete puts his hand on Gordy's shoulder. "I'm going back there and get him out of here."

"Yeah. Good. Get him out." Gordy watches Pete make his way down the aisle toward the back door and Ronny. When Pete gets to Ronny, he can see Pete take Ronny's arm and then the two of them exchange words. He hears the gavel and turns back to the front.

"Please. Please. Can we come to order?" Martin Glendenning says. "Now." He waits for a few seconds and then gavels again. "Order. Order. I'm calling this meeting to order." The noise in the room slowly falls as people break off their conversations and find their seats. "We have a lot of business to get to this evening, and I know there is considerable interest in the events of the past few days. So that everyone can have a fair say, I'm asking that we dispense with the minutes of the November meeting. There are copies up at the front table, which you may take and read. Call the town clerk's office if you have corrections to the minutes, and those will be made for the January meeting. So that we can get to matters at hand, I'm going to ask that we start with reports from public works, the fire department, and then the police department. Warren, can you start off with the report from public works?"

Warren Anders stands up and makes his way to the front of the room, holding a couple of sheets of paper. "Town plow and sander number three is out of commission due to a broken clutch plate. Since there is snow forecast for tomorrow, I have asked Bernie Saunders to take over that route as a private contractor, which is Route 417 north from mile eighty-eight, and the streets that intersect that up to the state line. We're still within budget right now. Whether we stay on budget depends on the weather, which seems ahead of schedule as far as snow is concerned, and if the cost of repairs on plow three comes in close to estimate. Larry."

Several people laugh and Larry says, "I just fix the plows. You want to keep costs down, talk to the guys who break them."

"Warren," Tod Shanley says. "Would you ask Bernie to put the blade on his plow all the way down on Ramsneck Road? He always leaves about an inch of snow on the road."

"Ramsneck Road is like plowing an alligator's back. It's so rough, if I put the blade all the way down, I'll rip up a good half of the macadam," Bernie says.

"Who paved that road?"

"I did."

"Were you drunk at the time, Bernie?" More laughter.

Martin gavels the room back to order. "Let's keep this moving. We have a lot to get to tonight."

Gordy feels his stomach start to tighten.

"Fred Lemke will give the fire report."

"Fire department report for the month of November. The fire department issued eighteen permits for the burning of leaves during the month. There was one call-out for a brush fire on Porter Road that was extinguished by crew number two, with the help of the pumper truck. There was no property damage. That's all of the activity for November. Respectfully submitted, Fred Lemke."

"Thank you, Fred. Next, I'll call on Chief Gordon Hawkins to give the police report. Please let the chief give his report before you start to ask questions. Also, remember that you are not to speak until I have recognized you. Chief."

Gordy stands up. He has delivered these reports every month for ten years. But now he can feel his hands trembling, and his mouth is going dry. "Police report for the month of November. The Lydell Police Department made twenty-three arrests during the period—nineteen driving under the influence, one assault, one disturbing the peace, one breaking and entering, one possession of a controlled substance with intent to distribute. In these cases, all have been arraigned. Twenty-one have pled out, and two are currently awaiting trial.

"The police department issued thirty-one citations for failure to control speed, six for failure to come to a complete stop at a traffic sign, one for failure to produce proof of insurance, four for illegal dumping on public land, and three for discharging firearms on posted property. Twenty-seven warnings were issued, fifteen for inadequate vehicle lighting, and the rest for excessive speed. The police department answered four calls during the period for vehicle–deer encounters. Let me remind you all, the deer are foraging and you have to be careful. Remember that when you see one, there's probably a couple more coming. And if you see a deer on the side of the road, or if you hit one, please call it in. There was one on the side of the road on 417 for a couple of days. It's not the kind of thing we want drivers coming through here to see. We had two calls for domestic violence, and eight for the theft of tools and equipment from various barns and sheds. Let me say here that we have a little crime wave going on. It's in your best interest to keep your sheds and barns locked and secure, especially until we can identify the perpetrators here." Involuntarily, he looks over at Martin.

"Revenues for the period amounted to five thousand, three hundred and eighty-seven dollars. Expenditures came to six thousand, two hundred and twelve dollars. Nine hundred and seventy-four dollars and eighteen cents was spent on repairs to cruiser number four, a 2003 Crown Victoria with two hundred thousand and sixty-eight miles on it. We will be coming to the council for money to replace this vehicle as the cost of maintenance on it is exceeding its value now.

"We have two pending investigations. The before-mentioned break-ins and thefts that have been going on for a couple of weeks, and the hit-and-run accident that occurred on Route 417 on the night of December seventeenth. I can tell you that we have now recovered the vehicle that we believe to be the hit-and-run vehicle. We're waiting on the state crime lab for confirmation of that. We have a suspect in custody for the hit-and-run death of Matthew Laferiere. Once we get the crime lab results, we're confident we can conclude this investigation in a timely and orderly manner. This concludes our report."

Jean Burke immediately moves to accept all three reports, and Tony Bracco, also of the council, seconds.

"Is there any discussion?" Martin asks.

"What about the news report?"

"Again," Martin says, "if you wish to ask a question or make a comment, you must be recognized by the chair."

"Sid Maclin." A man in a tan barn coat and jeans stands up. "There was a report on television last night that said Matt Laferiere and Ronny Forbert were fighting and that Matt got shoved into the road where he got hit. Is that the way it happened?"

Gordy looks over at Martin.

"You are recognized for the remainder of the meeting, Chief. You can respond to all questions asked of you."

"That is an unsubstantiated report. I had heard nothing of that before I saw it on television, the same as you."

"Roger Wilkins. You have a suspect?"

"We do. We're withholding his identity for the time being, but he is a twenty-year-old from Waynesville who has indicated that he was driving the car that hit Mr. Laferiere. He has been arraigned in Warrentown."

"You have a confession?"

"Not an official confession as such. The man in custody is conferring with his lawyer before signing a confession, but there has been an acknowledgment. Yes. We're confident we have the driver of the hit-and-run vehicle."

"Art Samuels. If what the television is saying is true, what's our liability in this case?"

"I don't know. You'll have to ask the town solicitor. And we certainly don't know that the report is true. It contradicts everything we know to be true in this case."

"Stan Woodridge, town solicitor. It's too early to speculate on whether the town has any responsibility in this matter. This is an unsubstantiated report, and, to my knowledge, there have been no claims filed against the town."

"Gayle Laferiere. There will be a claim. We're suing for wrongful death. Our lawyer is making up the papers right now. That officer murdered our son, and Hawkins is covering it up. The whole police department is in on it. We have proof of that. We can prove it. We will prove it. Ronny Forbert's a murderer, and they're all protecting him."

There's a clamor of shouting, talking, and whispering as Gayle Laferiere sits back down. Gordy starts to speak, then thinks better of it and stands back, letting the audience work off their energy. Martin Glendenning begins to bang the gavel on the table in front of him. "Order. Order. We must have order."

When the noise has died down, Stan Woodridge responds. "The revelation of impending action doesn't really change anything. Filing an action is not the same thing as winning one, and I would hope the Laferieres are well counseled on that point. Filing a legal action can be a costly and risky process.

"There is still no evidence that Patrolman Forbert has done anything actionable, anything, in fact, beyond his sworn duty as an officer of the law. The news report last night, which I did not, I regret to say, see, was made by an unidentified person who claims to be a witness to the event. This witness has not come forward to the police or any other authorities. The very fact that the witness has gone first to the television news challenges his credibility. Witnesses do not hide their identity. Persons hide their identity when they have something to hide.

"Personally, I think this whole thing stinks, and I will be filing papers tomorrow to make the station reveal the identity or to cease and desist further reports based on his testimony and a retraction of the original report. Fair is fair, and we need a fair hearing, not one based on accusations from someone who won't show his face."

"What if he is afraid of police retaliation?" Sam Colvington asks.

"Police retaliation? That's preposterous."

"If I may," Gordy says. "We are in the middle of an investigation that is proceeding very rapidly. If there is a witness, we want to hear from him, not shut him up. This may, in fact, be a tactic to stall the investigation."

"Let me get this straight," Roger Wilkins says from where he sits.

"Stand and be recognized."

Wilkins stands. "I was already recognized. Now, let me get this straight. The police department is investigating an incident involving one of its own officers."

"That's correct."

"And the police are being represented by the father of the officer's girlfriend."

"I represent the town of Lydell," Stan Woodridge says. "Not the police department. And if there is an action against Patrolman Forbert, I will recuse myself."

"It's wrong," Wilkins says. "It's all wrong. It's not an investigation, it's a whitewash."

"No, Mr. Wilkins. Roger," Gordy says. "It is an investigation.
It's very much an investigation, and it's being done by the police
department because that's our job. We're trained in investigation.
Who would you rather see investigating this incident?"

"Anyone but the police."

"Because you think it's a whitewash. I think your insinuation
and premise is, at best, insulting and probably slanderous. I have
been chief of police in Lydell for the past ten years, and a member
of the police department for seventeen years. In that time, I have
never given anyone a reason to suspect my integrity or the integrity
of anyone else on the force. This department and I have served this
community faithfully and honorably for a long time. We don't, any
of us, deserve this vicious and idiotic slander."

"Chief. Chief. Let's keep this debate on a civil level. There's no
call for name-calling. And, Roger, there's no call to be accusing the
chief of police in this matter. Now, please. All of you. This meeting
is a discussion, not a trial. Let's have no more incivility." Martin
Glendenning looks around the room and nods.

Art Samuels stands. "I want to commend the chair and agree
that this is a meeting where civility and cooler heads are needed.
I want to add something to the discussion, though, in regard to
Roger's point. I agree that the chief of police should be in charge of
the investigation of this tragedy. The chief is right about that. But
would it be wrong, or out of order, if there were a couple of townspeople involved in the investigation, too? It just seems fair."

"Do you want to make that as a motion?"

"No. I don't think so. I just want to know. Would that be all
right?"

"The investigation is winding up," Gordy says. "I don't see what purpose adding civilians to the process would serve."

"Just some extra eyes on what's going on."

"Again," Gordy says, "we're trained in investigation, and investigations necessarily require confidentiality. A case can be compromised when some piece of confidential information leaks. I wouldn't want that to happen here. We need to know what happened and just how it happened. I understand the need for answers in a relatively short time, and we're getting those. So, no, I wouldn't be in favor of that."

"A motion, Art?"

"OK, yes."

"I should add," Gordy says. "Once our investigation is complete and the case closed, it will become a matter of public record. Anyone in town can come in and review the materials of the investigation, with the exception of material that may violate the privacy of the individuals involved. There are photographs of the scene, for example, that no one needs to see." Gordy looks back to where Pete is standing close to Ronny. He watches them for a couple of seconds. Pete's stance is a gesture of protection and warning. No one can get close to Ronny, but Ronny can't move, either. Fatherly, Gordy thinks.

"Does anyone want to make a motion to appoint someone to serve with the police on this investigation?"

"There's already a motion on the floor," Stan Woodridge says.

Sam Colvington says, "Would you do it, Martin?"

"If the citizens of Lydell wish me to do that, I will. Yes."

"Then I move we authorize Martin Glendenning, president of the council, to sit in with the police on the investigation into the death of Matthew Laferiere."

"Second."

"All right," Martin says. "It has been moved and seconded. Before we proceed to a vote, is there further discussion?"

"It has not been moved and seconded," Stan says. "There is a motion already under discussion."

"With all due respect," Gordy says. "This is a political move. While Martin has the interests of the town at heart, I'm sure, he has no training for this. His contribution will necessarily be a political one. And I don't think the pursuit of justice is a political action. Let us do our job. We do it fairly and impartially."

"Are you saying you're not political?"

"I don't run for this office. I serve at the pleasure of the town council."

"I think you need to listen to the chief," Stan says. "I served on the council for many years, and I serve the council as solicitor. I know Chief Hawkins is a good and honest man who, above all, serves the needs of the community. Adding Martin Glendenning to the investigation will add nothing, and it's likely to slow things down."

"A politician is a politician is a politician. And Gordy Hawkins is a politician who takes our money and then denies us the right to have input into the major affairs of the town. We need Martin Glendenning to be a part of this to look after the best interests of the town," Roger Wilkins says.

"That's right," someone says. "Now the police chief is telling us we can't have any say in how our town is run. It's just a matter of time before he's coming to our houses to demand our guns. That's how this shit works."

"Stand and be recognized," Martin says. "And mind your language. This is the town council, not a barroom."

Art Samuels stands again. "I think that putting Ronny Forbert on the police force was a huge mistake by Gordy. We need to cut him loose before any lawsuit is brought. This is his fault, not the town's."

"Irrelevant," Stan says.

"It's not the time to bring this up," Martin says. "That's another discussion. We're discussing the motion to appoint the town council president to investigate the death of Matthew Laferiere."

"When I had an accident last year," a woman says, "Gordy Hawkins helped me with the paperwork and even got someone to bring me meals when I was laid up. I don't know how anyone can say Gordy doesn't have the interests of the town at heart. He does. And I don't trust anyone who claims he doesn't."

There's a smattering of applause as she sits down.

"Can I call the question?" Sam Colvington asks.

"You may. I don't think this discussion is going anywhere, anyway. Do I hear a second?"

"Second."

"All right. The question is called. If there is a two-thirds majority to cut off discussion, we will proceed to the vote. All in favor, please say aye."

There's a loud chorus of ayes.

"I think that's two-thirds. We'll move on to the vote."

"I don't think that's two-thirds majority," Stan Woodridge says. "You never called for the nays."

"Very well. All those opposed, please say nay."

There is another chorus, this time of nays.

"The ayes have it. We will proceed to vote on whether to appoint me to the police investigation."

"That's not a clear majority," Stan says. "You need to poll the room. Paper ballets or a show of hands. This is out of order."

"You're out of order. All those in favor of the motion please say, aye."

Another chorus of ayes, louder this time.

Martin looks at Stan. "I hear a clear majority. Do I need to ask for the nays?"

"Of course you do."

"All right. All opposed, say nay."

Another chorus of nays.

"Motion carries."

"For Christ's sake."

"Don't take the Lord's name in vain, Stanley. I warned that gentleman about language, and I'm warning you."

"What? You're threatening to throw me out?"

"I hope not. But I will."

Gordy hangs his head and shakes it. He sees where this is going. The motion to fire Ronny will come up again, and Martin will ram it through. Stan will object that it's not a legal vote, but it would be up to Ronny to take action against the town for lack of due process. He will have neither the money nor the will to do it, unless the union steps up for him. But with a town as small as Lydell, that's unlikely. Gordy catches Pete's eye and motions with his head to leave out the back door. With Ronny.

Gordy looks over at Stan, who's looking grim but determined. He doesn't know how Stan feels about Ronny, though Ronny has been dating his daughter for nearly a year now, and they're generally seen as a couple. He guesses that Stan is being the good possible future father-in-law, standing up for the boyfriend. But Stan is also one of the good guys, one who believes that things should run according to the rules of reason and compassion. He's the sort Martin Glendenning would like to see run out of government altogether.

Gordy feels an energy growing in the room, and it's not a good energy. There's an agenda that's not on the xeroxed agenda that's been handed out. And that agenda is coming to a point where it will simply gather steam until it's unstoppable. Probably it's already at that point, though he will have to fight as if it has not gotten there yet.

Kyle Withers raises his hand and, without waiting for recognition says, "I would like to make a motion if I may."

"The council recognizes Kyle Withers."

"From what I'm hearing, we're dealing here with a bad cop. Maybe not an evil cop, but one who can't control his temper, and maybe can't follow police procedures. Seeing that we're facing a lawsuit, it would seem wise for the town to distance itself as far as it can from this officer. Therefore, I would like to make a motion that we dismiss officer Ronald Forbert from the force."

"Second."

"This is preposterous," Stan says. "This is asinine and malevolent. You just passed a motion to put a member of the council on the investigation, which is, I believe, illegal, and now you're dictating the outcome of the investigation. You can't fire that young man before the investigation is complete. There is such a thing as due process."

"I believe we can," Kyle says. "With what we heard on television last night, it's obvious that something went very wrong on Route 417 that night. The longer Officer Forbert is allowed to remain on the force, the more vulnerable the town is to a very expensive legal action."

"Stan is right," Gordy says. "This is a clear violation of due process. It's wrongheaded and illegal. There's a police union in this state, and Officer Forbert is a member of that union. You're guaranteeing a lawsuit from the union. One you have no hope of winning."

"That's right," Stan says. "We'll be sued, and we'll lose. This is a violation of due process. There is no doubt about that."

"Due process is unconstitutional," someone yells.

"Due process is guaranteed by the Constitution. Both the Fifth and Fourteenth Amendments contain due process clauses."

"Then they're unconstitutional."

"They are the Constitution. They can't be unconstitutional, you moron."

Gordy takes Stan by the arm and tries to calm him down.

"Stanley," Martin says. "Please refrain from name-calling. I believe you're right that this would be a violation of due process. Kyle, would you be willing to retract your motion?"

"And if you're going to use the Constitution, read the damned thing," Stan says.

"I won't retract it."

"Kyle, it's a bad motion. Retract it."

"All right. I retract it. But I still think it's a good idea."

Art Samuels stands and is recognized. "I understand that it would violate due process to fire Officer Forbert before there is a full investigation. But it wouldn't be a violation to cut his position for budgetary reasons, would it?"

"Budgetary matters are handled at the spring town meeting, not in town council," Stan says. "To cut an existing budget, you would have to wait until spring, or call an emergency town meeting, which requires thirty days' notice."

"Is there no other way to cut a budget?"

"No."

"No way at all?" Martin asks. "I believe there is a clause that allows us to do that in the case of an emergency."

"But there's no emergency."

"What constitutes an emergency, Stanley?"

"We would have to consult the town charter for that."

"Does anyone have a copy of the charter?"

"I have one in my office," Stan says. "I can report back at the next meeting."

"I want to get this settled tonight."

"I have one in my office," Lois, the town clerk, says. "It's just across the street."

"We will suspend business for ten minutes," Martin says, "while the clerk gets a copy of the charter. We will reconvene at seven forty-five."

People begin to stand, looking around and stretching as if they have just woken from sleep and found themselves in an alien place. There's a low murmur of voices that begins to increase in volume. Gordy puts his report back into his briefcase and turns for the door.

"Sorry, Gordy," Stan Woodridge says. "Can you believe this shit? They'd lynch this kid if they could."

"I know. It's uglier than I even thought it would be. Thanks for standing up for Ronny. He doesn't have many friends here."

"Technically, I'm standing up for the law. Sorry. I was trying to avoid letting them know about the emergency clause. I read it today. I'm going to start calling people and asking them to get down here. Maybe a show of strength can defeat this, or at least stop it from coming to a vote. We don't need a lot of people to keep them from calling the question. It's all illegal, anyway. This is just a cluster-fuck."

"That might work. I don't know," Gordy says. "Excuse me. I need to run back to my office real quick." On his way, four people stop to express their support for him or their disdain for the council.

Ronny looks up when Gordy comes through the door.

"Why are you here?" Gordy asks.

Ronny shakes his head. "I just want to know. I have to know. They're going to fire me."

Pete looks to Gordy and shakes his head.

"I won't lie to you," Gordy tells Ronny. "They're trying. But trying and succeeding are two different things. You should know that Vanessa's father is calling people right now, trying to round up enough voices to put a stop to this. He's on your side. We're on your side. And there are lots of other people who are, too."

"There's more that aren't."

"We've become the enemy," Pete says. "They resent that our service isn't free. They don't see what we do for them. They only see that they have to pay us. We're so far below cable TV and Internet porn, they can't even see us anymore."

"There's a whole new ideology that government, in any form, is an unnecessary evil," Gordy says. "There's nothing that's looked at without suspicion. Used to be, everyone kind of pulled together. Now it's everyone pulling in separate directions. I've got to get back, but we're not going to let them get away with this."

Gordy starts across the street. The meeting is set to resume in two minutes, but he sees Stan talking to Lois, crowding her, pushing in, making motions with his hands, and, no doubt, talking fast. Gordy realizes that Stan is stalling for time to get more people to the meeting. Already two cars have pulled up.

Back in the hall, Stan goes to Martin. "You're making a big mistake here. You're going to get sued, and I won't be able to help you."

"If we make a mistake, we'll correct it at the next meeting."

While Stan and Lois go over the charter, Gordy watches as more people file into the room. There are probably half a dozen new people. He can't really tell, but he doubts there are enough to stop them from calling the question and voting the motion through.

Finally, Stan addresses the hall. "Lois and I have gone over the charter carefully. It appears that a fiscal emergency occurs when the town council votes that it has occurred. There are no specific circumstances indicated."

"Thank you, Stanley and Lois," Martin says. "It would appear that the council will have to vote on whether this is a fiscal emergency. Stan, is there an indication of how this should proceed?"

"No. I guess the council simply proceeds with a motion and a vote based on its infinite wisdom."

"'Infinite wisdom.' I like that. Will someone on the council please make a motion?"

Sam Colvington offers a motion that the current situation in the Lydell Police Department constitutes a fiscal emergency. That's seconded by Ben Sibilski. There's little discussion. Gene Fuller calls the motion and the very idea of it a travesty. The council votes, and the motion is passed five to two. Ben Sibilski asks that the town clerk be instructed to read the minutes of the meeting so far, so any new people can be caught up on the proceedings. The request is granted and Lois reads two and a half pages of notes.

"Now," Martin says. "Do we have a motion on an action to be taken to relieve the town in this fiscal emergency?"

Sam Colvington makes a motion that the town immediately release Officer Ronald Forbert from the force. It is seconded.

"I would like to make a friendly amendment to the motion," Martin says. "I don't think it's a good idea for the council to be dictating to the police department on personnel issues. I would like to amend the motion to request the chief of police to reduce his staff by one person. It will be his decision as to who will be released."

"Second," Sam says.

"No. First you have to say whether the amendment is acceptable to you."

"Of course it's acceptable. I just seconded it."

"Just say it."

"Acceptable."

"Now it can be seconded."

"Second."

"Thank you. Discussion?"

"It will be Chief Hawkins's decision?"

"It will be, as it should."

"I would rather do that than tell the chief who he has to let go."

"Just to clarify things," Stan says. "This is no favor to the chief. It's an insult. It allows the council to wash its hands of the whole nasty affair and make the chief do the dirty work. It's a slap in the face. Though I presume that's what you want to do."

"But it doesn't strip the chief of his authority."

"Yes it does. It just makes it seem like it doesn't. He has no real choice in this matter."

"I would like to hear from the chief himself."

Gordy steps forward. "I don't like it. Not one bit. There is no fiscal crisis that warrants the laying off of any staff from the police department. We're well within our budget for the year. This is completely unnecessary. It will not save the town from a lawsuit. It will, in fact, guarantee a lawsuit. All it does is place blame on a young police officer without even hearing the results of the investigation, which will, certainly, exonerate him. This is plainly and simply an attack on the police department. And yes, if you're going to ask, this does feel very personal to me. If you pass this, you will be doing a grave injustice to a young police officer who carried out his duties as best he could."

"And that wasn't very well," someone yells.

"Thank you for your thoughts on the matter, Chief. I'm sure the council will give your concerns adequate consideration. Is there more discussion?"

An old man rises. "I'm James Archer from Plain Mills Road. I have lived in Lydell my entire life, and that's a long time. I'm eighty years old. And I support the police department and our chief. Gordon is a good man who runs a fine department. In your hearts, you know that. If Gordon says something is so, I think something is so. And I can't, for the life of me, understand why everyone is so ready to insult him. I live pretty much on Social Security, and that means I don't have a lot of money. But I pay my taxes. I pay them like everyone else, because I use the services of the town, and that includes the police department. I believe in paying for what I get. Why do you all believe that the good things of Lydell are too expensive and need to be done away with? I know you spend a lot of money on your computers and your phones and your fancy cars and motorcycles and boats and such. But are those things worth more than your safety, the education of our children? Are they so important you will steal money from the people who keep you safe? I don't understand this at all. I really don't. That's all I have to say, except I'm ashamed of what's going on here."

"If there's no further discussion, I would like to proceed to a vote. It's getting late here."

A man Gordy doesn't recognize stands and says, "I hope everyone pays close attention to what's going on here and remembers it on Election Day."

"All those in favor of the motion to direct the police chief to reduce his staff by one please say aye."

There are the same five ayes.

"The motion is carried."

"Chief Hawkins, the council directs you to reduce your staff by one by the end of next week."

"Great," Gordy says. "Just in time for Christmas."

"Do I have a motion to adjourn?"

"Moved."

"Second."

"The motion has been moved and seconded. This meeting is adjourned."

AS PEOPLE LEAVE THE HALL, GORDY STANDS IN THE REAR. HE WANTS to leave, but to just walk out feels like further defeat, and he's had enough. It had occurred to him that the council might try to scapegoat Ronny Forbert, but he hadn't expected anything like this. The treachery and cowardice of Martin Glendenning never fails to surprise him.

People come up to him and express their disappointment and shake his hand, assuring him that they will work to get this overturned. They won't. They will want to, but the sting will fade, and this will become less and less of an issue for them. He smiles and thanks the well-wishers.

Stan Woodridge stands to the side, smiling and nodding at the townspeople. When the last person has shaken Gordy's hand, he moves next to Gordy. "I'm sorry," he says. "This is just the shits."

"Is there any way to fight this?" Gordy asks.

"Yeah. Sure there is, but you're going to have to go through with it. Work with the police union to file a civil action against the town. There's an outside possibility you might be able to find a judge who would be willing to grant an injunction, but it's not a good possibility. Next year will begin the election process, and the sentiment around the country doesn't favor government or personnel. I'm afraid I can't help you, either. I'll be representing the town, unless Martin gets rid of me, too. I don't like it, but the pay I get for this helps keep my practice going. If the union does file an action, I'm going to be hoping they kick my butt."

"DIDN'T GO WELL, DID IT?" PETE ASKS WHEN GORDY GETS BACK TO the office.

"No. It didn't go well. They cut one position from the department."

"I'm fired," Ronny says.

"No. You're not. And if I can help it, you won't be. Not sure how I'm going to get around this, but I'm going to figure a way. No matter what you hear or read about what happened tonight, no one from this department is facing termination. I'm not going to let that happen.

"And right now, I'm getting out of here before I have to talk to anyone else. Pete, don't call me unless it's a dire emergency. Underline 'dire.' Ronny, I'll take you home."

"My truck's out back."

"Can I trust you to go home and stay home and not talk to anyone tonight?"

"Yeah. I guess so."

"And you should know that Stan Woodridge stood up for you and fought for you. So go on home and don't worry. Otherwise, Pete's going to cuff you, and you're going home in the trunk of my car."

"I'm going."

GORDY SITS WHERE NO ONE CAN GET AT HIM. HE'S LEFT HIS CELL phone in the house and is out here in the shop, sitting practically on top of the space heater, eating frozen M&M's, where he can't hear the house phone. He's trapped. Martin has done exactly what he wanted to. Gordy's going to lose Ronny, and he'll have to betray him in the process. Ronny is the only one he can let go, as Martin well knows. He thinks, briefly, about reducing everyone's hours by a third, so he can keep Ronny on. But Pete, Steve, and John all have families. They can't take a pay cut. The only one who doesn't have a family is Ronny. Trapped. He wonders if this is not part of Martin Glendenning's plan, to get the police department to voluntarily resign so he doesn't have to try to disband it himself.

It occurs to him that he can go in the house, unplug the phone. He could eat the fresh M&M's he bought for dinner, but this seems right. The house is still too empty for him, and he's guessing he's now addicted to frozen M&M's.

RONNY DOES AS HE HAS PROMISED AND DRIVES DIRECTLY HOME. There's really no place to go. Every place in Lydell will be full of talk about him. He's through. Gordy will do whatever he can to save him, but, Ronny thinks, there won't be anything he can do. The news report that he killed Matt Laferiere has ruined him.

He wants to talk. He picks up the pieces of his phone from the living room floor. It doesn't look that bad. The back has popped off and the SIM card is out. The battery has also come out. The screen has two big cracks that meet at the side of the phone. He reinstalls the battery and SIM card and tries to reattach the back. It, too, is broken. He goes to the kitchen and gets the Scotch tape. He holds the back down and carefully tapes it around the edges. Then he tries it. Nothing. He looks around the floor for any pieces he might have missed, finds a couple bits of black plastic, but nothing more. He squeezes the back tightly and pushes the power button. Again, nothing. He lays it on the coffee table and looks at it for a minute, then takes his hand and sweeps it off the table and onto the floor. It comes apart again. He leaves it that way.

He thinks briefly of going to Citgo and buying a cheap phone, but he's pretty well tapped out. He's stuck in his apartment for at least another day. When he gets back to work, if he's not fired before he even goes back, which seems the most likely to him, he still will be broke.

He again goes over the list of who might have done this to him— Stablein, Cabella, or Colvington. All seem possible, none seems right. He senses the presence of Matt Laferiere, even though he's underground by now. Still, he can almost hear Laferiere laughing at him. Somehow, Matt has reached out from his grave and fucked him up, big time.

HE GOES TO THE BEDROOM CLOSET AND TAKES OUT THE DESERT Eagle, brings it to the kitchen and unlatches the case. It's an amazing weapon. He doesn't know how he's going to pay for it, especially now that he's losing his job. He should probably find Purcell and give it back. He picks it up and holds it in his hand. He's beginning to like the feel of the gun, even if the laser sight makes it slightly out of balance. He pulls the slide back, pulls the trigger, and feels it come back together with a smooth, clean authority. Everything in the world should work as simply and as well as a gun.

He sits at the table in the kitchen, disassembling the gun, carefully laying out each piece before going to the cabinet under the kitchen sink and getting his cleaning kit. He oils each piece, rubbing each down with a soft cloth until there is only the thinnest film of oil. Then he reassembles the gun, and slowly and carefully wipes it down to get any excess oil.

He should probably take the gun back. He still owes seven hundred dollars on it, and it's money he doesn't have and isn't likely to get. He holds it in his hand. It's such a lovely thing, despite its bulk and awkwardness. He should take it back and see if he can get his money back. Probably he can't. He finally decides that it doesn't really matter anymore.

Then he puts it to his head and pulls the trigger.

"Bang," he says. "Just, fucking, bang."

WHEN HE'S OUT OF M&M'S, GORDY GOES BACK INTO THE HOUSE. HE doesn't turn on the lights, but walks back to the bedroom by feel and practice. The red lights on the alarm clock next to the bed read 10:44. In the dark he undresses, crawls into the bed, and pulls the covers over himself.

The problem is simple. The conversation he started with himself in the shop begins again. Martin has boxed him in. He has to get rid of Ronny Forbert, and he has to be the one to make the decision to do it. Certainly Ronny fucked up. But it wasn't a significant fuckup. Matt Laferiere died, but that wasn't simply the result of Ronny's failure to get backup. It wasn't the lack of backup that killed Laferiere. Two officers might have been able to subdue Laferiere, but it was also likely that Laferiere, drunk, would have fought both the officers, just as he had Ronny. And there's the distinct possibility that he still would have gotten killed, and maybe taken one or more of the officers with him.

But that's idle speculation. What happened is what happened, and the effects of it rippled out continuously. How could you stop the rippling of water? As far as he knows, only time can do that, and he doesn't have much time.

CHAPTER 8

(DAY FIVE)

GORDY WAKES IN THE MORNING. HE GETS OUT OF BED AND STANDS slowly. His back is stiff and painful and his stomach feels overfull and queasy. Why did he eat the full bag of M&M's? He had hoped things would be clearer in the morning, but they're not. He slowly moves over to the sink, rinses out the coffeepot and starts a new one. Then he goes to the bedroom to shower and brush his teeth.

While he dresses, he turns on the TV. The big news is snow, more snow.

"That Alberta Clipper that we've been tracking will be coming through here, probably late this afternoon or early this evening. Now, this is a clipper, not a nor'easter, so we're looking at a short intense storm that will be out of here by morning. Right now, my best guess on accumulation is three to six inches over most of the area, unless this little front hits the high pressure right here and stalls. But I don't think that's going to happen. I think it's going to slide right on past, drop its three to six inches, and be out of here before the morning commute.

"There will be some shoveling for you in the morning, but the primary roads should be plowed in time for the commute, and the secondary roads not too long after. So all in all, it's not much. A lot of snow coming down for a short while and then a slow steady snowfall heading toward morning, completely gone by sunrise I think.

"And there's good news. It looks like we're going to be in for a stretch of cold weather for the next several days. So even if there isn't another snow by next Tuesday we're headed for a white Christmas."

Gordy thinks that he probably had better get some gas to get the snowblower going while he's out for the day. Three to six inches isn't much, and he guesses that he can probably get away without clearing the driveway tomorrow if it stays more to the three-inch level. But Vickys aren't great in the snow, even with snow tires. Better safe than sorry. He should make sure the shovel is right next to the door and pack in extra firewood as well.

"A bit of a boisterous town council meeting in Lydell last night," Renee Lawson says, "as Lydell residents gathered to weigh their options in the light of the hit-and-run death of a Lydell man in police custody last week. We'll have that story when we come back."

He sits down heavily on the bed. He didn't see anyone from the television station at the meeting last night. Where are these people getting their information?

Two car commercials and an Applebee's spot later, Renee is back, standing in front of the darkened town hall. "Lydell residents faced off last night over the horrific hit-and-run accident that left Lydell resident Matthew Laferiere dead Sunday night while in the custody of Lydell patrolman Ronald Forbert. Forbert, who is under suspension, was the subject of an unsuccessful attempt to fire him in light of the evidence around the suspension. The motion to release Forbert did not carry, but a motion to reduce the town's police department by one person did carry, and town council chair Martin Glendenning ordered Police Chief Gordon Hawkins to reduce the force by the end of next week.

"I'm here with town council president Martin Glendenning. Mr. Glendenning, what's your reaction to what happened last night?"

"Well, I'm still deeply saddened that such an event could take place in a town like Lydell. But I was proud of the way the town came together last night to support a resolution that did not single out an individual for responsibility in the affairs of the police department, which have, for a time, bothered me. I think the town showed great wisdom and courage in what they did last night."

"Do you think the result of this resolution will be the removal of Officer Forbert?"

"I don't know. That's not up to me. We addressed a budget issue last night, and we left the specifics of the action to Police Chief Gordon Hawkins. He is the chief, and this is his responsibility as long as he is."

Renee Lawson looks back to the camera. "There it is. Here in Lydell, the town is still reeling from the hit-and-run fatality last Sunday night. We'll keep you posted as things progress here in Lydell. This is Renee Lawson for Channel Eight *Newswatch.*"

"As long as he is," Gordy thought. "As long as he is."

RONNY FORBERT TURNS OFF THE TELEVISION AND PICKS UP HIS KEYS. Outside, he gets in his truck and drives to the station. As soon as he walks in, Pete says, "Aw, for fuck's sake. Don't you ever learn any-thing? Get out of here before Gordy gets in. He's just about had it with you hanging out here."

"Has he said anything about firing me?"

"He hasn't said anything about firing anyone."

"It's going to be me, isn't it?"

"Man. I don't know. I'm not the boss of this outfit. It could be any one of us. So your guess is as good as mine."

"It's got to be me," Ronny says.

"That's what Martin Glendenning wants. Gordy doesn't like to do what Martin Glendenning wants him to do. John or Steve or me are maybe more likely than you, just so that Gordy can piss off Glendenning."

"He wouldn't fire any of you guys. He likes you guys."

"Are you suggesting that Gordy doesn't like you? Are you crazy? Gordy's been caring for you for like five years. He groomed you to be on this force. He risked his career putting you on this force. And you think we're supposed to feel sorry for you because he doesn't like you enough? Get out of here." Pete picks up a piece of paper, wads it up, and throws it at Forbert.

"Hey, hey. I'm sorry."

"You ought to be. One of us is getting cut loose. It's going to be like losing an arm or a leg. No one wants to be the one cut loose, but more than that, no one wants any of us cut loose. We're more than just a police department, this here is a brotherhood, and we look out for each other. So don't go around thinking that anyone is feeling good about somebody else losing his job. Whatever way it comes down, it's a bad deal. If I'm not the one who goes, I may feel some relief, but I'm going to be a long fucking way from celebrating when the decision comes down.

"Now get out of here, you little shit, before Gordy comes in and chews my ass for letting you hang around. And he will chew my ass. Believe that, man."

RONNY GETS BACK IN THE TRUCK AND HEADS FOR WARRENTOWN. HE hasn't had a workout in a couple of days and he feels overdue, jumpy and flabby. He's working with the free weights when the grunter comes in. He's called that not because he grunts during his workouts, but because that's pretty much all he does. As Ronny stands before the mirror doing curls, he watches the grunter start stacking weights onto a barbell. He has what looks to be a hundred pounds on one end of the bar. He goes off somewhere for a bit and comes back, this time with his kidney belt on, and his lifting gloves. He adds plates to the other end of the bar so that it's at least level, and then he goes off again, leaving the barbell unusable for anyone else.

That's his routine. He stacks plates on bars and machines. He builds apparatus, but never actually lifts them, or if he does, never lifts more than once or twice. And he does it all accompanied by loud grunting and dropping the weights so they clang through the gym. Everyone knows he's there, but no one ever sees him actually work out.

It disgusts Ronny. It's fraud, and the guy is just putting on a show while he lets himself go. You don't have to look very hard to see that a lot of his bulk is flab. The only thing he really lifts is beer bottles. And everyone knows that he's faking it all. He isn't fooling anyone. But tomorrow he will have a job, and Ronny won't. He hates the guy. There are layabout cops like him all over the state. And they keep their jobs, while the cops who really work, who do their jobs, just get fucked over. It's the way of the world, the drunks and the fuckups and the layabouts just fuck things up for everyone else.

He's finishing up when Purcell walks in. "Hey, man. How's the Mark VII working for you?"

"Don't really know," Ronny says. "I haven't fired it since that day at the range with you."

"Yeah? You don't like it?"

"I like it just fine. Just haven't had the time, that's all."

"Well, listen, if you don't want it, I'll buy it back from you. I was in a little tight space here for a while, but it's good now. You want to sell it back, let me know. Or I might be able to trade you for something you like better. Hate to see a customer unhappy."

Ronny figures that Purcell had somehow turned up a motivated buyer.

"No. I guess I'll hang on to it."

"All right, man. Do what you want. But listen. I'll give you more than you paid for it if you want me to take it back. Like you might want a smaller gun and some cash. I know things must be a little tight for you right now. Whenever you decide it's not your best weapon, just give me a call. I'll give you a hundred more than you paid. You know. Goodwill."

"I'm going to keep the gun, but maybe I'll leave it to you in my will."

"Whatever you want, man."

"DON'T BE SO GLUM," GORDY SAYS TO PETE AND JOHN. "I'M GOING TO draw a name out of a hat. You've got three out of four chances to keep your jobs, whether you deserve them or not."

"Oh, that's just cold, man. You should get a job at the hospice, giving everyone odds on how much longer they're going to last. You'd be a comedy sensation."

"I just may do that," Gordy says.

"You're awful cheerful, considering."

"No. I'm not cheerful. I'm just not going to give Martin Glendenning the satisfaction of knowing how much this is bothering me."

"No, man. I mean you don't even look bothered."

"I've made a decision. And I'll let you know pretty soon. So I'm not still trying to work things out, that's all. It's pretty much decided. I'm going to talk to Martin later this afternoon. Either of you want to resign?" Gordy looks from Pete to John and back again. He smiles. "I didn't think so. I'm going to be in my office for the rest of the morning. You two hold down the fort. I don't want to be disturbed."

"You got it."

GORDY EMERGES FROM HIS OFFICE ABOUT AN HOUR LATER. "OK. EVerything in there is taken care of. Anything out here I need to know about?"

Pete starts to say something, catches himself and shakes his head. "No, man. Everything here is copacetic."

"Good. I have some errands to run. I probably won't be back until two or so. I'm not telling you where I'm going because I don't want anyone to know where I'm going, and you two won't have to lie when you say you don't know."

"Got it," Pete says.

When Gordy is gone out the door, John says, "I don't much like being in the position I'm in, but I bet it's a hell of a lot better than the position he's in. I got a seventy-five percent chance of surviving this. He's got no chance of not pissing off a lot of people."

HE MAKES HIS WAY DOWN THE ROCKY AND RUTTED ROAD. HE HASN'T been down this road since the day they found the white Lexus, but he's maneuvering it better, as if something buried in his brain has come to the surface and he's driving the road on years-old memory.

He stops in front of the house and knocks on the door. She doesn't answer, but he suspects she rarely spends much time in the house in the daytime. She'll be out back somewhere, attending to something. Her truck's here, so she's here.

"Need a hand?" he asks when he comes into the barn where she's breaking down bales of straw for bedding.

She looks at him for a bit. "I think I got it. Been doing it for a long time." Her hair's coming undone from her feed store cap and hangs down at the side of her face. She reaches up and tucks a strand of it behind her ear. "You need something?"

"A bit of your time. A cup of coffee, maybe."

"I don't drink coffee anymore. Tea?"

"Yeah. Tea."

"I'll go in and start the water. You want to spread this straw in these two stalls? I got girls getting ready to kid." It wasn't a question.

"Yeah. Glad to."

"Do a good job. A doe is someone's mama."

WHEN HE'S DONE, HE WALKS INTO THE HOUSE THROUGH THE KITCHEN where the teakettle is steaming away on the stove. Nearby are a teapot and two thick ceramic mugs.

She walks into the kitchen from the hall that leads to her bedroom. The barn coat and cap are gone, and she's rolling up the sleeves of a denim shirt. Her hair is pulled back into a ponytail.

"You look nice," he says.

"You look like shit. And don't get your hopes up. Sometimes I just feel the need to brush my damned hair."

"Just came over to talk." He smiles.

She pours the water into the teapot and brings it and the mugs over to the table. "What do you take in your tea?"

"I don't know. I really don't drink tea."

"Well, if you did, what would you take in it?"

"Probably nothing."

"There's goat's milk and sugar, if you want it."

He smiles. They had once battled over goat's milk. He refused to drink it, expecting it to be thin and bitter. He had finally drunk some on a bet and had been amazed by the smooth creaminess of the milk.

"What's up?" She leans back in her chair and puts her feet up on the one vacant chair.

"A crossroads. Came to a crossroads, and now I'm dithering. This way or that way."

"And you came to me?"

"You're the only one I could think of who isn't either working for me or dependent on me in some other way. And you won't bullshit me."

She smiles and shakes her head. "Goatshit you."

"Whatever. You won't."

"So you think. You don't know. Maybe I've changed a lot in the last few years."

He looks hard at her. She's a little heavier, her hair touched with gray, and her mouth and eyes lined. But on the outside, she really hasn't changed much. He suspects the same is true for the rest of her.

"Well, I'm here. Mind if we talk for a while?"

"No. Let's talk."

PAM POURS HIM A CUP OF TEA, AND HE PICKS IT UP HOLDS IT TO HIS nose and feels the steam come onto his face. He takes a sip. "So we go on. Whatever way we go on, we just do. That's all."

"Well," Pam says. "That sounds about the way it is. You do just go on."

"Are you happy?"

"Me? Yeah. I'm happy. Maybe I could be happier, who knows. But I'm happy enough that I don't worry about it. I take it that's not the case in your situation?"

"It's a tough time. The toughest time I've ever had, or at least in the top two. I need to make some decisions here, and I don't feel like I have enough information to make them."

"What information do you need?"

"Do you get lonely?"

"Are you coming around offering a miracle cure for loneliness, which is really your loneliness?"

"No. I really want to know. You live out here by yourself, and you seem to do fine."

"Myself and forty-six goats. More than that in the next couple of days. Yeah, sometimes I wish goats could talk. But mostly we get along just fine without the talking. Loneliness is not a state of being, you know. It's a reaction to a state of being, which is simply being alone. And you choose both of them. I don't have to live alone. I could find someone to live with. It wouldn't be that hard. Men are pretty damned easy to find. I just haven't found one who's better than not having one, which is a state I find myself more and more contented with."

"Contentment is a pretty wonderful thing. I was pretty content for a long time, then the apple cart went over."

"Apple carts do that. But tipped apple carts don't have to stay tipped. Or if they do, you can go on without them. Find another. I kind of think that contentment was always there, I just chose to chase after other things. When you finally find yourself content, it's like you always were, but you just forgot to think about it."

"Buddhism?"

"Goatism."

They look at each other for a bit. Where there was once so much to say, now there is so little, or maybe too much.

"I am sorry about Bonita. I really am. I didn't really know her, but I know she was very well thought of in town. And of course, I'm sorry for you. Vic died nearly thirty years ago, and I still miss him. Maybe not every minute or every day, but he's always not here."

"Vic?" He has never heard of Vic.

"Before your time. Vic and I came here back in the eighties. He died of a staff infection, really just a very, very bad cold. Hadn't even been here a year. I had burned a lot of bridges, and I had nowhere to go. So I stayed. Me and the goats. It's been an odd life, I guess, but a good one, all in all. Don't know where I'm going with this. Except that you get through things. You think you're not going to, but you do."

"You know what happened last night?"

"No. What now?"

"The town council met for the unstated but perfectly obvious purpose of firing Ronny Forbert."

"And they did?"

"Actually, no. They put me in a spot where I'll be forced to fire him. Pilate washing his hands, I guess. So I'm in kind of a bind everywhere. Bonita's gone, my job is turning into its own private hell. You know what bothers me most? The one thing that really fries me? It's when someone sees a tragedy as an opportunity to advance themselves. The complete lack of decency. That's what kills me."

"My father used to say that people are like goats. What they can't eat, they shit on. Actually I've found goats to be a lot more noble than people. It's a bad rap on the goats. And what are you going to do?"

Gordy smiles. "Well, I can't eat it."

"You want some more tea?"

"No. I better get going. I just needed to talk a little, and you're a great one to talk to. Hope I didn't take too much of your time."

Pam shrugs. "What's time? Another thing I've learned from goats. Time is just something people make up to worry about. The goats will get fed. I'll get fed."

"Well, thanks for the tea."

"You're welcome. Anytime. Whether I have tea or not. Gordy. Don't do anything stupid."

"What's stupid? That's got to be as relative as time."

BACK IN THE CRUISER, GORDY PHONES MARTIN GLENDENNING AND sets up a meeting for lunchtime. "You've made up your mind, have you?" Martin asks.

"I believe I have. Yes."

RONNY GETS OUT OF THE SHOWER, DRIES AND DRESSES IN HIS DUTY gear, tucking his pants into the highly polished nine-inch combat boots. He thinks again about getting a new phone or finding a pay phone. But the need or desire just isn't strong enough. Maybe he doesn't actually want to talk to her. He isn't sure.

He drives through Lydell, past the center of town and down Snake Farm Road, until he comes to the pull-over, where he parks his truck and gets out, puts on his coat and the holstered Mark VII. Everything looks the same, as if he and Max were out here only days ago, not years.

Someone, probably a hunter or two, has been here ahead of him. The snow is packed, and boot prints cover boot prints. He walks over the latest set and into the woods. It's quiet, beyond quiet, silent. Most of the birds have migrated and many of the animals are hibernating. But there are always winter birds—juncos, titmice, chickadees, and turkeys. Deer and rabbit are abundant in the winter. Probably everything is hunkering down for the storm tonight. He can feel it coming as well. It's still and warm, not windy and cold as it had been earlier. The storm is moving in.

He walks on down the thin but well-packed trails. Everything is covered with a layer of ice that was once snow. The rocks are treacherously slippery. Twice his boots slip on the rocks, and once he nearly goes down. He has to climb over one big oak that has come down onto the trail, and he ducks under the branches of a smaller beech that has been uprooted in a storm.

Clearly no one is working on the trail anymore. Hunters would be too single-minded to bother clearing it up, and he guesses that kids are too busy with video games and other electronic stuff to come out to the woods. How long has it been since he has really walked through these woods? Years. He guesses he can't hold anyone more blameworthy than himself.

The small stream that he and Max used to dam up to catch crawfish and minnows is still there and running. It has made small openings in the ice cover where he can see the water moving. He sits on a granite boulder and watches the water go by as the ice glistens in the last sun.

It's peaceful here, and there is something here that he has lost—an ability to just exist and accept. There's a feeling in the woods that the world is right, and that he is a part of it, and is, therefore, right, too. But then, he doesn't live in the woods. He isn't sure that there is a way to even begin to set things right. The world beyond the woods has methodically collapsed around him, and he can do nothing, probably, to stop it. Here, it's all right. Here, those matters seem small, but he knows that once he steps out of the woods they will grab him again.

He unholsters the Mark VII and looks at. He still wants to think it's a beautiful gun, but it isn't. It's too big, too ungainly to have any beauty to it. It's a sledgehammer or a bolt cutter or pick-ax. It's useful, it's efficient and powerful, but it isn't beautiful.

He opens his mouth and takes the barrel of the gun into it, letting his tongue slide over the end of the barrel. The taste is oily and metallic. But somehow he can exert no pressure on the trigger of the big gun. This is a place where he wouldn't mind dying. At least so he once thought. But here, now, with the Mark VII in his mouth, ready to blow his skull to bits, he doesn't want to die. He thought he did, but he doesn't. He isn't afraid. He just doesn't want to do it. Maybe this is the wrong time, the wrong place, but, whatever, it's wrong.

He takes the gun from his mouth and reholsters it. He listens to the water below his feet as it makes its way past the smooth stones. He smells the air as if he could smell the coming snow the way animals can. He slides off the rock and begins walking out, picking up trash and moving deadfall from the trail.

"GORDON," MARTIN SAYS WHEN GORDY WALKS IN. "IT'S GOOD TO SEE you. Are you doing all right? The council meeting must have been very unpleasant for you. I wish that hadn't happened. I tried to make things a little easier on you."

"I had the impression that the meeting went exactly the way you planned it to go, Martin."

Glendenning smiles. "Nothing goes exactly as you plan it. You have to adjust to the currents, so to speak. I bear you no ill will, Gordon. I hope you know that. I admire what you have done for Lydell over all these years. I hope that was clear in my amendment to give you the authority in all of this. I didn't want the council to be dictating police matters to you."

"Martin, if we could bag you and sell you by the pound at a gardening center, Lydell's financial problems would be a thing of the past."

"We talking manure here, Gordon?"

"We're living it here, Martin." Gordy takes the envelope from inside his coat pocket and hands it across the table to Glendenning.

"This is your decision? You could have just called me or sent me an email."

"No. I think it has to be this way."

Glendenning opens the envelope, unfolds the letter, and puts on his reading glasses. Gordy watches him as he reads.

"Gordon. This is a letter of resignation."

"Yes it is."

"But this is not right. No one has asked for your resignation. No one wants your resignation."

"I did what I thought was best for the town, Martin. You wanted to cut the payroll, and I cut out the biggest single item—my salary."

"But we have to have a police chief."

"Then have one. Promote Pete. He has seniority. And he's the best cop in the department. You don't really have a problem here."

"I don't know that I could work well with Peter Mancuso. I mean, not like I work with you."

Gordy smiled. "It will be a different experience for you. One I wish I could watch, but I'll be off somewhere being retired. And you know you and I have never worked well together. You just throw shit on me."

"And you throw it back. But Forbert. This leaves Forbert in the department. This is not acceptable."

"I told you. He's a good cop. Pete will go on making him a better cop. And you and I both know that you were after Ronny to get at me. Now you don't have to go after anyone. I'm gone as of the end of the year."

"But the witness that has come forward. Forbert is not a good cop."

"Do you know who the witness is, Martin? Never mind. I know you do. And I know that whatever the witness saw, it'll be a tough sell in court. There's no question that there was a struggle, and there's no question that Matt Laferiere was seriously impaired. And I've asked the state police to take over the investigation. It'll be fair, and Ronny will be exonerated."

"I will refuse to accept this." Glendenning holds up Gordy's letter.

"Doesn't matter if you do. I dropped another copy off at the town clerk's office. I will be retired on January first."

Glendenning scowls and then seems to regain control of himself. He stands up and extends a hand to Gordy. "Then I will accept this with only the greatest regret."

Gordy smiles. "I wouldn't have wanted to give you anything less. Enjoy your time with Pete."

UNDER THE TRUCK, WHERE HE IS HIDDEN FROM VIEW, WHERE HE crawled to start working on the rusted nuts that hold the rear axle shackles in place, Sammy hears someone come into the garage, and he slides out from under the truck, just his head, and he sees Ronny Forbert. Then he hears the angry voices, and he scoots back under the truck. He has a three-pound hammer in one hand that he's been using to hit the bar, trying to crack the rust on the nut and bolt. He stops breathing when he hears the first shot.

Then there are more shots. And red dots swirling on the floor. He knows from TV that those are laser dots from a gun sight. And after each shot there is yelling and groaning and he sees two of his friends drop to the floor as though they were puppets with their strings cut. And right after each shot, he hears the small brass chime of a bullet casing hitting the concrete floor. And though he knows what they are, he cannot help his brain from repeating the line, as he remembers it, from the old movie about the guy who wishes he'd never been born, that they show every Christmas. *God just made another angel.*

And then there's silence. Even after he hears the truck start up and back away from the garage he doesn't move. He can see Paul, beyond the truck, on the floor, facing him, his eyes wide and staring. Dead. Sammy just tries to start breathing again.

HE LIES STILL FOR A LONG TIME, WAITING, TOO SCARED TO MOVE. And when he does move, he's sore from holding every muscle in his body stiff. He moves one leg first, pulling it toward him, then pushing with his arms until he's sliding his body across the floor and out from under the truck.

He's amazed at what he sees. The bodies of his friends. Paul, Bobby, and Paul's little brother, Elliot, are all on the floor, all splattered with blood. They're dead. He knows that. He has to call someone. The police, probably, though that seems exactly what he should not do. He still has the hammer in his hand. He drops it on the floor.

HE DOESN'T HAVE A PHONE. HE'S WANTED ONE, AND HAD ARGUED that he needed a phone, though his father had refused to buy him one or make the payments that would come every month. He thought he could find enough work with Paul and Bobby to afford one, though he was also trying to make payments on this beater of a Silverado he is trying to buy from Paul Stablein.

He goes to Bobby's truck, parked next to his, also up on ramps. Maybe Bobby's phone is in the truck. But it isn't and he knows then that the phone is in Bobby's pocket, and Bobby is dead. And he can't touch Bobby, even to get the phone. He looks around the garage. The phone is in the office, and the office is locked. They are allowed to use the garage, but they can't go into the office.

HE WALKS TO THE OFFICE AND LOOKS IN THE WINDOW IN THE DOOR. There is the phone, sitting on the desk. The door is locked. He goes back and gets the three-pound hammer and swings it through the glass, reaches in and unlocks the door.

"NINE ONE ONE. WHAT IS YOUR EMERGENCY?" THE DISPATCHER ASKS.
"There's been a killing," he says.
"Who is this?"
"There's three of them. Shot dead."
"Where?"
"Baxter's. On 417."
"Baxter's Garage on Route 417?"
"Yes."
"Three dead?"
"I think so."
"What's your name?"
"Kevin," he lies.
"Are you there? Are you on the scene?"
"Yes."
"Kevin what?"
"Just that. Kevin."
"Is the shooter still there?"
"No."
"Are you safe? Kevin? Stay there. I'm sending a car."

THEY ARE SENDING A CAR. THE POLICE ARE ON THEIR WAY. HE PUTS down the phone and walks back into the garage. There is even more blood now. It's leaking out of them. His friends. The police are coming. He thinks maybe he can hear the siren in the distance.

He has done this, he thinks. He and his father. If his father hadn't pushed him to do that bullshit interview, none of this would have happened. He killed his friends as surely as if he had shot them himself. He and his father. His fucking, rat-ass father.

He goes to the window and looks out. It's snowing hard now, but he doesn't see anything or anyone in the parking lot out front. Slowly and carefully, he opens the door, just a crack. When nothing happens, he cautiously sticks his head out the door, waits, then opens it farther. He throws the hammer into the garage, puts his head down, and runs out into the night, away from the garage, his friends, the police.

EPILOGUE

GORDY'S DRIVING HOME IN THE LATE MORNING WHEN HE HEARS it. "In news at the eleven o'clock hour, convicted mass murderer Ronald Forbert has died. Forbert, a former Lydell police officer, was convicted in the shooting deaths of three young men in December 2010. Officials at Attica Correctional Facility say that Forbert, who was awaiting execution for the murders, was found dead in his cell this morning. No cause of death has been identified, but sources say that drug overdose is suspected. An autopsy will be performed.

"In other news . . ." Gordy turns off the radio. He's feeling the cold vacancy of sudden shock. He makes a quick right at Hanley Burroughs Road and heads for the police station.

He hasn't been here since shortly after the murders and his retirement. He's not sure why, except that this seems not to have anything to do with his life anymore. Walking into the office he feels a warm familiarity. There are some new posters on the wall, new institutional gray carpet, and in the photo gallery on the wall inside the entrance the face of a new officer he doesn't know.

"Gordy," John North calls. "Gordy, good to see you."

"Morning, John. How've you been?"

"Good, Gordy. Good as gold. How about you?"

"Fine. I'm doing just fine."

"How's retired life?"

Gordy thinks for a minute for the right word. "Blissful. It's blissful, John. Makes all that working worthwhile."

"Hope I get to find out one day."

"You've heard?"

Gordy turns to Pete, who has come out of his office and is standing a few feet away.

"Pete." Gordy walks the steps toward Pete, extending his hand. Pete takes it and pulls him in for a hug.

"Good to see you, Gordy. Though not such a good occasion. You heard about Ronny."

"Just now. On the radio. What do you know?"

"Not a lot," Pete says. "Pretty certain it was an intentional OD."

"Suicide."

"Yeah. Suicide. He'd been trading blow jobs for barbiturates according to the captain of the guard."

"Oh, God."

"At least they didn't kill him," Pete says. "He wasn't going to let that happen. You want some coffee? Our new guy, Andy, makes some pretty decent coffee. Starbucks."

"Yeah. I'll take a cup. Been drinking tea in the morning. I'd love some good coffee."

"Sit." Pete motions to the chair as he turns to the coffeemaker. "Unless you want to talk in the office."

"This is good. Good to see John. How's everyone else?"

"We're all good. Steve is out on patrol. Should be back shortly. He'll be glad to see you." He hands Gordy a mug of coffee. "You keeping busy?"

"I am. I'm a part-time goat farmer, now."

"With Pam Garrity."

"Yeah. I'm over there most of the time these days. Just helping out whatever way I can. Starting to do some of her deliveries now."

"You know you're always welcome here."

"Yeah. I do. Sorry I haven't been around. Just don't feel like this is really part of my life anymore."

"I spend a lot of time wishing it wasn't so much of mine. So you're RWG, now?"

"RWG?"

"Retired with girlfriend. That sounds all right."

"We're keeping separate places, but we spend a lot of time together. It's a pretty nice life. Keeps me out of trouble."

"We have some more news. It hasn't been released yet, so you'll need to keep this under your hat for a day or two. Martin Glendenning has been arrested. The Staties stung him. Found a lot of equipment in Roger Laferiere's outbuildings. Matt had been storing it there. Roger flipped in about ten seconds. He's going to testify. But here's the best part. Martin's attention to detail? He kept records on every piece of equipment there. Dates, where it came from, where he sold it. Everything. He tied his own noose."

"Are they going to try Roger?"

"He'll get a suspended sentence. No jail time."

"Good job, Pete. That's great. After all those years of trying to get him."

"It was all the Staties. How's that for irony? The guys he wanted to replace us with. Sometimes life is just rich."

"Yeah," Gordy says. "Sometimes."

ACKNOWLEDGMENTS

I wish to express my gratitude to my late brother George O. Cobb IV and to Paula Webb for sharing their stories, to Shane Fowler and Paco Kelly for their information and encouragement, to my editor Henry Ferris, and to my last grad students—Katie Brunero, Robert Lafebvre, Sherry Roulston, and Dave Shifino—for their sharp eyes and good judgment.

And more gratitude than I can adequately express to Amanda Urban and to Randy.

Author photograph by Eugene St. Pierre

ABOUT THE AUTHOR

THOMAS COBB is the author of *Crazy Heart,* which was made into the Academy Award–winning film starring Jeff Bridges. He is also the author of the novels *With Blood in Their Eyes* and *Shavetail,* both of which won Western Writers of America Spur Awards. He grew up in Arizona and currently lives in Rhode Island with his wife.